JACK BYRNE was born and raised in Speke, Liverpool to an Irish immigrant fath … advocate of Irish and Liverpudli … ilogy followed two gener … their journey from Irelan … *ouse* is the first novel in a …

Follow Jack on Twitter @Jackbyrnewriter

And find him on www.jackbyrne.home.blog

BURNING DOWN THE HOUSE

JACK BYRNE

NORTHODOX PRESS

Northodox Press Ltd
Maiden Greve, Malton,
North Yorkshire, YO17 7BE

This edition 2025

1
First published in Great Britain by
Northodox Press Ltd 2025

ISBN: 978-1-917005-18-0

This book is set in Caslon Pro Std

Printed and bound by CPI Group (UK) Ltd,
Croydon, CR0 4YY

To all who have thrown sand.

Wherever you are, whatever sand you can throw in the gears of genocide, do it now. If it's a handful, throw it. If it's a fingernail full, scrape it out and throw it. Get in the way however you can.

Rasha Abudulhadi

CHAPTER ONE

PAUL

Tuesday, January 7th, 2020.

Look at him, with his floppy hair and skinny body. Who does he think he is? He and his kind will never save the world. *We* will protect the Lord's creation from *them:* the immoral, the greedy, the unclean and ungodly. Paul watched the youth climb into an old banger.

"As righteousness leads to life, so he who pursues evil pursues it to his own death."

Proverbs 11:19–21 (NKJV)

CHAPTER TWO

MATTHEW

Tuesday, January 7th, 2020.

For an environmentalist, Julia drove a disaster of a car. Matt watched the blue apparition chug its way down the street.

'Morning.' He slid into the passenger seat. 'You know, I could have got the bus.'

'Might as well carry two people as one.' Julia's eyes were bright. 'Anyway, I wanted to make sure you got there safe and sound.'

'I can get to town on my own.'

'You could catch your death in this. Goes right through you, that damp. Ten minutes standing in that and your bones'd be rusty.'

'Okay. Well, thanks.'

Julia turned to smile at him, her silver-grey pony tail swished. She was alone except for Sammy, her dog, and climate activity was her attempt at making sure the grandchildren she rarely saw had a planet to grow up on. She waited for a gap in the traffic and threw the car around in a U-turn. 'New start today. You excited?' She looked across at him.

'More nervous. I hope they turn up.' Matt had been to speak to the Rail Maritime and Transport union the week before.

'They said they would?'

'Yeah, we had a good meeting. They were a bit sus' at first, but when I said it was a straight up protest, no direct action, they were fine.'

Julia gave him a quizzical look. 'How many are you expecting?'

'Just a couple, I think they want to check us out.'

Julia joined the stream of commuter traffic and, for a mile, they crawled along Halewood Road, before turning off into Hunts Cross train station. Julia opened the hatchback and sorted among the paraphernalia of protest. She took out two big bags full of handmade signs. 'Andy said he'd bring the banner.'

'OK, as long as we have enough flyers.'

'Yeah. Here, can you take these?'

Matt swung his rucksack free, balanced it on the car and packed a box of flyers into it.

They made their way through the ticket office and down the ramps. Schoolkids and commuters clogged the open platform, coats and hoods pulled tight against the damp morning air. Somewhere the sun was getting out of bed and its bright rays were breaking through the mist. The train appeared down the track and the waiting passengers shuffled toward the edge of the platform.

Within ten minutes they were part of the stream of humanity flowing from the trains up escalators, funneled through the electronic barriers and onto Liverpool Central station concourse. The station had three exits; a sharp right to a set of steps out onto a side road, the two busier exits to the left and a slight incline out onto Bold Street, and one straight ahead onto Ranelagh Street. Bold Street was the best spot, people left the station and joined the foot traffic down toward the centre. Matt was surprised to see Andy and the others on the station concourse. Andy's dreadlocks swung as he twisted and turned, handing out flyers.

'Why are you here?' Matt was pissed. 'We were supposed to be outside the station.'

Two people held the banner, and half a dozen others were mingling with the commuters handing out flyers.

'Oh great, you brought the megaphone.'

'Andy?'

'It's fine, don't worry about it.'

Emma, a key member of the team, bounced over and gave Julia a hug. Matt nodded.

They were stationary in a sea of movement, the commuters flowed around them.

'Fuck,' Matt grimaced. Two men in high-viz vests came in against the stream and headed toward them.

'Do you know these?' Andy pointed.

'Yeah, they're from the union.'

Matt stepped forward. 'Morning. Stuart, isn't it?'

The taller of the two spoke. 'Yeah. Alright, lad?' He looked around. 'What are you doing here?'

Matt turned. 'I'm not sure, to be honest... Andy?'

'There's more people. We get more attention.'

'You're on station property. They'll have you kicked off.' Stuart looked around again as if he expected to see the police.

'Transport Police have been over. Told us to move.' Andy shrugged. 'We said 'No, we're staying', and they left.' He smiled.

Matt swung his rucksack over his shoulder. 'We should move outside on to the street.'

Stuart spoke to Matt. 'Look, we agreed to support you, but we can't do this on station property. We'd be risking our jobs. We're not here for arrests and headlines.'

'I'm sorry, mate. I didn't realise.' Matt glared at Andy.

'No problem. We're going to get off though. This isn't for us. It's a shame, lad, we want to start working together. It's our future too.'

'I know. Leave it with me. Thanks for showing up. Sorry about this.'

Stuart led his mate away.

'What the fuck, Andy? Come on, we agreed... no direct action... a bit of leafleting, petition... speaking.'

'What action?' Andy held up the flyers in his hand. 'Leafleting.' He pointed to the megaphone in Matt's hand.

'Speaking. What are you waiting for?'

Matt dropped his rucksack and slid it over behind the banner. He raised the megaphone and began to speak. 'Every day, we see wildfires. In Australia, California, and now here in the UK. Climate change is happening all around us, we have to take action to stop fossil fuel, coal, oil, and energy companies from destroying our environment.' Matt let his arm and the megaphone drop.

Julia had moved across to stand beside him. 'You were doing fine. Why stop?'

Matt shook his head. 'For the first time, we had the union guys with us. What the fuck is Andy is up to?'

'Ego. Silly ego.'

'I hope that's all it is.' As Matt raised his megaphone he saw a black shape slicing through the stream, moving quickly toward them. He resumed speaking, 'The world is burning...'

CHAPTER THREE

CHARLIE

Tuesday, January 7th, 2020.

'The world is burning.' The voice rang out over the station concourse. Amplified by the megaphone, his tones were harsh and metallic - scratchy denunciations delivered into the cold morning rush hour. 'It's here… we don't have to wait... it's not about our future. Wildfires in… Australia... America and now the UK. Our world... is burning. We're burning down the house. We are dying.' The speaker's face strained, and the words tumbled out as he exhorted the commuters to join him, to join the protesters.

With the red half of the city, Charlie was happy and looking forward to getting to school and work. He walked quickly towards the station exit, head down, ears full of '*The Anfield Wrap*' podcast. It was a great start to the new year, a Liverpool kids' team had beaten Everton one-nil in the Football Association Cup's fourth round. Bragging rights had been well and truly established. Charlie's world was good today.

A group of climate protesters waved hand-painted placards and banners. He ignored them. Liverpool Football Club was on fire, but not in the way they were moaning about. He wanted to enjoy the last few minutes before he started work. A shrill and panicked voice cut through the cold air.

Charlie's eyes jumped to a police snatch squad of six officers. They moved swiftly, slicing through the commuters. A screech of feedback filled the air as the speaker, a young man with a soft round face and loose hair, was taken down. He hit the floor, hard.

Charlie was shocked at the speed and violence. The black uniforms had pierced the crowd, focused on their prey. A well-rehearsed routine, it was precise and clinical. He couldn't help but be impressed.

One officer bent low, and his arm swept away the speaker's legs, sending his upper body falling backwards. The fall was partly broken by arms that held him down. Within seconds, the guy was on his back, legs held firmly, arms pinned to the ground. The detained man pressed the button on the megaphone as his only means of resistance. It produced the feedback that cut through Charlie's podcast.

'Shut that fucking thing off!'

Following orders, another officer wrestled with the megaphone, attached by a strap to the man's wrist. Charlie's sight line was clear; he made eye contact. In the seconds before the protester was flipped over onto his stomach, he stared at Charlie. Charlie could see fear, pain, and anger in his eyes.

As he lay defeated, head held down, he mouthed, 'We are dying.'

It stopped Charlie in his tracks. *What*? What the hell was going on?

Commuters jostled him as they rushed past. He pulled the pods from his ears. He watched as a bizzie placed a knee on the man's back and pushed his face into the ground. The other protesters were stunned and passive. By the time someone produced a phone to record it, the speaker was face down, immobilised, and in pain.

Eric Garner, Eric Garner, the name flashed through Charlie's mind. *Who the fuck is Eric Garner*?

Another bizzie, arms spread, protected his colleagues behind him. Charlie approached him pointed and asked. 'Is that necessary?'

Charlie knew it was useless to ask, but he had to do something. He looked around; people streamed past like the whole scene was invisible.

The guy's distorted face pressed against the tiled floor of the concourse was flushed and red.

The officer's reply was cold and sharp. 'Move on.'

'I'm asking if he needs to do that?' Charlie pointed again.

The policeman swatted Charlie's hand away. 'None of your business. Keep moving.' He pushed Charlie to the right.

Charlie met the bizzie's eyes. They were cold and contemptuous. He recognised the aggression from crowd control at football matches, barked commands, and shouted orders. The bizzies were trained to dominate people and space.

'I said, move on.' It was an order that came with another push, a warning delivered with the hint of a smile. 'Or you're fucking next.'

Unbalanced, Charlie moved a little. He didn't know what to do. Adrenaline pumped through his veins.

The screech died, and an officer wrenched the megaphone from the protester's hand. To sharp commands, the man was lifted face down, legs and arms restrained as they carried him out of the station. The squad moved in step and cut through the morning commuters. Charlie followed, watching. The detainee gasped for air. His face strained, eyes bulged, his body wracked for breath. A police van waited at the kerb, and Charlie heard the thud as the body hit floor. *Bastards.*

The officers climbed in and the doors slammed. The van pulled out into the traffic. Charlie moved on to work, but the look in those eyes haunted him; pain and anger, and then the words, '*We are dying.*'

Charlie left the station and walked down pedestrianised Church Street. His feet knew the way; he didn't have to think. Rough sleepers were stretched out like corpses in every other doorway. The air was fresh, a breeze blowing in off the River Mersey a few streets away. The day would be nice as soon as the sun got its arse into gear.

The workers' entrance was through the main door. The shutter was half up, and after ducking under it, Charlie was in the store. He went through the shop area and a side door that led to the warehouse. The images of the arrest disturbed him - and the name Eric Garner swirled around his mind.

'Hey.' He waved to the half dozen workers sitting around, waiting to start. He took his coat off and slipped on his hi-viz vest.

Gary grinned. 'One nil.'

Charlie high-fived him. 'Were you there?'

Gary met his hand midair. 'Nah, couldn't afford it. Saw it on the telly.'

'Same,' said Charlie. 'Saw summat weird a minute ago, in Central Station.'

'What?'

'The bizzies arrested a kid.'

'What for?'

'Dunno. Some kinda protest.'

'Yeah I saw them.' Gary said. 'Probably hippies.'

'Yeah, I guess.' Charlie slipped his card into the scanner, it would record his arrival, his every movement while in the building, and his departure. Even this was better than the last place, a huge distribution centre for online orders: handheld tablets monitored every minute. Zero Hour contracts and three strikes and you were out. It all meant high pressure, low pay and no security.

He was a couple of minutes early, so he got a beef soup from the machine. The tea was awful. At least the beef drink had a distinctive taste.

'How long have you got left?' Gary said. 'Heard anything?'

'No, waiting for a text. How about you?'

'Same. Hope they give me some notice. I think we'll be here till the end of the week.'

'Till the January sales finish?'

'Yeah, the agency will move us after that.'

Charlie turned to face him. 'Who's Eric Garner?'

Gary thought for a moment. 'Dunno, mate. Do I know him? I mean, should I?'

'The name's in my head. Probably nothing.'

'He was killed by police in New York.' The voice came from among the workers at the table behind them.

'Sorry?' Charlie turned, but didn't see who had spoken.

'Strangled for selling loose ciggies. Killed by the police.' The speaker was a mixed race woman with bright eyes.

'Thanks,' Charlie said.

She raised her eyebrows, 'Thanks?'

It felt like an accusation. 'I mean for telling me who he was.' Charlie turned back to Gary before she could see his face flush.

~

The shop was halfway between a mail order and a High Street store. Catalogues were displayed in the retail area, and customers filled in a form with the product number and paid the cashier. This product number was displayed on a large screen in the warehouse together with the employee number responsible for collecting it from the shelf and delivering it to the conveyor, which brought it out into the shop.

'Gary and Charlie, you're on overnight orders, so you can start,' the supervisor said.

Charlie didn't mind this. Those orders were placed the night before, online, so they could work their way through the list at their own speed for the first hour of the day.

The ten-hour shift was timed from the first order scanned. They were allowed a thirty-minute lunch break. The temperature-controlled, windowless warehouse was a perfect place for Charlie to disappear into zombie space, and the piped radio through overhead speakers helped set a tone of monotony - get the code, find the parcel, scan it, put it onto the conveyor, start again. He remembered the precise movements of the police in the station.

The day wore on, and the images from the morning diminished. Charlie was able to enjoy the Liverpool victory again. That curling ball in from the left, the desperation as Everton scrabbled for an equaliser that never came.

The tinny words of the radio newsreader broke through, '*Liverpool... protest... arrest... death...*'

Charlie stopped. His stomach sank as the reporter explained.

'There has been a death in police custody. The deceased, although unidentified, is believed to have been a climate protester detained this morning in Central Station. Police have made no official statement at this time. Unofficial reports suggest the death was due to natural causes. We will bring you more information as soon as it is available.'

Charlie's thoughts swirled like a leaf in the wind. *How did he die? Was he diabetic? Maybe he had asthma or something? The kid died?* He remembered the face pressed against the floor, the fear in his eyes. *He spoke to me... he knew he was dying.* He felt a growing dread and the words of the copper hit him like a brick. *'Fuck off or you're next.'*

THREE MONTHS EARLIER

CHAPTER FOUR

MATTHEW

Saturday, October 12th, 2019.

A gaggle of protesters ambled down pedestrianised Church Street. Andy, a young man with dreadlocks, led the way. They carried drums, blew whistles and sent whoops through the chill of the afternoon air to bring attention to themselves. The protesters were live on YouTube and Facebook, filmed by Julia, a rainbow ribbon tied her silver-grey hair. She danced backwards while filming and speaking.

Her high-pitched voice was a little tremulous. 'Calling all rebels. Calling all rebels. We are on the move. Come down and join us in Liverpool City Centre. We're in Church Street. Enact your principles with us today as we turn morality into action. Join us. Calling all rebels. Come and join us.'

Thirty feet behind the group, Julia's camera caught a man of medium height with short brown hair, beige chinos and a brown zip-up corduroy jacket. He maintained the same distance from the group even as shoppers moved past him.

The drums followed a rhythm, and members of the troupe improvised with rice shakers and banged sticks to add to the arrangement. A mix of men and women distinguished by the earthen palette of loose jumpers, cardigans and trousers dressed warmly against the October air.

Matt, younger than most and a new recruit, was near the rear of the group, half-heartedly carrying a sign that called for

Climate Action Now. In jeans and a hoody, he cut a disparate figure among the dancers.

Emma, an organiser, had long blonde hair, tied in ribbons of different colours, and a loose pale green dress over brown trousers with an open orange and yellow woollen coat, everything pulled in at the waist by a white scarf. 'Hey, come on, keep up. We don't want to lose you!' she said above the drumming.

Matt gave a half wave in response. His blue jeans and black hoody identified him more with the shoppers than the protesters. Most pedestrians gave the group a wide berth, although some rocked to the drumming as though a circus had arrived in town.

A narrow row of market stalls selling Liverpool and Everton FC memorabilia ran down the middle of the street. The group reached the centre of Church Street between Marks and Spencer on one side and opposite the fashion store Next on the other, with the stalls in between.

Andy raised his loudhailer. 'Whoooaah,' he called as if reigning in a team of horses.

The dancing, shuffling musicians formed a circle with Andy at the centre.

'We are on the edge of catastrophe.' He declared.

'You're on the edge of my fucking pitch,' a stallholder shouted.

Andy moved the circle towards Marks and Spencer.

'Time is running out. The planet is warming. There is no time for half measures. No time for excuses. No time for words. We need action, and we need it now.'

The drummers provided a soundtrack and rhythm for Andy. Breaks in the speech were greeted with whoops, shrieks, and shaking hands. Andy lowered the megaphone, and a song began to go around the circle, its lyrics like a record stuck in a groove.

'The river is growing, flowing down to the sea
Nature can carry me,
A child I will always be.'

Matt stepped back from the circle. He held his sign but wasn't singing. Andy moved out of the centre and led the way further down Church Street. Emma appeared at Matt's side. 'Are you okay?'

'Yeah, fine, I'm not sure about this stuff.'

'What's the problem?'

The group moved slowly down the street, the gap between Matt, Emma, and the group widening.

'Like a river flowing? Carry me like a child to the sea? I am here to protest, not sing about being a fucking child. This isn't me. This is bollocks.'

Emma reached out and held Matt's arm. 'Please let the negative energy go. We are here with positivity to save the planet. It is the negative energy that is killing us.'

'It's not negative energy, it's pollution that's destroying the planet. And singing isn't going to stop it.' Matt moved his arm away, and Emma let go.

'Just wait. We can have a chat after the action.'

'What action?'

'We're moving on to Liverpool One. Come on, let's catch up.' Emma walked ahead, and Matt followed.

Liverpool One was five acres of new shopping and high-end retail development between Church Street, the old retail centre and the renovated Albert Dock on the River Mersey. Recently completed at the cost of billions, advertising hoardings proclaimed it the *North West's Premier Shopping Destination.*

Andy and the group reached the bottom of Church Street and turned left into Paradise Street. Five security guards emerged from among the shoppers and formed a semi-circle facing Andy. Matt and Emma caught up to the group.

'Hold up, mate.' The lead security guard had his hand out, palm facing Andy, and his other hand held a crackling radio. 'Where do you think you're going?'

'We are spreading the word on the destruction of the planet,' said Andy.

'Not here, you're not, mate. This part of the planet is private property.'

'We are non-violent and peaceful,' Andy said in his projected voice, speaking over the guard.

'Then you can peacefully turn around and go back the way you came, and you with the camera, no filming without permission.'

Julia lowered her camera.

Andy spoke for the benefit of the shoppers around them. 'We have the right of assembly and peaceful protest.'

'I guess you didn't hear me the first time. Not here, you don't. This is private property. This land does not belong to Liverpool Council. It's the property of the Westminster Group. You have no right to assemble or protest here.'

'The Westminster Group is owned by a duke.' Emma said. 'Are you telling me that he decides if we have the right to protest?'

'That's right, love, and the grand old Duke of York here...' he pointed at Andy, 'can march you lot back where you came from.'

Andy raised his megaphone and turned to address bystanders. 'More than half of all carbon releases ever, have been since 1990.' The drumbeats began quietly at first and built, in intensity, as Andy spoke. 'We are facing a national and international disaster. Human existence is threatened by climate change, and we've known this for decades. But it's not too late for bold action to prevent catastrophic temperature rises and ecological collapse. Join us! Help save the planet - planet before profit!' He turned and led the troupe back up Church Street.

When they reached the top, Matt turned to Emma. 'That was the action, was it?'

'What do you want? We are nonviolent, non-confrontational.'

'You might as well add non-existent. You need to have an effect and impact,' said Matt.

'You're right. We need to strategise. You should come to the meeting.'

'Where's that then?' The man in his thirties, wearing chino's and corduroy jacket, who had been at the rear of the group had sidled up to Emma. 'Where's the meeting?' he asked.

Emma gave him a quizzical look. 'Are you interested?'

'Yeah, of course,' he replied.

'It's in Saint Peters in Woolton. I don't know the exact address, but I will text it to you. Are you near Woolton? What's your name?'

'Simon. I'm in my car so, yeah, anywhere is good.' He held out his hand.

Emma shook it.

'Simon,' he repeated and extended his hand to Matt. 'Good to meet you, brother.'

'Whatever,' Matt replied.

Andy walked over. 'Hey.' He threw his dreadlocks over his shoulder. 'Didn't think we'd get onto Liverpool One, but it was worth a try.'

'Yeah, I guess,' said Matt.

'Are you coming to the meeting?' Andy directed his question to Simon.

'Yeah, definitely.'

Andy looked at Matt. 'And you?'

'Maybe,' Matt said.

Andy turned to Simon. 'Okay, mate, can you give us a minute? I need to speak to these guys.' He turned back to Emma and Matt. 'Maybe we can get a coffee?'

Matt was impressed with Andy's direct manner.

Emma walked off with Andy, leaving Matt and Simon together. Matt moved away from Simon and feigned interest in the football stall. Simon stood alone, waiting.

After they spoke to the group, Andy and Emma returned. 'Sorry, mate, who are you?' He asked Simon.

'Simon. I heard your protest. I think it's cool. I was saying to the girl, the woman-'

'Emma,' she interrupted.

'Yeah, Emma, I was saying we have to protect the earth.'

'That's great,' said Andy. 'I tell you what, you give me your number, and I'll text you the next meeting. You can come, meet everyone, and have a proper chat. How would that be?'

Simon smiled. 'Yeah, great.'

'The thing is, I need to speak to Matt, organisational stuff, really boring. You know what I mean?'

'Yeah, of course, no problem. I'll take your number,' said Simon.

Andy swiped his phone and displayed his number.

After taking it down, Simon said, 'Okay, great. I'll call you.' He raised his hand to Matt. 'I'll see you.'

Matt watched him walk away. When Simon reached the corner, he turned, looked back at Matt and waved again.

Matt ignored him.

'Come on, let's go.' Andy led the way. 'Did you know that guy?'

'No, he came up when me and Matt were talking,' said Emma.

'You got rid of him pretty quick,' said Matt.

'Yeah, he's probably genuine, but you never know.'

'Know what?' Matt asked.

'Undercover coppers,' said Emma.

'Or just creeping over Emma,' said Andy.

'Isn't that a bit paranoid?' Matt asked.

'No. They've admitted it.' Emma said, 'The police, I mean. They had something called the Special Demonstration Squad. They were doing it for years. Undercover cops even had kids with women in the movement, did all kinds, for years.'

'How do you know I'm not?' Matt gave Andy a quizzical look.

'What, a cop?' Andy smiled, 'Too young, too cynical.' He changed the subject. 'Let's go to Organic. Is that okay with you?'

'Sure.' Matt didn't know what it was, but it sounded harmless.

~

They walked up Church Street, this time merging with the shoppers, a part of the ebb and flow of humanity in the town centre on Saturdays. The sky had darkened and a greyness swept in from the river and slowly covered the land. At the bottom of Bold Street, they passed the side entrance of Central Station. Matt looked down as he always did, drawn by the image of people disappearing into a void.

Organic was a cafe. The development of Liverpool One had a knock-on effect of damaging retail in the rest of the town centre. Bold Street was once the main shopping area, but time had taken developments downhill and back to the river's edge.

In Bold Street, whispers of the past survived. A few hand-painted shop signs from its post-war heyday. It was now home to the second string retail, cafes, independent bookshops, craft stores, and the newly trendy second-hand furniture and clothes.

Matt noticed the physical ease of Andy and Emma, the light touches and quick looks; he assumed they were an item.

They ordered and collected drinks from the counter and found a table near the window. Andy launched into his spiel. 'What I said on the street is true. I don't say this stuff because it sounds shocking or to win people over or wake them up. I said it because it's true. Our world is dying, and we need to do something to stop it. That's the bottom line, and you are either with us or against us on that.' Andy took a drink of fair-trade organic coffee and sat back.

'I'm with you that things have to change. That we are destroying our ability to live on the planet.' Matt paused and knew this would wind both up a bit, but he had to say it. 'We are not destroying the planet. The planet will survive. It might be uninhabitable for us, but it will still exist as a spinning entity.'

'That's true, but that's not the point, is it? We have to get people to wake up,' said Emma.

'It is the point because if people don't believe you - if they think you are exaggerating, they won't accept anything else you are saying.'

'Ninety-five percent of scientists agree-'

'I know, I'm not disagreeing with you.' Matt said, 'I'm saying that presenting it as the planet itself is dying, when that is factually untrue, doesn't help convince people you are not hyperventilating hippies. The singing and dancing?' Matt lifted his hands in exasperation.

'It's expressing ourselves,' said Emma.

'Yeah, whatever,' said Matt.

'No, come on, what are you suggesting?' Andy leaned forward, ready to hear Matt out.

'I don't know, but there has to be something more we can do. It shouldn't be about expressing ourselves. We're here to win people. No, not just win people, win the struggle. Stop the destruction of our environment.'

Emma clapped. 'Oh… my… God, we need you, Matt. We need someone with fresh ideas, not afraid to challenge things. You have to come to the meetings.' She leaned across the table and put her hand on his.

'Yeah, mate, we want you involved.' Andy added, less effusively. He looked around before adding. 'Things are gonna change, mate; get serious. We've been discussing new strategies.'

'Let me think about it,' said Matt.

~

Matt walked down Bold Street. He was on edge. If he went to the meeting, he would be getting involved. Everything around him was tangible and real; the shops, the pavement, the people, the cars, the buses. All of that. Could he really affect it? Change it? Change how people thought and acted?

A group of girls came out of an accessory shop. One opened a bag and snapped a glittery cat into her hair. Her friends admired it and the group moved on. Matt knew that next they'd be buying a t-shirt or skirt made in Bangladesh, or a new phone case made in China. Was this what society had come to? Glittery plastic shit made by kids for other kids to buy? He didn't want to be like Andy and Emma, making a lifestyle choice to claim moral superiority but achieving nothing more than self-satisfaction.

His stomach sank, and he felt like shit as he mumbled, 'Sorry, mate,' to a homeless guy next to the station entrance.

He dropped his money into the ticket machine and thought he saw a familiar face in its polished reflection. *The guy from the protest?* He turned around but couldn't see him. Matt followed the stream down the escalators, shoppers leaving town, arms full of their spoils, football supporters arriving in red and blue. Matt thought of bread and circuses.

The train drew into the station and he climbed aboard. He chose a window seat. In forty minutes, he would be home.

The train began to fill, the doors closed and it started to move.

Wait. Matt turned his head, and there he was again, on the platform: the weird guy from the protest. He told Emma he was driving. There was no question it was him this time. *Did Simon follow me into the station? Maybe he's going the same way? Then why didn't he get on?* They made eye contact before Simon ducked behind a pillar. *What the hell is he up to?*

CHAPTER FIVE

PAUL

Wednesday, January 8th, 2020.

Paul's uniform was dry cleaned and hung in its plastic shroud. The iron was heating and he could wait. Patience was a virtue until the time to act, and then precision, timing, speed and force combined to produce victory - in any field of endeavour.

The light on the iron flashed. He raised the hot steel and felt the searing heat. He brought it closer. He could smell the danger, feel it close to his flesh; the hot air stung his nostrils. He turned it on its side and spat. The splat of saliva bubbled and hissed. It was ready. His shirt lay stretched over the ironing board, newly washed and pristine. He smoothed it with his hand, pure white cotton.

He looked at where his saliva landed. It had evaporated and was now a faint grey tinge. How completely things could vanish, the solid could turn to air and the real become unreal. Everything in God's world was transitory because He made it so. Life was the most transitory gift of all.

He laid the iron flat on the cloth and let it glide. It smoothed away the wrinkles and memory of folds. All the lines and creases disappeared. What remained was pure, clean, smooth, white cotton.

That was his role, his purpose, to remove the wrinkles, clear away the creases, and apply heat until nothing but a pristine surface remained.

'You know I can do your ironing for you.' Mrs Taylor watched as Paul stood in the centre of the living room.

'Thank you, Mum, but a man should be responsible and in control of his own life.' His consciousness was heightened as the events of the previous day coursed through his veins. He didn't need to remember or think. The muscle memory and the sensations flowed through him like electricity, constant and energising.

'I was only offering to do your ironing, that's all,' Mrs Taylor raised her teacup to her lips. 'Someone's going to be a very lucky lady when they get you for a husband.'

'No time for that. There's work to be done.'

'I know, dear, but don't you forget about yourself now. Every man needs a good woman, and every woman a good man.' She licked her lips to remove the tea droplets. She would typically follow with talk about his father, who was now sitting on the right hand of Jesus and deservedly so, as one of the most god-fearing, upright men to have walked the city's streets. It was a source of consolation in her empty days to know he was seated with the Lord.

Paul was comfortable with the mood music of her devotion. It made the house a special place of retreat.

He stepped out into the grey January day and closed the front door. The air was damp. He was buffeted by the wind, and heard a high-pitched squeak, the sound of a squeezed rubber ball. He looked down. In the corner, behind a drainpipe, was a kitten, a tiny black thing with matted wet fur, closed into itself out of fear. Away from its mother, it was terrified.

It squealed again. Paul turned and headed up towards Park Road, the busy main road dissecting the area. The streets were narrow, Victorian two up two downs, modernised to include bathrooms. The roads ran downhill from Park Road to the river, or the docks that once lined its banks. Housing developments and boutique hotels now dominated the riverside, where dockers once waited for work, huddled against the cold and rain. The cobbled streets now warehoused the city's professional class, instead of cotton and barrels. Mercedes and BMWs now waited in line.

Paul walked up, away from the Mersey. Beyond Park Road, everything opened into the wider plateau of Liverpool Eight, home to the multiracial community that had existed in Liverpool for centuries. The streets of what was now celebrated as The Georgian Quarter led to Hope Street Police Station, his base of operations. He swiped his ID and registered to enter the building.

He was already in uniform, so there was no need to change, but he went into the changing room to lock his jacket away.

'Shit's hitting the fan about yesterday.' PC Martin was getting changed.

'Bound to, but everything was by the book. Not down to us if the guy had a dodgy ticker.'

PC Martin clipped on his tie. 'IOPC will be down on this like a ton of bricks.'

'Stop worrying,' said Paul. 'Paperwork, and bureaucracy. They've got to look like they're doing something.'

'I hope you're right because if you think I'm risking my career for you, you've got another thing coming.'

'Stop panicking. What did I tell you? Everything by the book. If... there's an inquiry, it'll be for show. I'm not asking anything from you.' Paul slammed his locker shut. He walked to the door, stopped, and turned. 'But it's good to know who's side you are on.' He marched through the corridors to the stairs and took them two at a time to the second floor. He knocked and opened the door. 'He's expecting me.'

'He is, but you can wait.' The Chief Superintendent's secretary indicated the chairs opposite her desk.

He removed his helmet and sat. She pressed a button on her desk and started typing. Paul guessed she was letting the boss know he was waiting.

In the antechamber of the Lord, waiting would be longer for those impure in spirit. Purgatory was not for him. He would ascend in the rapture after the Lord returned to the Earth to lead His army against the forces of darkness.

'You can go in.' The secretary broke his reverie. 'Sergeant Taylor...'

'Yes?'

'You can go in.'

'Of course. Thank You.' Paul crossed the office, knocked, then opened the door and entered. He strode the short distance to stand in front of the Chief Super's desk.

'Wait there, please.' The voice was calm, measured and in control. When Paul looked, all he could see were the signs of power, the pips and crown on his epaulettes.

Paul saluted. His salute was acknowledged.

'Superintendent Johnson will be joining us.'

'Of course, Sir.'

Superintendent Johnson entered the room a few seconds later, his cap tucked under his arm.

'I have your report from the incident yesterday.' The Chief began.

'Yes, Sir,' said Paul.

Superintendent Johnson intervened, 'Is this a full and accurate statement?'

'Of course, Sir.'

The Chief leaned back in his chair. 'We will have to issue a referral to the Independent Office for Police Conduct.'

'Why…Sir?' Paul looked between the two officers, conscious of their disdain.

'Because there has been a death in our custody.'

'Everything was done according to the book, sir. I swear on the bible.'

'You'll have plenty of time for that later. For now, you are being suspended from duty on full pay. You will be notified of the requirements of the IOPC.'

'That's not fair... Sir... in God's name...'

'You do realise a young man has died? Do you understand the seriousness of this situation?'

'Of course, Sir. But, if I may, the target was a known agitator-'

The Chief slammed the papers down. 'Are you stupid?'

Paul stiffened.

'It does not matter who the deceased is or was. It is you and your actions that will be under the microscope. I suggest you spend your time making sure you have all your Is dotted and Ts crossed. Check and recheck your report and paperwork. If something is wrong, correct it now before the IOPC arrive. Do you understand me?'

'Yes, Sir.'

'Good, collect your belongings, leave your warrant card here and be ready to respond as soon as you are contacted. Is that clear?'

'Sir.'

Superintendent Johnson shook his head. 'I should've known.'

'Sir?'

'You... sanctimonious... self-righteous, do you think you are the only Christian in this station? What gives you the right to lecture and judge others? Go on, out.'

'Yes, Sir.' Paul spun on his heels and left the office.

In the corridor outside, he looked left and right, turned and then gave a sign of benediction to the office and officers he'd left behind.

~

'Back so soon?' PC Martin was buttoning his jacket.

'Formalities, IOPC has been called in.' Paul turned his key in the locker door.

PC Martin turned to leave. 'Told you,'.

'Like I said, a formality.' Paul pulled out his jacket and waited till PC Martin left the changing room before he slammed the locker door.

As he walked through the station, he felt his colleagues' eyes following him. He walked tall and proud, even a little slower than usual. He wasn't afraid of the scrutiny. He savoured it. His time was coming, he could sense it, feel it, and the events of the last few days had only confirmed it for him.

He left the station for home. He didn't take the most direct route; he wanted to enjoy the fresh chill in the air. The traffic and its emissions couldn't harm him, and he didn't hear the noise, didn't taste the fumes. He passed through streets he owned without fear, without consequence. Other people were barely present. They dodged and moved aside. He was the force around which all entities spun. Jesus was with him and in him. His pace was brisk, and he enjoyed it. The inquiry would do what it did. He didn't care. The death was not on his conscience. If God wanted him to live, He would have breathed life into him. He didn't, and so he died.

He turned the key in the lock on his front door and heard the squeal again.

'Still here?'

He bent down. It was a miserable creature, tiny and weak, its fur hanging in clumps, and it shivered with the cold and damp. It must have sensed his presence as its cries and meows increased in volume. It was begging for its life.

Paul lifted it. 'May God's mercy be upon all creatures.'

His step-father had provided the house before he was taken from life. A heart attack at a young age had removed him from Paul's world. His mum was left comfortable and able to provide for Paul's physical needs. They had adopted him at the age of thirteen from Paradise, a huge house in Crosby, away from the city. Dozens of boys were looked after for months or years when families were going through problems, difficulties that paled beside those inflicted by the carers within the home.

'You're early,' Mrs Taylor cried out from the kitchen as he entered the living room.

'Yeah, shift change,' he lied, 'special assignment.'

'Shall I do you some lunch? I was about to put your laundry

in, but it can wait. I've changed the bed linen. How about an omelette? I've got some fresh mushrooms. Would you like that?'

'Thank you. That would be fine. Could I have a glass of milk with it?' He turned and walked into the hallway, his steps silent on the carpeted stairs. The shivering body in his hand was quiet now.

Mrs Taylor shouted from the kitchen, 'I'll leave it outside your door when it's done. You get some rest.'

Paul closed then locked his bedroom door. He put the kitten on the floor, rummaged through his drawer, found an old jumper, and made a makeshift bed. He removed his shoes, took off his jacket, removed his tie, and then his shirt. He was disrobing, removing the uniform of the state. He was comfortable in it because it brought power and status in the physical world. In boxer shorts and a vest, he sat in an armchair next to the bed.

He closed his eyes and remembered an earlier time. He could feel the weight of the body. He remembered how it swayed and swung as he carried it to the van. When the body was secure in the van, he applied the bite guard. Other officers held the man's arms and legs; Paul was at his head.

He released and tightened the guard to allow him to breathe. The snorting and spit were expelled as the chest and lungs heaved. He controlled the flow, allowing for the movement of the van, the struggles of the body. He sat in the dark and let the feeling of power return…

Then he remembered an earlier time, his face pressed down into the blankets, the weight on his back, he remembered when the power was used to control him and with the memory his tears flowed. In the dark of night, among the silence of sleeping bodies, he was held... he was pressed... he was forced.

'Your omelette is outside, fresh mushrooms, just how you like. Don't let it get cold now.'

CHAPTER SIX

CHARLIE

Thursday, January 9th, 2020.

Charlie walked past Central Station. Some placards from earlier in the week were discarded in a corner. Like the speaker he saw arrested, their appeal was now silent. The words of the copper "*Fuck off or you're next*" still echoed. Charlie guessed he was the last non-police contact the guy had. He died in Charlie's eyes, not his arms. Instead of going home to his life, he was transported to a police station and death. Charlie carried on. *This is stupid. None of my business.*

He didn't know what he expected. The radio said there was a protest outside Hope St Police Station where the twenty-three-year-old had died. *The same age as me.*

He was due to meet his mate Terry in the pub but was now heading in a different direction.

The quickest way to Hope Street was up Bold Street and past the bombed-out church. Four roofless gothic walls were all that was left of St Luke's, a memorial to the bombing of Liverpool in 1941 that left thousands homeless. There had been no bombings recently but homeless people dotted the route. They were indistinguishable if he didn't look closely, so he didn't.

Buses and cars filled the street with sound, movement and fumes-evening rush hour. He trudged up Hardman Street, with every step getting closer to Liverpool's Universities and the cafes, kebab shops and pubs that served their students. Before turning the corner into Hope Street, a scratchy amplified voice reached him. 'We want justice and truth for Matt. No cover-up! No lies! Justice for Matt!'

Around twenty people milled about in front of the police station.

A woman approached Charlie. Her hair was tied in a bun on top and she had one strand of bright blue among the blonde. 'Will you sign our petition, please?'

'What is it?'

She was attractive, in a hippy student way. 'We want an investigation into the death in police custody on Monday. I don't know if you heard…'

'Yeah, that's why I'm here.' Charlie took the petition from her. 'I saw him being arrested.' The next question was difficult. 'How did he die?'

The woman led Charlie away from the centre of the pavement. She spoke softly. 'His family have been told it was a heart attack. Nothing is official yet, there will have to be a coroner's report, maybe even an autopsy. I'm not sure.'

'A heart attack? He was a young guy.'

'Twenty-three, and yeah.' A tear slid out of her eye and she moved quickly to brush it away.

'I'm sorry.' Charlie reached out instinctively to touch her arm. 'I guess you knew him?'

'Yeah. Thanks, and no, don't be. Sorry, I mean. Come over. I'll introduce you to some people.'

'I'm not sure...' Charlie moved back. 'I don't know why I'm here.'

She reached out and held his arm. 'I do.' For a second, her eyes met and held his.

He looked away, embarrassed. 'You do?'

'Yes... solidarity.'

'What's that?' It was a serious question, but she ignored it.

'My name's Emma.' She held out her hand. 'Nice to meet you.' Her smile was sad but engaging.

'I'm Charlie.' He wanted to know her.

'Let me introduce you to Andy,' she turned and led Charlie to the guy with the megaphone.

Charlie wondered if it was the same loudhailer the dead guy used. Across the road from the police station, people were arriving at the Philharmonic Concert Hall. A series of taxis dropped passengers at regular intervals, most in evening attire. Suits and black ties for men and evening dresses for women. The busy road separated the two disparate groups. Andy appealed to them over the megaphone while petitioners moved between the concertgoers asking for signatures.

'Hey,' Andy, lowered the megaphone.

'Charlie was there,' said Emma. 'He saw Matt get arrested.'

'Matt? That was his name?' Charlie asked.

Emma nodded.

'You're a witness,' Andy said.

Charlie took a step back. 'I guess so. I'm not really sure I saw much, though.' As he said this, an image came of the copper's knee in Matt's back and his face pressed into the ground. 'Yeah, I was there.'

'Are you going to be a witness? Get his name and address,' Andy said to Emma.

'I'm not sure,' said Charlie.

'You can't let them get away with it.' Andy threw his words at Charlie like a challenge.

'Yeah, I know, but...' Charlie didn't like being pushed around.

Andy raised the megaphone into Charlie's face. 'No justice! No peace! No lies. No cover-up. Investigate the police.'

Charlie winced. *What the fuck.*

Andy turned again and spoke to growing number of concert-goers across the street.

Confused, Charlie took a step back. 'What was that?' he asked Emma.

'He's just upset about Matt. We all are.' She moved away from Andy and pulled out her phone. 'Here.'

A cameraman and reporter hurried towards the group.

Emma held her phone up with the number displayed. Charlie rang her to make sure the connection was made.

The reporter reached them. 'Can we speak to someone about the protest?'

Andy brushed past Charlie towards the reporter. Charlie moved further away and walked off.

'Wait!' Emma shouted.

He turned to face her.

'Are you okay?' she asked.

'Yeah, fine.' He wasn't comfortable at the protest.

Emma kept eye contact longer than was necessary, and Charlie felt its warmth. 'I'll call you,' she turned away.

For the second time that week, a look had stopped Charlie dead.

She was pretty. Blonde hair framed a round face with no sharp lines. As she walked away, Charlie was bereft; her presence had energy and connection, and he recognised its loss. 'Wait!' he called out.

She turned and headed back.

He didn't know where the question came from. 'Why do you need me? The other people can give statements.'

'If they were at the protest, they'll be seen as partisan. You're independent, objective.'

It sounded like praise, and he felt good.

'Move.'

He was shoved in the back and fell forward into Emma. Her eyes widened in fear and she held onto him. They were pushed to the side as police officers in riot gear rushed past them.

The police formed two lines on the pavement in front of the police station, creating a corridor to the entrance. Andy and the band of protesters were on the other side of the police lines. Emma was still holding onto Charlie on the other.

'Can we get through?' Emma asked an officer.

His reply was curt. 'No.'

'I thought I told you to fuck off.' A look of recognition passed between Charlie and the copper who pushed his shield forward.

'Come on, move back.' Charlie pulled Emma to the back of the group. 'He was one of the police there on Monday morning.' He told me to fuck off or I'd be next.' Charlie looked around.

'Does he know who you are?'

'No. Why would he?'

'That's crazy,' said Emma.

Charlie saw a group of people coming toward him. They had all the equipment of those on the other side of the police lines; placards, a banner and at the front with a megaphone was the mixed race woman who told him who Eric Garner was. She stopped when they reached him.

'What's going on?'

'The police have just come out. You were at work... the other day?'

'You two know each other?' asked Emma.

'I'm Amina,' she answered.

'You told me who Eric Garner was,' Charlie said.

Amina looked straight at Charlie. 'Tamir Rice. Mark Brown. Philando Castile in the USA. In the UK, Joy Gardner, Mark Duggan. And here in Liverpool, Mohammed Mzee. A few of the Black people who've died at the hands of the police. And yes, Eric Garner.' Amina's voice was clear, her gaze direct. She had an energy that nearly knocked him over. Charlie didn't know what to say.

'Look for Andy. He's the organiser,' said Emma.

'I will.' Amina said to Emma, but she was looking at Charlie as she moved past him, followed by five youths.

As they moved toward the police lines, Amina's voice was soon ringing out across the street. 'No Justice! No Peace!' She was at the front, Charlie could just see her among the moving heads, she had turned away from the police and raised her megaphone to address the protesters.

The crowd was getting bigger, louder, and the pushing and shoving at the front more intense. The police had been using shields to smash into protesters. Amina was pushed in the back, she held her ground and continued speaking. He lost sight of her, but saw an officer draw his baton.

'Shit!' Charlie surged forward pushing his way through. He reached the front as the metal baton flashed through the air. Charlie shoved his arm out and took the full force of the blow before crashing into Amina.

'Fuck!'

Someone grabbed the baton and was stopping it being raised to hit again. Amina pushed Charlie and the crowd parted to let them through. Amina was supporting him now. His right arm hung down at his side.

'Are you okay?' she asked when they were clear.

'Fuck, that hurt.' Charlie raised his arm gingerly.

Emma joined them, 'How bad is it?'

'He'll live.' Amina said, 'What the hell were you doing?' Her eyes met his and he saw fire in them.

'Come on, we need to get you out of here.' Emma guided Charlie away from the protest. They crossed the busy road and stood outside the Philharmonic pub. Emma's phone beeped and she swiped to unlock it. Her fingers danced over the screen. Charlie was still thinking of Amina.

'You shouldn't go back. I've told Andy we'll meet him at the hub. We can look at your arm there. What happened?' she asked.

Charlie winced as he raised his arm, 'I don't know. I saw the baton and panicked.'

They were on the corner of Hardman and Hope St. Charlie looked toward the Catholic cathedral known as 'Paddy's wigwam'. He nodded. 'Which end are you?'

It took Emma a minute to understand. She pointed toward the Anglican Cathedral at the other end of the street. The two cathedrals were emblematic of the dualities within the city; red or blue, black or white. In this case, orange or green differences always present. At least in this case they were joined by Hope Street.

'My parents, though, not me.'

'Same here,' said Charlie. 'Parents, that is, we're this end.' He indicated the Catholic Cathedral.

The chants of the protest echoed through the streets. Charlie looked for Amina, he couldn't see her now, but knew he would see her again.

~

Emma led the way towards the river, down Duke Street. Charlie followed her past the battered shop fronts and old warehouses. The Baltic Triangle was between the town centre and The Dingle was so called from the timber yards and warehouses of Norwegian wood that once filled the area. Liverpool was finally coming to terms with its history, and Jamaica St that ran through the Baltic was a reminder of the gold than ran through traders fingers' from sugar and slaves.

Charlie had tramped these streets behind his dad, who conducted historical walking tours. Greenland Street linked Liverpool to the most powerful beasts of the sea, as whales were landed, decapitated, and processed. Blood filled the gutters as blubber, meat and bones filled the workshops. Walking this area in its heyday would have been to dice with death, as ropes and nets swung high above the carters and horses filling the streets below. The murder and mayhem hadn't disappeared but power and time had shifted it.

The modern Baltic was the city's new arts and design centre. Digital startups, bars, and cafes breathed new life into the warren of streets. Retro bars and raves were springing up, adding a new page to the area's long story. Behind Duke street, they turned into Henry Street, a cobbled street framed by run down warehouses one side, and modern box workshops on the other. At the end of the street The Pagoda a community centre marked the area as home to the historic Chinese Community.

'This way.' Emma pulled aside a tarpaulin sheet, revealing an opening in the metal fence. They walked around the edge of the wall, turning into a gap between it and the next building.

Charlie looked up and was surprised to see walkways connecting the two. Emma raised a boarded-up window frame, ducking so they could enter through the bottom half. She let it drop after Charlie got in.

'Is this legal?' Charlie asked.

'We're squatting. They need a court order to get us out.'

The walls had been whitewashed at some time in the past. The large windows, boarded at the ground level but still glazed above, let the light in, creating an unlikely bright space. Music drifted down the stone staircase Emma led them to. The solidity, space, and expanse of the building were impressive.

On the first level was an open central area with several sofas and armchairs. The walls were covered with a combination of half-formed murals of varying skill and graffiti. Against the wall on one side, a line of tables held desktop computers and printers.

~

'We've got a first aid kit somewhere.' Emma began searching. 'Organisation maybe not always our strong point.'

Charlie took off his jacket raised his sleeve. 'Not much a first aid kit can do for this.'

Emma joined him. 'That looks nasty.'

His arm was swollen in a diagonal line, and shades of purple and blue were spread across it.

'Can you move your wrist... fingers?'

'Yeah.'

'It doesn't look broken, but it might be fractured, you should go to the hospital. Get an X-ray.'

'I'll survive.' Charlie shook his head. 'Fucking bastards though.'

'What do you think happened?' Charlie asked.

'With Matt?'

'Yeah, a heart attack, really?' He was processing the names Amina had quoted. He guessed they were Black but Matt wasn't.

'I don't know; stress, restraints, maybe he couldn't breathe, who knows? I mean, at this point, we don't know anything. He could've been beaten up, suffocated.' There was pause before she asked. 'So, you came for the protest?'

'Yeah. I think I needed to know who he was. I'm not sure...'

'Matt was a good guy. He hadn't been around that long, just the last three months, really, but he had a big impact.'

'How do you mean?'

'In our group, he knew what he wanted. He was quiet if you spoke to him, but he wanted change. And more than anyone else I have ever met, he knew how to get it. He had a strategy, not for protest but for social change. We do things differently as a group because of him. For a quiet guy, he really made a difference.'

Charlie was shaking his head. 'He shouldn't have died like that.' At the time, he had subconsciously made the connection with Eric Garner. Now, Amina had started to fill in the picture. 'Eric Garner... was strangled, or choked by police in the States for selling loosies.'

'Loosies?'

'Single ciggies. It's fucked up.' After a few seconds of silence, he asked. 'What do you study?'

'You're sure I'm a student?'

'A guess.' Charlie was pretty sure he was right.

'Geography. Development and resource management, including our response to climate change.'

'Do you like it?'

'No, I hate it, actually. It's a constant reminder of how we are fucking the world up. It's important, and I'm glad I'm doing it, but I can't really say I enjoy it.'

He nodded.

'What about you?'

'I work. Really crap, for an agency in town. Been there since before Christmas. But we'll probably get finished this week.'

'What will you do then?'

'I don't know. I'll have to see where they send me, if anywhere. I can't get benefits because I live with my parents.'

'Are you going to make a statement to the police?'

'I don't know.'

'Hey.'

Charlie heard a voice behind him.

Emma greeted Andy as he joined them. 'How did it go?'

'Good. The railworkers Matt knew turned up. I did an interview on TV. The reporter said she thought The IOPC would be called in.'

'Who's that?' Charlie asked.

'Police complaints' said Andy. 'Don't put any faith in them, but it's part of getting the story out. But you should definitely give a statement,' said Andy.

'He is,' Emma said.

Charlie didn't respond. Andy was pretty full of himself.

'Did you see they guys from L8?' Andy asked.

'Yeah, Charlie knew them.'

'Really? They were good. Loud and well organised.'

'I kinda know one of them,' Charlie said.

'She looked like the leader,' Emma added.

Andy ignored Emma and moved beyond the computers. 'Here, let me show you what we do.' Charlie followed him. 'Our own screen printing setup. Pretty basic, but it works.' As proof, the walls in this area were covered with posters, crude but effective messaging and imagery. 'Come on, look.' Andy lead the way upstairs to the third floor, crossed the main room and stepped out of a full-height window onto one of the walkways Charlie had seen from below. 'This is our escape route if we get raided.'

Emma motioned Charlie forward. 'Have a look.'

Charlie crossed the room. Avoiding metal studs that dotted the floor, he stepped through the window. He had to duck. The cast-iron window frame was held in place by a piece of wood wedged in the frame. One pull on this and the window would crash down.

'Careful,' Andy said as if reading Charlie's mind. 'Don't knock the wood.'

'What is this?' Charlie looked down over the railing to the alley below.

'We can kick in the door. It's usually open but stiff. I won't do it now because we need it to look completely closed. But, with a kick, we can get through that building and back out onto the street. A pull on the wood, and anyone chasing has to get the window open before they can follow us.'

'I mean, why the walkway here?' He stamped his foot, and the cast iron rang out.

'Careful,' Andy said. 'It's a bit dodgy in places. These are old warehouses, they moved stuff from one building to the other and lowered stuff down onto carts below. Clever though, eh?'

Charlie climbed back through the window.

Emma was waiting. 'The hope is everyone can get out before the police start to arrest people.'

'Not hope.' Said Andy. 'Hope is the enemy of action. Good planning.'

Emma didn't respond.

'Yeah, impressive,' Charlie lied. 'It looks like you've got a lot going on. But...I've really got to get going. Got mates waiting for me in the pub.'

Andy stood, arms folded. 'Well, when you want to take control of your life, you know where we are.'

'Sure thing.'

'Emma will show you the way back down.' Andy walked off.

'Come on.' Emma pulled his good arm.

~

Back on the ground floor, Charlie took a deep breath. 'Look, sorry, I hope you don't mind me asking. Are you and Andy an item?'

Emma smiled. 'We're poly.'

'Oh, right.'

'I'll call you,' Emma turned back toward the stairs, as Charlie climbed out of the ground floor window.

When Charlie climbed through the fence, he knew he was leaving behind a world that wasn't his. As he crossed into Bold St and made his way to Central Station, two questions were on his mind. *What the fuck is poly*? *How can I find Amina?*

CHAPTER SEVEN

MATTHEW

October, 2019 - The Meeting.

The entrance to the meeting hall was through the churchyard. Matt had to pass under the lychgate that protected the entrance to the cemetry. The impressive wooden and slate structure had a cross mounted on the top. Wealthy businessmen had built Saint Peter's Anglican church in the middle-class suburb of Woolton. It hardly seemed an appropriate location for the cradle of a climate revolution.

'Hey, good to see you?' Andy greeted Matt.

Matt nodded and added a general wave to others in the room.

Emma approached him. 'Glad you could make it.'

The white walls and high vaulted timber ceiling created a feeling of space and freedom. Voices carried and bounced off the sandstone walls.

'We'll be starting soon,' said Emma.

Matt held her eyes until she looked away. A couple of people were arranging chairs. Julia, who he'd met in town, organised the tea at a table to the side.

'What shall I do?' asked Matt.

'Nothing, we've got it covered,' said Andy.

Matt looked around the room. Most of the people at the event in town the previous week were there. More people arrived and took their seats. Simon walked over from the back of the room.

'Hi.'

'You remember Simon?' Andy asked.

'Yeah.' Matt stared straight at Simon, looking for something, not sure what.

'Your first time, too?' said Simon.

Matt ignored him.

Emma and Andy traded glances.

'Can you give us a hand with the chairs?' Andy asked Simon.

'Yeah, anything to help,' Simon looked directly at Matt.

Matt turned away to Emma. 'What's happening tonight?'

'Andy will give a talk, introducing the group for new people. That okay for you?'

Matt shrugged. He didn't reply because the question was stupid. What if it wasn't okay? He walked over to the side table, where Julia was preparing tea.

'Cuppa?' she asked.

'Yeah, why not.' Matt looked at a painting on the wall behind her: four young figures, two sitting, two standing. The painting was adequate but with nothing to make it exceptional.

Julia turned. 'The famous meeting.'

'What meeting?'

'You mean; you don't know?'

'No. Should I?'

'Of course, you should.' Julia's mock outrage and pained expression forced a half-smile from Matt.

'John Lennon and Paul McCartney met in this very hall on the 6th July 1957, the start of a revolution in music.' Julia pulled the lever on the tea urn, and a steady stream of a brown liquid filled the cup. She put it on a saucer and handed it to him.

'Thanks.'

'You're welcome, young man. You're new to the group?'

'Yeah, a bit. I saw you in town.'

'You're not so impressed, are you?'

Matt pulled a face. 'Just a bit embarrassing. No offence, but the singing, whooping...' He rolled his eyes.

'Hah, I know what you mean. Look at me... an old lady who should know better. I should be in my twin set and pearls, and here I am, looking like a hippy chick.'

Matt smiled.

'We're all a bit ridiculous. The key is recognising it, and...' She looked around furtively. 'Not giving a shit.'

Matt liked her. 'The other thing that gets me, though, is all this talk that things are sacred... moral... like it's a cult or crusade or something.'

'It is,' Julia said 'Here's milk and sugar.'

'What?'

'The milk and sugar are here.'

'No, you said, *It is.*'

'Well, in the sense of a group, cut off from the rest of society, with its own language and norms. We're in our own little world. Yeah, we are a bit of a cult. The only thing missing is a charismatic leader. The speakers I've seen have less charisma than my old dog, and she stinks. It's not her fault she has a stomach disorder, but the results, phew.' Julia waved a hand in front of her nose.

'If you think that, why are you here?'

'What choice have we got? I've got five grandkids. I don't want the planet to be destroyed. These are good people, and at least they are doing something.'

'Singing in town?' Matt raised his eyebrows.

'The truth is, I'm too old to be embarrassed - embarrassment no longer exists in my world. If these people need to sing, whoop and scream, then so be it. That, my boy, is the source of our power.'

'Your power comes from not being embarrassed?'

'In a way, yes. We don't care what people think. That's what makes us so powerful. How's your tea?'

Matt took a sip. 'Good, thanks.'

He liked her approach; he thought it more honest and realistic than the warnings of doom and appeals to heroism.

When he turned back to the centre of the hall, a circle of chairs had been drawn up and Andy was about to lead things off.

'If you have something to say, then don't hold back,' Julia said.

'Yeah, maybe,' he said. He took a seat.

Andy called out. 'Okay, can we get together? Thanks to everyone who took part in our recent outing in the town centre. Although we didn't quite manage to get onto Liverpool One, we did have an impact and raise awareness. So, if you were there, give yourself a clap. And if you weren't there, how about showing some support for those who did make it.'

The room applauded itself.

When the noise died down, Andy continued, 'And as a result of Saturday's activities, we have two new friends. Let's welcome Simon, here, who was inspired by that action to join Earthquake, our affinity group with Extinction Revolution, and a big welcome to Matt, another new face.'

The second round of applause echoed through the hall. Simon acknowledged the clapping by raising his hand. 'Thank you. We have to protect Mother Earth.'

'Indeed, we do,' said Andy. 'As everyone here knows, at the current rate of C02 emissions, we have twelve years to limit climate change before irreversible decline sets in. Before we pass ecological trigger points. If we can't keep the increase in global warming below one point five degrees, we set in train a disaster for humanity from which there will be no return.

'Make no mistake; we are talking about the end of civilization. We are already at one degree above pre-industrial temperatures. We have a moral responsibility. We have a duty, a *sacred* duty, to save this planet. We hold the future in our hands, in *our* hands.' He raised his hands. 'What we decide determines the future of the planet because no one else is going to save it. No one, not the politicians, not the media, no one. So, are you ready to protest?'

Various volumes of 'Yes' rang out. Matt shifted in his seat and didn't respond.

'Amen,' Simon said.

'Are you ready to put the planet first?' Andy's voice became more strident.

'Yes.'

'Are you ready to save the planet from dying?'

'Yes.'

Andy focused on Matt. 'Then you are in the right place. We are the warriors. We are the saviours. We are the people who can and will save the planet.'

'Matt, are you ready to save the planet?'

'Sorry?' Matt was genuinely surprised by the question.

'Of course, he is,' said Emma. 'We all are.'

'Are you ready to save the planet?' Andy repeated, looking directly at Matt.

'The planet is not dying,' Matt said. He didn't want to make a scene, but he wouldn't allow that statement to pass.

Emma sighed. Andy raised his voice. 'We need people who are committed to put the planet first, not their careers or their social circle, but the fight against climate change. Because if we don't have a planet, what do we have? Would you like to say something, Matt? Don't worry, we are all friends here.'

'Go on.' Julia urged from behind the tea table.

Matt stood and spoke in a clear, if monotone, voice. 'The problem you've got is that if politicians aren't going to combat climate change, then it's not going to happen. You can argue the system needs to change or the politicians are no use; but the acceleration of climate change will only be stopped by governmental and universal action. It will not be stopped by individual choices or minority actions, however imaginative or creative.' He paused to let his words sink in. 'I told Andy the planet won't die, so we can't save it. The planet is an aggregation of physical and chemical elements. It doesn't live, so can't die. It doesn't care if temperatures destroy the ability of humans to live on it. The point is, if we want to *save* society, then we have to *change* society.'

He shook his head as he looked through the audience of concerned boomers with a few Gen Z scattered about. 'The system is set up for private use and control of natural resources. It can only produce private solutions to public dangers. Governments must constrain private industry, set the parameters that society demands. Until we show how illogical it is to have private control of all these resources, we will not be able to seriously impact the growing environmental crisis. The bottom line is; you guys have to decide whose side you're on. What's more important: profit, or humanity? If it's humanity, then join with the only people fighting profit; organised workers.' Matt sat down.

There was a moment of silence as people absorbed his words. Julia began to clap, slowly at first, but then increasing in pace as others joined her.

Emma applauded, as Andy moved to the centre of the floor. 'Thank you, Matt, for that... incisive and... thought-provoking contribution.'

'There is a short film a little later. But first, I would like to go through the activities over the next few weeks, and then we-'

There was a loud rattling as the door was shaken open.

'Hi, y'all.' An American accent rang out, and a bald head popped round the door. 'We're just here to visit Eleanor Rigby and see the painting.'

The head popped back out, then a young, sharply dressed woman entered. 'Hello, sorry to disturb you. We have an agreement with Saint Peter's... access to the tour group. I hope you don't mind. We won't be too long.' She didn't wait for a response and opened the door wide.

'We were having a meeting,' explained Andy.

'Don't let us disturb you, love. You just carry on. We won't be long. We've got Strawberry Fields and Penny Lane next.'

A large group of tourists came in. They moved around the hall, admiring the architecture, the timbered roof and sandstone base. A few gathered opposite the painting above the tea table. Cameras and phones clicked and buzzed, and selfies and posed photographs were taken.

Julia was smiling, posing with a cup of tea beneath the painting. 'Anyone like a cup of tea? Proper English tea, just a pound a cup.'

'That's a bit steep, isn't it?' asked the tour guide.

'Saving the planet, love. All for a good cause,' Julia said. 'No, let me correct that.' Julia looked over to Matt and winked. 'Fighting climate change.'

'Oh, right.'

Andy stood. 'Why don't we take a break.'

Matt was first out of his seat and headed toward the door. Emma followed him. The churchyard was also the graveyard and full of headstones.

Emma caught Matt. 'Let's walk a bit.' She led him between the stones. 'There's a bench at the other end. They're here for the Eleanor Rigby grave.' She indicated back towards the hall.

'Yeah, I heard.'

'What is it, Matt? Something's bothering you?'

They picked their way through the headstones. Matt avoided stepping on any graves. He reached the bench first and sat. Emma joined him.

'Why?' He was confused by her interest.

'We want you as part of the group. We support people, especially those who want to help.'

'Hey, there you are!' Simon moved through the headstones towards them.

'What do you want?' Matt asked as Simon arrived.

'Nothing. Just thought I would join you.'

'No thanks,' said Matt.

The rejection cut through the air like a blade. Shocked, Simon stopped moving forward. 'Right. Private, is it?'

'Yeah, as it happens, it is.'

Emma looked sideways at Matt. 'It's nothing important.'

Simon raised his hands palms forward. 'Okay, no problem, I was just being friendly.'

'Can you give us a minute, Simon?' said Emma. 'I'll come in and find you.'

'Okay.' He glared at Matt a second before turning and moving back towards the hall.

Matt had held his stare; but looked through him. He waited for Simon to go.

'What was that about?' asked Emma

'I don't understand.'

'You were rude to Simon, and not for the first time.'

'No, I left the hall. You followed me to start a chat, then Simon followed you. I've got nothing to say to him. I'm not interested in him. In fact, he's weird. I'm sure he followed me to the train station last week.'

'That's not very inclusive.'

Matt shrugged. 'True.'

'We try and welcome everyone.'

'Maybe that's your problem.'

'First, you criticise Andy's strategy, and now you're rude to Simon?'

Matt turned to face Emma. 'What's going on? Is this group for lonely people? Support to build people's confidence? Or is it a campaign to change society?' He didn't say but could've added, '*Or a pool for you to fish in*?'

'I'm not sure. Why can't it be all of those things?'

'Because you'll achieve none of them if you're not clear about your aims.'

Andy appeared with Simon just behind him. 'Is everything okay?'

'Fine, thanks,' said Matt.

Emma remained silent.

Simon chipped in, 'Matt here has a problem... he's not very sociable.'

'Your comments were a bit sharp,' said Andy.

'Okay, well, I was invited here on the basis that you welcomed open discussion. If you think new ideas are a threat, then I've obviously come to the wrong place.'

'There is no need to be like that. Your ideas are…'

'Why can't you show respect? asked Simon.

'Respect for what?' asked Matt.

'You don't respect anything or anyone. You're arrogant. You set yourself up as above everyone and everything, but you are not.'

Matt shook his head. 'I know I'm not.'

'We don't judge people's motives,' said Andy. 'Everyone is welcome.'

'So I hear,' said Matt

'Andy?' Julia appeared. 'We're ready. The wandering Americans have wandered.'

'Okay, let's get back to things.'

Andy and Simon turned, and with Emma close behind, they walked toward the hall.

'Did I interrupt something?' Julia asked.

'I'm not sure,' said Matt. 'But I'm glad you did.'

'An argument?'

'Maybe.'

'Look, if it's about policy or strategy, why don't you have a debate? We can set it up for the next meeting, you and Andy. Andy!' Julia shouted ahead.

He stopped and turned.

'The next meeting... can we have a debate on strategy. You and Matthew? What do you think? Informal. No votes or anything, just an exchange of opinions.'

'If it's what Matt wants.'

'Yes, he does,' said Julia.

Andy turned and walked ahead.

Julia walked in front of Matt on the narrow path. 'There,' she pointed at a gravestone. 'What all the fuss is about. You really don't know your Beatles, do you?'

'No,' said Matt. 'I missed the nostalgia class at school.'

'Okay, smart arse. Eleanor Rigby, the grave, there it is.'

'Should I care?'

'*All the lonely people, where do they all come from*?' Then, after a moment, she said, 'And yes, to answer your question, you should care. But never mind, you've got plenty of time to learn.'

CHAPTER EIGHT

PAUL

Wednesday, January 15th, 2020.

Paul waited. These were the forces of earthly power. No match for the eternal, but in this life they held sway and needed to be resisted. A woman. Of course it would be a woman to carry out the emasculation. Superintendent Smith. Paul, accompanied by his Police Federation representative, was given advance notice of the interview. The federation rep had told him to give as little information as possible until they knew the case against him.

In the interview suite of Hope Street Police station, Paul placed his notebook and bible on the table. The blonde woman opposite had cold eyes and clear skin. Paul noticed her thin lips. *Frigid*, he thought, before he saw the gold ring on her finger.

'Sergeant Taylor, I am Claire Smith, regional investigator with the Independent Office of Police Conduct, and this is my colleague, Detective Sergeant Micheal Molloy. As I am sure you are aware, if someone had direct or indirect contact with the police when, or shortly before, they were seriously injured or died, we are called in. However, forces only need to refer cases where the contact may have caused or contributed to the death or injury. Do you understand this?'

Paul nodded. She wasn't local, he could tell that. Her voice came from money and position. He doubted she had ever patrolled the streets.

'This interview is being recorded. Could you please speak

clearly.'

'Yes, I understand.'

'Thank you. Let me begin by saying we know you have a very difficult job, in very stressful circumstances, and we appreciate the job you do. I just want to make that clear.'

'Thank you, ma'am.' Paul tried to hide his disdain.

'I also want to make it clear that this is a fact-finding investigation and not part of any disciplinary or complaints procedure. That your attendance at this stage is purely voluntary. We have reviewed the CCTV footage and are in the process of interviewing everyone else involved in the incident. We want you to know we are not seeking scapegoats here. Our only task is to establish the facts, and to determine whether the policies and procedures of Merseyside Police were upheld; that Mr Whitney's rights were at all times protected and observed.

Her hair was gathered at the back, and he guessed it was shoulder length when let down. A strand had escaped and rested on the epaulet of her uniform. Paul found her words difficult to follow. Her lips moved and sound came out, but when she looked down at the document in her hands, the strand of hair moved and laid against her neck.

'Sergeant Taylor, can you confirm this is your four-page report dealing with the detention and arrest of Matthew Whitney at 8.45 am on Monday the 7th of January 2020 on the concourse of Liverpool Central Station.'

Paul focused and took the offered document. His eyes swept over his own typed words, he looked at the initial at the bottom of each page, and flipped to the end and saw his signature. 'Yes, I can confirm that is my report.'

'Can we enter document A453 into the record?' Claire Smith's clear tones cut through the air. Her words were sharp; she never ummed, erred or in any other way projected uncertainty. 'Mr Matthew Whitney, age twenty-three, died after being arrested, transported and detained under your authority.'

Paul launched into his statement. 'That's correct. Matthew Whitney died in police custody between the time of 9.15 am when he was left alive in his cell, and 9.30 am when he was checked by the custody sergeant. All due precautions and safeguards had been instituted here at Hope Street station. I am sure the custody Sergeant will confirm the deceased was processed in the normal and legal way.'

'Our problem, Sergeant Taylor, is that you were the last person to confirm that Mr Whitney was alive before you left him in Cell Number Nine.'

Paul spoke slowly and clearly. 'That is true. He was alive when I left him.'

'How do you know this?'

'He was carried in by myself and PC Martin. When PC Martin left and I removed the restraints, he was alive.'

Supt Smith's head angled, and her tone was questioning. 'No other officer is able to confirm this?'

'That is because no other officer was there.'

'So we only have your word for it.'

'That *is* your confirmation. My statement, my word, should be enough. Why do you need anything else?' Paul tried to read the sly grey eyes.

Superintendent Smith shifted her gaze and scanned the document in front of her. 'You joined the force in 2016.'

Paul leaned back. 'Yes.'

'You underwent Police Support Unit training in 2017, then again in 2018 and, earlier this year, you underwent Level 2, Mutual Aid Support Trained (MAST), as part of a full-time Matrix Disruption Team, becoming a unit leader.'

'That is correct.' He was looked at the light grey brick wall. Despite repainting, he could see scratches underneath initials, no doubt of real criminals, held in this room at some point in the past.

'So you have been a unit leader in the Police Support Unit here on Merseyside for approximately six months.'

'That is correct.' The stray hair was back on her neck, it brushed against the stiff,white collar.

'Why the PSU? The Matrix Disruption Team?'

'The challenge...' Paul shrugged, 'a higher level of training... more specialised.'

'Did regular police work bore you?'

'No, I wasn't bored.'

Supt Smith flicked the stray strand of hair from her neck. 'Are you married, Sergeant? Do you have children?'

'You can see from the file I am not.'

'Yes, that's right. In fact, no immediate family.' She raised her eyebrows.

'No blood family. That's right.'

'That must be very difficult.'

'No. I am used to it.' His eyes narrowed at the turn in questions.

'You were raised in a foster home?'

'Yes. I was in care first. Look, what has this got to with anything?'

'We like to get a sense of who we are dealing with, Sergeant.'

Why did he feel like she was playing with him?

'Can you tell us in your own words what happened that morning?'

'You have the sergeant's statement,' The Federation representative interrupted. 'I don't think it is in my client's interest to ad-lib on this.'

Paul shrugged.

'That is a pity. I thought the sergeant was a truth-teller,' The superintendent leaned back. Paul knew she was goading him. She looked the part; the tailored uniform, the straight upright posture. She could play the role, but Paul knew her type. Paul smiled as Supt Smith flicked at the loose hair on her neck.

'Excuse me?' The Federation rep cut in. 'I don't know what you-'

'No, no, it's okay,' said Paul.

Supt Smith smiled. 'I can see the sergeant holding on to that Bible like his life depended on it,'

'It does,' Paul said.

'I'm sorry?'

'My life does depend on it. So does yours. So do all our lives. The only difference appears to be that I know it.' He was more comfortable now and spoke freely.

'You have strong religious beliefs, Sergeant Taylor?'

'I have accepted The Lord Jesus into my life.'

'Yes, that's what I meant.'

'I'm not sure of the relevance of this?' The Federation cut in..

'Just curious how the sergeant marries his faith with his professional life?'

The rep turned to Paul. 'You don't have to engage with this discussion.'

'I'm proud to proclaim my faith.' Paul knew her game but wasn't afraid.

The Federation rep turned to Paul. 'I can't stop you, but I am advising you not to respond to questions outside the details of the arrest and detention procedure.'

'I understand. I do. It makes no difference to me. I am here to serve the Lord, and I enforce the law of the land.'

'Is there ever a difference between serving the Lord and the law of the land?' asked the Superintendent.

The Federation rep raised his hand. 'Superintendent, I must protest. This has nothing to do with the facts of the day.'

'Okay, Sergeant Taylor, can you tell us in your own words what happened on the morning of Monday the 6th of January at approximately 8.45am.'

Paul sat back and coughed to clear his throat. 'Am I allowed to consult my notebook?'

'If you need to.'

Paul read from his notes. His sentences were short and he kept his voice clipped. 'I was assigned to cover a public order incident in the concourse of Central Station, Liverpool. An unauthorised protest was taking place on private property. The protesters had been informed by officers of the Transport Police that they were committing the criminal offence of trespass and had refused to disperse. I arrived with my team. After making an initial assessment, it was my judgement that public order could be restored by removing the chief instigator and organiser of the action. This would allow officers to clear the concourse and restore order.

'In line with training and policy on target extractions, we deployed and detained the individual in question. In order to overcome the resistance, I authorised the use of lifting restraints and mouthguard. The subject was delivered to the vehicle and transported to Hope Street Police Station, where he was transferred into cell number nine.' He looked up from his notes and met her gaze.

'Mr Whitney was restrained during the journey?'

'That is correct.'

'And in the transfer to the cell?'

'That is correct.'

'You were not worried by the effect of the restraints?' Supt Smith leaned forward.

For the first time Paul caught a trace of sweetness. She was wearing a scent of some kind.

'No.'

'Was the subject offering resistance?'

'During his detention, yes.'

'But not on the journey?'

'No.' He knew the shift to quick-fire questions was one more way to try and catch him out, see if he would let something slip.

'Or his transfer into the cell?'

'No.'

'When the restraints were removed, did the subject respond? Did he say anything? Do anything?'

'No.' Paul remembered the pungent smell of sweat and fear, so different from this. He drew air in through his nostrils; he could almost taste the roses.

'You didn't think this strange?'

'No.' The questions were annoying him. He expelled her scent, breathing out.

'Why not?'

'The subject was subdued because we had, in fact, subdued him. The purpose of restraint is to restrain.' He knew he was matching her step for step.

'Is the purpose of restraint to kill?'

'No.'

'And yet he died.'

'He did.'

Supt Smith had slowed back down. 'No remorse?'

'He's with the Lord our God. There is no need for remorse.'

'The bite guard... why?' She paused between each question now, as if to imply full answers were required. 'You were aware there are warnings about its use?'

'No.' Paul wasn't playing her game.

'Why was it deployed?'

'Because I considered there was a danger of the detainee biting.'

'Had he tried to bite you or any other officer?'

'No, because I deployed the bite guard.'

'Before you deployed the bite guard, had Mr Whitney attempted to bite you or any member of your team?'

'No.'

'Are you aware that there have been other incidents in which this piece of equipment has caused injury?'

'No.'

'Was Matthew Whitney booked in by the custody sergeant?'

'He was.'

'But he did not give his name or take part in an interview?'

'No, because of his resistance. I gave his details to the custody sergeant who approved his detention.'

'We have viewed the footage, and Mr Whitney appears to be struggling. His body is moving and he is difficult for the officers to hold.'

'Yes, as I said, the subject was resisting.'

'Maybe he was fighting for his life?'

'He was resisting restraint.'

'He was dying. He was fighting for breath.'

'He was resisting.' He ignored her attempt to goad him.

'He was fighting for his life...' She took a sharp intake of breath. 'You gave the subject's name to the custody sergeant?'

'Yes.'

'How?'

'Sorry?' Paul was confused What was she up to?

'How did you know? He didn't have any identification on him. His property is here... a set of keys... seven pounds and fifty-four pence... a watch, and a telephone. There is no ID. You gave his name to the desk sergeant?'

'Yes...' Paul stretched out the word as his mind scrambled.

'Did you have any contact with Matthew Whitney before his arrest?'

'No.' As he shook his head, he realised he was probably overdoing it.

'How did you know his name?'

'Sorry?' He was playing for time.

'You gave his full name to the desk sergeant, but Mr Whitney had no ID. How did you know his name?'

'It was used by his friends, his co-protesters as we arrested him.'

Superintendent Smith leaned back. 'That sounds strange. Can you describe how that happened?'

'Someone said 'I am recording Matthew Whitney being arrested.' I distinctly heard his name. So, this was the name I gave to the desk sergeant.'

'This is not in your report. You are aware that we will

interview everyone who was at the protest?'

Paul shrugged. 'I didn't think it was relevant.'

'Okay, Sergeant Taylor. I would like to thank you for your cooperation.'

'You're welcome.'

The Federation rep closed his file, and Paul pushed his chair back.

'Did you agree with him?' Superintendent Smith asked.

'Agree with who?'

'Mr Whitney.' Smith was scanning the pages again. 'It appears Mr Whitney was an environmental activist. Did you sympathise with his views?'

'I didn't consider his views.'

'You knew. You were aware that the protest was related to Climate Change?'

'Yes, I knew.'

'You were not interested?'

'No, I'm not interested.' The interview was over and he wanted to get away from this woman now.

'So... no saving the world for you?'

'I really don't think this line of questioning is productive,' said the rep.

Paul pushed his chair back further, the metal legs screeched against the concrete floor.

'*The world is burning*. That is a direct quote. I have it here. Matthew Whitney was repeating over the speaker. *The world is burning*. He was trying to save the planet, save the world and save people. What do you think of that?'

Paul stood. 'Is the interview over?'

'Yes, you can leave. Go, if you have nothing to say, that's fine. Matthew Whitney was out there trying to save people while you sit in your room with your little book.' She pointed at his bible. 'Matthew understood the brotherhood of man. He fought for it.'

'He couldn't save people. God is in control, not man.' Paul

had had enough.

She laughed. Actually laughed, her mouth open, white teeth flashing.

'Don't laugh at the Lord or His works!' he snapped.

'You are ridiculous, Sergeant Taylor. No wonder you are a loner. No friends. No family. No one wants to be near you.'

Paul looked at the rep who cut in, 'You can't say that.'

'I just did. No one likes you. Your colleagues think you're weird. Your supervisors don't trust you. How does it feel to be rejected?'

The Federation rep put his arm around Paul's shoulder to guide him out the door. Paul brushed his arm aside and turned to face the Superintendent. His fists clenched, his muscles tense, his face strained. 'You know not of what you speak.'

'I know, we all know,' she smiled.

'You know nothing!' Paul shouted, 'You ignorant, stupid, evil woman.'

'We all know you have been rejected by everyone and everything in your life. Is that why you hurt Matthew? A young man, who was a leader, was loved, accepted, looked up to, respected? Don't you want to be saved? Oh, I am sorry you *are* saved, isn't that right?'

'Yes. I am saved.'

'Don't you want the rest of us to be saved too? Isn't that part of your plan? Or God's plan? Or doesn't that matter?'

'You don't have to answer these questions,' the rep insisted.

'That's right, you don't have to answer to me, but you do have to answer to someone else. Don't you, Sergeant Taylor? You couldn't live with a guilty conscience, could you?'

The federation rep interrupted. 'What is this? Where is this going?'

Paul lifted his hand. 'Stop.'

There was silence in the room.

Paul raised his voice. He wasn't shouting; it was just loud

and clear, well-modulated. His preaching voice. 'The day of the Lord will come as a thief in the night.'

'Does that mean you can break the law too?'

'The heavens will pass away with a great noise.'

'Is that the end of the world? Is that it? Was Matthew stealing your thunder? Was he?'

Paul built the tempo and pitch, 'And the elements will melt with fervent heat; both the earth and the works that are in it will be burned up.'

'*The world is burning* - did you want to take those words out of his mouth? Were they your words? Was he stealing your sermon? Is that why you killed Matthew Whitney, Sergeant Taylor? Is that why you killed Matthew Whitney? You got angry with this godless heathen preaching your sermon?' She paused. 'The bush fires in Australia. A terrible business, don't you think, Sergeant? Was that God's work? Or the work of Man?'

'You don't have to answer these questions,' the rep insisted again.

'I'm not stupid,' said Paul. 'I know you are trying to rile me. Let me tell you; it won't work. I am saved, and when the time is right-'

'Did Matthew Whitney know it? Do you hear the word of God? Did Matthew Whitney's life depend on the word of God?'

'All life depends on the word of God.'

'Who do you serve, Sergeant Taylor? Merseyside Police or your God?'

The federation rep held an arm out in front of Paul. 'I am terminating this interview, Superintendent, and will be making it clear that this line of questioning is an abuse of process. Sergeant Taylor attended this interview voluntarily.'

'If you do wrong, be afraid.'

The Superintendent's eyes widened. 'I should be afraid? Did you really say that?'

'Romans 13,' Paul quoted. 'If you do wrong, be afraid, for rulers do not bear the sword for no reason.'

'Thank you, Sergeant. You have given us plenty to think about and we will continue this investigation. You can rest assured that we will speak to you again. This interview is concluded Wednesday January 15th 2020.' She checked her watch. 'At 15.10.'

Paul picked up his notebook and Bible. He slipped the notebook into a jacket pocket then raised to the Bible to his lips and, keeping eye contact with Supt Smith, he kissed the Bible. Then left the room.

CHAPTER NINE

CHARLIE

Wednesday, January 15th, 2020.

Charlie now knew that *poly* went before *amorous* to mean he had a chance with Emma.

'Hey, thanks for coming.' Emma stood and moved towards him. She fitted the hipster cafe they were in perfectly. Her woollen cardigan, light blue summer dress and boots matched the eclectic second-hand furniture. She gave him an enthusiastic hug. Charlie winced.

'Oh sorry, how's your arm?'

'Recovering.'

Emma sat on a sofa. Charlie took the armchair opposite. 'Did you get an X-ray?'

'No, it's okay. Bruised, that's all.'

'It's good to see you again.'

Charlie wasn't sure why she wanted to meet. 'It sounded important.'

'Yeah, it is. I think you should speak to Matt's mum.'

Confused, his stomach sank. 'Why would I want to do that?'

'You saw him arrested; it might help her.'

He didn't know if it was disappointment that she hadn't arranged the meeting just to see him, but he didn't hide his annoyance. 'How can it help? Me telling her I saw him get slung in the back of the police van. I'm not sure about this.'

'I thought you wanted to help?' Emma turned away; her

blonde hair swished through the air.

'I do... but I don't know how this will help.' It was a question and appeal, and both were ignored.

Instead, Emma simply acknowledged the *I do*.

'Thanks, that's great.' She reached out and touched his hand.

Charlie pulled it back and looked around instinctively. 'Where is she?' *Was he being played?*

'She's not here. I said we would go to her house.'

Charlie's eyes narrowed. 'So you've already spoken to her?' He felt like a dog on a leash.

'Of course. I knew you'd do the right thing.'

~

Emma went up the path first. The garden was overgrown, and the privet hedge and grass needed trimming. Charlie was right behind her. He reached out and broke off a stray twig.

They reached the front door, and Emma pressed the bell. She turned and flashed her eyes at Charlie, and he was struck, as ever, by the depth of colour, the life, and energy in them. She smiled with her whole face, not just her lips. Charlie stripped the twig of leaves and each fell to the ground around his feet. He wasn't sure what was behind the door. He pushed the leaves aside with his foot and threw the bare twig into the garden.

The door opened and a thin woman with lank brown shoulder-length hair stood in front of them. She wore a beige woolen cardigan over a loose brown dress. She looked blankly for a second before animation reached her face. 'Emma. Come in, come in, it's nice to see you. I don't get to see anyone...' She turned her head away from the unfinished sentence and stepped back to allow them in.

Charlie nodded 'Hi' as he stepped passed her into the living room. The room was in a half-light, the curtains closed, and a weak side lamp illuminated a corner of the room containing an armchair. She followed him in and switched on the overhead light. Charlie thought everything took on a piss stain yellow.

'Please sit.' Matt's mother held her hand out, indicating the sofa.

Charlie lowered himself, Emma next to him, but so close that he had to shift a little, and they were still touching. He felt weird; they were sitting like a couple. Emma was in the middle of the sofa; she had the space to move if she wanted. It wasn't that he didn't like it. He didn't understand it.

'Charlie, this is Mary.'

'Nice to meet you, Mary.'

'It's so good to see Matt's friends.'

'I'm sorry. I really didn't know Matt.' He shifted, creating a bit of space between him and Emma.

'Charlie saw Matt get arrested,' Emma explained.

Mary turned and looked directly at Charlie. 'Is that right?'

'I was on my way to work. He was talking over the loudhailer about Australia. I remember him saying, 'the world is burning.' Next thing you know, the police had him on the floor. He was still mouthing it, even without words.' Charlie hesitated before saying the next bit, unsure what the reaction would be. 'He said, 'We are dying.''

Mary held a handkerchief to her face. 'He was right.'

Charlie spoke quietly but firmly. 'One copper had his knee in his back. It must have hurt, you know, the full weight of someone in your back. His face was pressed against the floor.'

'The police told me all this,' said Mary.

'They put some kind of straps around him,' Charlie continued, 'I don't know, like they were carrying a log. He was face down as they carried him out to the van. He wasn't struggling. I don't think he could. It was all pretty quick. They kinda slid him into the back of the van, the coppers jumped in, and then they were off.' His eyes scanned the room and came to rest on a photo on the mantelpiece; a simple chrome frame held a picture of a smiling boy of around fifteen, arms outstretched, measuring the one that got away.

Mary picked the photo up and brought it over to Charlie. 'There are few pictures of him as happy as that. He wasn't a happy child. He seemed to carry the weight of the world on his shoulders. Such a shame. He went fishing with his dad somewhere in Wales. I guess it just wasn't meant to be. I didn't deserve him. It was my punishment for the first.'

Charlie held the photo. 'It looks nice.' He didn't know what else to say. Or what 'the first' meant.

Mary sat back down, and Charlie placed the photo on the coffee table in front of him.

'Always worried about other people, other things, never looked out for himself. But no one cares, do they?'

'Matthew did. That's why he was demonstrating,' said Emma.

'Yeah, well, maybe that was his problem. He should have been more selfish. Maybe if he cared less, he would still be here. Do you go to these demonstrations and protests?' Mary looked at Charlie as she spoke.

'No, it's not my thing.'

'What is your thing?' she asked.

'I don't know... football? I'm not political. I don't really understand it.'

'I wish Matthew was like you. Then I wouldn't be sat here with a stranger filling an empty space.'

Charlie looked down at his hands, embarrassed to be in this grieving woman's house.

'I'm sorry. Seeing another young man, his life in front of him...' She shifted back upright. 'What are you here for?'

The question was to Charlie but Emma answered. 'To get justice for Matt.'

Charlie stood up. 'I'm sorry, I have to go.'

Mary shook her head. 'What justice?'

Charlie held his hand out. 'I'm sorry for your loss.'

Mary held his hand in both of hers. 'I'm sure you're a good

lad.' She held onto his hand.

Charlie pulled gently but she kept her grip. 'You saw him die.'

He pulled his hand free. 'No, I saw him get arrested.' He was nauseous, and wanted to get out of there. The room was stifling; he couldn't breathe. He closed his eyes as tightness gripped his chest. His heart was pounding and he struggled for breath. He was light, weightless. 'Fuck.' He reached out, moved forward, stumbled over the coffee table and crashed to the floor.

~

Outside in the fresh air, Emma held him up. 'Are you okay?'

'I'll be fine.' The air was cool; it rushed in and filled his chest. He squinted in the bright afternoon sun. His head was clearing. 'What happened?'

'You kinda passed out. Fainted. Has it happened before? We were going to call an ambulance.'

'No. I'm fine. What the fuck?' He shook his head and leaned on the gate.

'Do you want to go back in? Sit down.'

'No, the fresh air's good.' His arm was around Emma's shoulder, and her arm was around his waist. 'I'm sorry. Jesus, I don't know what happened.' He looked around at the mid-afternoon scene. A mother pushed a pram along the pavement and cars coughed their way along the street.

'Don't be silly. There's no need to be sorry. It was an emotional moment.'

'It wasn't that. I don't know - it just felt weird- I felt like it was me.'

'What do you mean?'

'It was Matthew.' The voice rang out from behind them.

Charlie turned and saw Mary in the doorway. 'It was Matthew. I felt it when I held your hand. Matthew was showing you how he suffered.'

Charlie wiped his face. He let go of Emma. 'I've got to go.' He walked away up the road. Emma caught up and walked along beside him. Charlie headed for the main road and a bus out of there.

'She's upset,' Emma said.

'She's crazy,' said Charlie.

'No, she's not. She's lost her son. Killed... murdered... who knows?'

'I know. Okay? I fucking know.' Charlie stopped walking and turned to face Emma. 'What is it? Are you trying to guilt-trip me? You set this whole thing up. She didn't want me there. What the fuck are you up to? Is this how you get your kicks? Messing with people's lives?'

'No, of course not.'

'Then get off my back.' He walked off again.

Emma caught him and pulled him around. 'I thought you cared.'

Charlie stopped and threw his hands in the air. 'I do, I do care. What the fuck? I didn't see him die. He died later in the police station. Why did she say that?'

Emma put her arms around him. Charlie didn't resist. He let his head fall onto Emma's shoulder.

'The thing is, I think she was right. Weird as it sounds, I could feel Matt being arrested. The panic, the suffocation, and then a kind of acceptance... peace.'

'We can do it together.' Emma said.

Charlie looked back, Emma stared at him.

CHAPTER TEN

PAUL

Wednesday, January, 15th 2020.

'We're in Indian territory,' a past commanding officer had told Paul. The double-doored entrance of Hope Street Police was the opposite of fortress-like modern constructions. The essence of the new station designs was strength and defence. Hope Street's glass-fronted office architecture was no longer suited to its purpose.

Paul was a fortress against all that was wicked and evil. He was the wall upon which sin would break. He wasn't alone in this task; it would be trite to say he had God on his side. It would be more accurate to say God was his side.

The interrogator... the woman... sent to trick and trip him up, would fail, not because he had truth on his side, but because he was the truth. It was not enough to *have*, the point was to *be*. He decided to leave via the front; he didn't question why but accepted God's grace in everything.

Suspended from active duty, Paul was checking on his pay and benefits, and pressed the button to open the connecting door to the front desk. He saw a flash of blonde hair before he heard her, and a street rat. He pulled back quickly but kept the door from closing. Did she see him? He watched through the glass panel on the door. Emma always had the look of dissolution, and today was no different: unkempt hair and shapeless clothes. That was no exercise in modesty, as the bright scarf in her hair and the way the shapeless dress hung off her curves proved. She stood closer than was necessary to a young buck, clad in the black uniform of the street; sports casual. The darkness of the uniform matched the souls of the soldiers. *'By their clothes shall we know them.'* Paul opened the door a little to hear better.

'I saw it. I want to make a statement,' the youth said.

'You have to give me your name and address, and then we can deal with whatever you want to say, okay?' PC Martin looked closer. 'I know you... don't I?'

The youth didn't respond.

PC Martin spoke in clear, measured tones. 'You were there in the train station, and at the protest. What's your name and address?'

'Charlie Connolly. 4 Enisworth Road, Allerton.'

Emma spoke up, 'He saw Matthew Whitney get arrested.'

'Thank you, miss. I'm sure Mr Connolly here can tell us what he saw. Are you making a complaint? A witness statement?'

Emma spoke again. 'A complaint.'

'Let me deal with this,' the youth said. 'I would like to make a statement about the arrest of Matthew Whitney.'

Paul stayed out of sight. He knew Emma. This Charlie had the look of a wannabe hard man. Adidas trainers, a black North Face hooded top, and black trackie bottoms. Paul was surprised at the address. Allerton. So he was more of a plastic, middle-class kid, aping the look of the estates.

'Now I have your name and address, I will contact the officer responsible, and they will be in touch with you. Make sure you leave your email and number too.'

'Is that all?' He asked.

'For now, yes.'

Charlie filled out the form he was given.

'Really?' Emma asked.

She was every inch the hippie; a slut. Vegan eco-campaigner.

Bearer of the original sin. It wasn't difficult to see the temptation placed in the way of Adam.

'Yes, really.' PC Martin said, 'Is there anything else I can do for you?'

Charlie finished writing and slid the form across the counter.

'Thank you.' PC Martin picked it up and examined it.

Charlie turned to leave.

'If no one gets in touch, we'll be back,' Emma said.

'You do that,' PC Martin replied.

Paul watched them leave, a half smile formed on his face. *Now I know who and where you are. Charlie Connolly. 4 Enisworth Rd, Allerton.*

TWO MONTHS EARLIER

CHAPTER ELEVEN

MATTHEW

November, 2019.

Matt arrived, brushed the rain off his jacket and shook his wet hair. Emma moved through the audience to meet him.

'It's getting on a bit. I thought you might have got the date or time wrong.'

'No, all good.' He made his way across the room and stood in line for tea.

Julia handed him a tea, 'You should have let me give you a lift.'

'Oh, it's okay. I waited for the bus but walked in the end. It's not so bad, fifteen minutes.'

'I hate driving that car by myself. Such a waste of petrol.' She refused the offered money. She winked. 'Perk of the job, I get to look after my favourites.'

Matt accepted the gift and went to find a seat near the back.

Saint Peter's Hall was full. Between fifty and seventy people had ventured out in the dark and wet to hear a discussion about strategies for combating Global Warming. Whatever Matt thought of the people involved, they were involved. They attended meetings and circulated petitions. Most of them took more individual than collective action, but that was part of the problem of the movement, not the individuals. Separating waste and recycling had become morality tests. He hoped to challenge a few of the assumptions made this evening.

Matt couldn't help but hear the embarrassed conversation

behind him.

'I've been waiting for this. You should beat him,' Simon said.

'It's not a competition, not that kind of debate, no winners and losers. We're discussing strategy,' Andy shifted from foot to foot.

'Yeah, I know, but he has no respect, he doesn't care, he needs to be taught a lesson. You'll win.'

Andy moved away from Simon towards Emma.

'Are you okay?' she asked.

'Of course, it's a discussion, an exchange of opinions.'

'Absolutely.' She reached out and stroked his arm.

Andy returned to his pacing, followed closely by Simon. The room around them had taken shape. Murmuring voices rose and fell in expectation. The South Liverpool group, Earthquake, was meeting in Saint Peters Church Hall in Woolton Village to discuss and strategise a response to global Climate Crisis. Of all the emotions in the room, humility was least in evidence.

Emma brought the meeting to order. She called Matt forward and positioned him on the left, Andy and Simon sat on the right.

The first activity of the evening was a video, '*Above Us Only Sky*' about John Lennon Airport. Speke airport, as it was known locally. Through a series of still images, the video showed the development of the airport, from a small private airfield, through the expansion of the Air Force base during the Second World War, to the commercial, regional airport it had become. Photos of The Beatles arriving back from their US tour in 1965 and Pope John Paul's visit in 1981 brought smiles to many faces. Using John Lennon's lyrics 'Above us only sky' to promote the airport was a popular move. Less popular were the holding company's attempts to expand into protected greenbelt land. The proposed expansion would also cut off access to the river and Oglet Shore for the thousands of people on the Speke estate. Or, as the speaker, Lynne, described it, shutting down the access would be like the estate losing its only lung. The audience was receptive and supportive.

The tension was building as people waited for the main event. The challenge to Andy. 'Tonight, we are hosting something a little unusual. Our discussions are always open to anyone to contribute, so we have decided to open the floor to alternative views. We would like a non-conflictual exchange of ideas, so please be respectful of contributors-Andy, what order are we taking?' She deferred to Andy as the unofficial leader of the group.

'Go, Andy,' Simon said.

'I'm happy with Matt going first, if he would like?'

'Matt?' Emma looked across.

'Sure.' Matt stood.

He moved forward a couple of steps and turned to face the audience. He was calm and relaxed as if speaking to a friend. He moved and spoke at the same time. Eyes followed him, and ears tuned in to his laid-back delivery. 'Hi. I want to carry out a little survey if you'll humour me? Can you raise your hand if you separate and recycle your waste?'

Every hand in the room was raised.

'Okay, thank you. Next question, how many people have a reusable bag for shopping?'

The majority of hands went up. Matt increased the speed of questions.

'Compost heaps? Solar panels? Use rechargeable batteries? Cycle not drive? Hybrid car? LED bulbs?'

Hands were going up and down, and it was no longer clear who was responding to what question. There were smiles and giggles as people enjoyed the confusion.

Matt paused and let the room settle.

'How many of you know you are being absolutely conned?'

No hands were raised. Matt continued, 'If everyone took all those measures, the compost heaps, rechargeable batteries, domestic recycling, every day for a hundred years, it wouldn't make a scrap of difference. Rotting away in your graves would be doing more good for the environment than the contribution of your lifetime of recycling.

'Okay, humour me here. Can you turn to your neighbour, slap him or her on the back, shake their hand, tell each other how good we are?'

Matt waited. Some followed his suggestion, others were more cautious. 'That is what this group currently is... a mutual masturbation society. A circle jerk.'

Some smiles disappeared, others giggled with embarrassment, and a few murmurs of disapproval grew.

Behind her tea table, Julia clapped. 'You tell 'em, Matthew.'

Simon stood, 'No. No, you're wrong. You're disgusting.'

Emma remained seated but raised her hands. 'Okay, can we calm down, please? Let him finish.'

Simon grumbled as he sat down.

Matt waited for Simon to quieten.

Andy interjected, 'You're just trying to offend people. Recycling is to re-orient people's lives. It's not proposed as a solution.'

'Yeah, you're right,' said Matt. 'I am trying to offend you. To wake you up because you need shaking out of this self-satisfied bubble of self-righteousness. The oil industry, the aviation industry, the arms industry... these people laugh at you. All your reusable bags, compost heaps, and rechargeable batteries are individual diversions from tackling the real problem of who controls society. Who determines when and where the oil industry can drill? Who says how many flights should come in and out of the country? Who decides what bombs are dropped where. Julia, how long have you been recycling?'

'Must be nearly fifteen years now,' she answered.

'And yesterday, the Israelis bombed Gaza, Palestine, again. This one act alone would have released enough chemicals and contaminants, not to talk about the direct loss of human life, to make your fifteen years of recycling look like pissing in the wind. You will hear Andy talk about the threat to human life in ten, twenty, thirty years, but what are you doing about the destruction of human life today?'

Matt walked from side to side. 'Andy was right... recycling is re-orienting your lives... to utterly useless personal gestures, and away from societal solutions. But then you don't want them, do you? Extinction Revolution doesn't actually have any policies. Doesn't have a programme.' He paused for a moment. 'Dealing with actual political change might scare people away.'

'Okay, enough.' Andy stood. 'This is not about strategy to combat climate change. This is whataboutery. What about this crime, or what about that problem? We are not here to create a league table of problems. We can all add to the list. What about racism? What about sexism? We are here combating a problem that affects everybody. If we don't get this right, if we don't take immediate action to stop or reverse the course of climate change, then all other arguments are a waste of breath.'

'Yeah, you tell him.' Simon stood and clapped. Others took up the applause.

Emma raised her hand. 'Please...'

'Immediate action, like slow walking, or dancing and singing through town..? Throwing paint at monuments, or pictures? Disruption for its own sake is a diversion. Unless you have a government willing to legislate and force companies to change, it will not happen. As long as you allow unrestrained capitalism to monetise the world, you will not turn this situation around. Action means regulating the polluters, forcing standards on the building industry, removing subsidies to aviation. We will never combat climate change through individual actions, and all your efforts will be wasted. Worse, you are leading people up the garden path, into the arms of charlatans and con men. Making people feel guilty, or self-satisfied as a result of personal behaviour, can produce volunteers and build a movement, but on its own won't change a fucking thing.'

Emma's role as moderator had been sidelined as Matt and

Andy swapped point for point.

Andy stood. 'Okay, thanks. It's becoming clear, you want to divert us down the path of politics. A path that has been tried. Tried and failed. How long have we waited for politicians? How many broken promises have we heard from the elite? It is time to take direct action into our own hands. Like the civil rights movement. Like Ghandi. Non-violent, direct action.' Andy paused for effect. 'You know the old slogan... *If voting changed anything, they would make it illegal!*'

There was sporadic applause.

Matt was quick to move in just as it died down. 'Power in our society is a function of economics. Nothing works without workers. If you want power, that's where it is. The bus driver, the cleaners, the nurses, the shop workers, the waiters, the binmen... without these people, nothing can function; not the banks, the hedge funds, nor the whole service industry. We need to go back to the mass industrial unions of a hundred years ago, all workers in one union. You need to win these people to your side. You can talk all you like about direct action, but Martin Luther King was killed while supporting a binmen's strike. He led the March on Washington, the smaller actions fed into the mass mobilisation for Legal Civil Rights. And if you think that non-violence won independence from the British Empire, then you haven't read your history.'

Andy cut in again, 'If people are talking about the problem, we are winning. If we block a road or stop a train, it fills the papers; people are talking about the issues.'

Matt clapped his hands together. 'I applaud the courage of those that take individual actions, chaining and gluing themselves, spraying paint.' Then stopped. 'But it's not enough. It's a distraction. It should be part of a broader movement. Don't just sit on the track, get the driver to stop the train. Don't block the motorway, unionise lorry drivers, tanker drivers. Setting up small scale actions for violent reprisals by the public, is dangerous. Secret actions lead to undercover police, conspiracy charges and longer jail terms. When members of the public are seen dragging you off the road, it lets people know protesters are fair game.'

Andy was on his feet again. 'This has nothing to do with climate change or how to fight it. It just shows the rabbit holes we start to go down if we broaden out our focus. We want a people's convention.'

'A convention is the form, the means; it's not a solution,' said Matt. 'Who will be at this convention? Where will they get their arguments and news? Who will they represent? Unless and until we include two principles in everything we do... humanity and solidarity, any movement, any party, any campaign, including climate change, will fail unless it operates on the basis of these two principles. Everything that has ever been won for working people, the eight-hour day, sick pay, weekends off, at the individual and level of society, health care, pensions, housing has been won through fighting and campaigning.

'I disagree with Andy, but we can have that conversation. Humanity is the solution, not the problem. There are Environmentalists who think too many people are the problem. For these people, it is never Western populations with air conditioning and SUV's that are the issue, it is always the growth of Asian, Indian or African humanity that threatens the globe. Or threatens 'our' borders, 'our' civilisation, 'our' comfort. Andy said I was talking about side issues unconnected to the challenge of climate control.'

Matt paused and let the silence hang, unafraid of the tension it built, welcoming the attention that focused on his next words.

'Without humanity and solidarity, we're all fucked. The low-paid, the unemployed, black people fighting for racial justice, women fighting for equality, migrants fighting for safety... without humanity and solidarity, we all lose. Because we will never have the power to stop the destruction of the planet until we harness the energy and talent of all of these people. If you think you can stop climate change while the polluters use race to divide us, or you think we can get the government to control the oil industry while we can't even get it to house the homeless or feed the hungry, then you are living in a recyclable bubble.

'Stop pitting yourself against working people and start trying to build with them.' Matt walked back to his seat but stopped before he sat down. 'Or... consciously or not you will be used against them. You will become everything you hate.'

The scattered applause grew until most of the room, including Andy, clapped.

Andy stood. 'I am not sure what to say. I could try and make a few points about the convention. I know I should defend XR, but you are all intelligent enough to go through the arguments for yourselves. I want to thank Matt for his contribution. It has certainly made me think. The organising group will welcome Matt's contributions to the practical activities we have planned.'

Emma stood and walked to the front. 'Thank you all for attending. Please look at the bookstall, keep Julia busy on the tea front and don't forget Lynne and the people from the Save Oglet Shore campaign are around and will be happy to have a chat. Thank you all.'

Scattered applause broke out, and the noise level rose instantly as voices held at bay for the past hour were free at last.

Julia left her tea duties in the control of a deputy and made her way over to Matt. 'I'm giving you a lift home - no arguments.'

'Thanks,' Matt said. He moved away from the small group surrounding him and made his way to Andy. 'I'm sorry if I sounded harsh.'

'Ha, yeah, you were, for some of it, but no doubt we deserve it.' Andy presented his fist for a bump. 'Well done, mate, I'm not kidding, I've been around for a while, and I think you really have something.'

Matt gave Andy a quizzical look.

'I'm serious. You can speak, you can hold an audience, but more than that, you explain things simply.' Andy paused. 'You know what, there's something else as well. You didn't pander to your audience. You challenged them, took them with you.' Andy shook his head. 'I wish I had that talent.'

'Talent?' Matt said.

'It's disgusting. You have no right.' Simon had moved over to join them. 'Who are you? Who do you think you are? This is not your group... this is Andy's. You can't take what doesn't belong to you.'

Matt stepped back.

'You can't replace people. You can't take his place.'

'Simon...' Andy placed himself in front of him. 'Chill out, mate.'

'It's not fair, he gets everything.'

'Come with me, come on. I'm giving you that lift.' Julia pulled Matt's arm. 'Let's get you out of here.'

Andy had his arms extended, stopping Simon from moving forward. 'Good idea. Thanks, Julia.'

Matt headed for the door. Others had joined Andy to calm Simon down.

Simon shouted. 'Jacob! That's who you are, a thief.'

~

The wipers scraped over the windscreen, producing a repetitive slap. The lights picked out the slanting rain, making it sparkle before it hit the ground.

'Jacob?' Matt asked.

'Another thing you don't know,' Julia smiled. 'Your Beatles or your Bible.'

'You got me there.'

'Jacob and Esau, Jacob stole Esau's birthright. A bit weird, Andy might lead the group, but he doesn't own it, so you can't steal it from him, but I think that's what Simon was on about.' Julia concentrated on driving as they wound their way through the road that dissected Woolton Golf course. 'I'll tell you one thing, though...'

'What's that?'

'Andy was right. You are special. You were born to do this stuff. A natural-born leader.' Julia laughed. 'You don't even know it, do you?'

'I know things need to change,' said Matt.

'You have great things ahead of you, son. You mark my words. We need people like you. We've been waiting for someone like you to come along.'

'Maybe that's the problem,' said Matt.

Julia drove on as the night grew darker.

CHAPTER TWELVE

PAUL

Friday, January 17th, 2020.

'Are we ready?' His mother spoke in the plural, partly from habit and partly from the oft expressed belief her husband was still with her. She was unremarkable as she shopped on Park Road, her 'little lifesaver' dragging behind her, its wheels wobbly but still able to turn. Mr Taylor, or 'Father', bought it when the potatoes became too heavy for her to carry home.

Mr Taylor was a good man, a godly man in an ungodly world. For fifty years, he worked in a transport yard, booking the lorries, arranging the custom notes, and contacting the clients. He spoke of drivers and loaders who were rough-working men. His was a sedentary job. 'Give me a pencil and a phone,' he would say, and he could transport any load from Timbuktu to Buckingham Palace.

Mr Taylor died when Paul was still young, a heart attack, probably due to that sedentary life. His only day of illness was the day he died. He had a broken finger that was never set straight on his left hand. He wouldn't go to the hospital or doctor out of fear. It was never said but Paul knew, so the finger was at a strange angle from the day they broke it to the day he died. Rough men from Garston, they wanted the manifest for his loads. They were all around. Dingle was famous for its dockers and railmen, thieves and seamen. Living in the Holy Land didn't make them saints. Paul knew from early on that the battle awaited him.

Mr and Mrs Taylor had saved Paul from the Papists. Though truth be told, he couldn't get out of there quick enough. Paradise House they called it. 'An abomination,' Mr Taylor called it.

'Are we ready?' she called out again.

She watched him descend the stairs. She called Paul her light and her life. He was thirteen when they saved him and brought him into their quiet home. They recounted the tale of how they'd given up hope until Mr Taylor saw an advertisement in the local paper.. 'Homes wanted for abandoned children.' After that, it all went smoothly, and Paul was so happy to have a home. He accepted everything; to them he was such a good child.

They walked the same route every time they visited the chapel. The biblical street names of the terraces built by Welsh builders harked back to an earlier period when non-conformist farmers settled the land.

Paul and his mother's walk to the ancient Chapel of Toxteth took them up to Park Road and then down through history to the bottom. The schoolhouse next to the chapel was built in 1611 by dissenting farmers. The preacher, Richard Mather, upset the church authorities, and was suspended so left via the Mersey to cross The Atlantic. Not the first or the last Scouser to get in trouble for speaking out of turn or to run away to sea.

~

The Unitarian meeting room was half full; about twenty-five people had come from all over Liverpool. The Disciples of Christ, The Christians, or The Church of Christ were all names used by the group. With no preacher or parson, no credo, creed, or denominational demands, the disciples could interpret scripture as they saw fit. They were a circle of believers; their commitment was belief in the Lord. Although leaderless in structure and design, Brother John articulated what held them together. Paul and his mother walked through the main meeting hall, its high ceiling crossed with timbers. A balcony ran around three sides but left the centre empty, light and space. White walls and wooden benches amplified the simplicity, creating an atmosphere of openness and honesty. Paul remembered his days in Paradise House, the dark chapel with its high altar, golden tabernacle, crucified Christ, the purple decorated robes of the priests, and the heavy gagging taste of incense.

When they entered the smaller side meeting room, John, a quietly spoken elderly man, whose hair had passed through the stages of grey and silver and now sat as white as cotton wool on his head, breathed the comforting words of Jesus from The Sermon on the Mount.

'Amen,' Paul was quick to interject when John finished.

As was the custom in their meetings, if someone felt the need, they could take up the lead, and so Paul did. 'Blessed are ye, when men shall revile, and persecute you and say all manner of evil against you... these words of George Fox, original dissenter, are true for all who defend the true meaning of Christ.' Paul spoke from his place in the circle and from his heart. 'We all suffer in his name, I speak out in his name, I chastise and correct, but I am not heard. I am truly reviled.'

He looked around the room and took on a sharper tone. He was moving the room from the 'blessed are the meek' of the Sermon on the Mount to angry denunciations. 'Not only creation, but destruction is also a power of the Lord. Floods and fires will indeed come. They are punishments for the sins of man.'

He recalled Revelation Chapter 1, Verse 7, 'Behold.' He raised his hands. John stood back and allowed Paul to take centre stage. 'He is coming with clouds, and every eye will see Him, even they who pierced Him. And all the tribes of the earth will mourn because of Him. Even so, Amen.'

The 'Amens' that would normally be forthright were now

hesitant and guarded.

'Let us not fear the flames. We are saved. Damnation awaits those who have fallen from the path of God.' Paul's voice sang out, strong and clear.

'We have seen the light, have studied the word of God given to us through the life of our saviour Jesus Christ. Accept him, and all things are possible.' It was not the quiet contemplation or the discussion of Christ's values that typically rose to the ceiling; this was boisterous and loud, each new appeal bouncing off the walls.

'Amen.' Was called in response.

'Through Him, all things are sacred.'

'Amen.'

'With Him, all things lead to eternal life.'

'Amen.'

Paul was well into his stride, unconcerned of the looks and shuffled feet. 'We do not fear the scourges of man; our future lies in the hands of the Lord,' he continued, unfazed. 'You may hear that the end is coming, and surely it is so. But do not listen to the false preachers who tell you we can avoid this end. There is one end. It is with God.'

John took up the call. 'Praise our Lord Jesus Christ. We thank Brother Paul for his words. As usual, they come from his Holy fire and spirit. We give thanks for you and to you. In our communion, may Jesus bless and save you.'

Mrs Taylor turned to her neighbour and clasped his hands in hers... 'May Jesus be with you...' she then broke the circle and crossed to John. 'Thank you, John. Your words always bring me peace.'

John bowed his head. 'Paul could be a preacher in a church ten times the size of this. His faith and voice, I'm afraid, are too big for our small communion.'

Paul joined them. 'Brother John, your mercy and compassion are the image of Christ in his turmoil. Not all of us can be so blessed.' Paul encompassed the elderly man's hands in his. 'My time will come, in the face of the world and its evils. My time will come; then, and only then, will my words be heard outside our communion.'

'A glorious day it will be, I'm sure.' John moved his hands free of Paul's, and bowed.

'Indeed, I am proud of my son before all,' said Mrs Taylor.

'A son in faith but not blood,' said Paul. 'Let us not practice to deceive our own hearts before those of others.'

John rebuffed the slight, intentional or not. 'We are all one family, one blood, my son.'

'Forgive me, John, it is true in this communion, in this church. In this life, my mother in all things is before us. But let us not forget that which comes from sin must be made pure.'

A look of concern crossed John's face. 'There are many roads to deliverance. It would be well to remember Matthew; *For with what judgment ye judge, ye shall be judged: and with what measure ye mete, it shall be measured to you again.'*

He smiled at *Matthew*. Paul's whole life was about judgement and meting out the measures of punishment, sometimes in the name of the law and sometimes in the name of the Lord. His calling was in knowing how to dispense the appropriate measure at the appropriate time.

The meeting was concluding, and congregants circulated, exchanging good wishes. John stood before Paul. 'You carry a great responsibility, representing our communion within the community.' He spread his hands to indicate the world outside the meeting hall. 'Surely, every act is personal and not on display, but we cannot hide our hearts or behaviour from the only one who matters. Remember: vengeance is mine sayeth the Lord.'

Paul stood back. 'Are you questioning me, brother?'

The chatter among the other worshippers had quietened as Paul's voice rose.

John bowed. 'I am aware of the content, the scripture you

choose to quote. I, like you, believe in the word of the Lord, but we must caution against choosing the words, valuing words above meaning. Every word, whatever the letters, should spell out God's love.'

'Amen,' said Mrs Taylor.

'I accept the Bible as the true word of God and don't need the wisdom of man to interpret them,' Paul's words surrounded John and reached the others.

'That is all we have, Brother. Until the resurrection, we are left with the word of God through man,' John said.

'The Bible is the word of God.' Paul looked around, expecting signs of support for this simple truth. What he found were looks of concern. No one avoided eye contact or looked away. This was their strength, and projection of anything except love and truth was seen as foreign.

'Through men,' John reminded him. 'Matthew, Mark, Luke, and John.'

Paul pointed to John's Bible. 'The text is written. What is in your hand, Brother? It is the word of God.'

'Did Jesus walk the earth speaking English?' There was no sign or instruction, but the circle had reformed, and congregants listened. John continued, 'No, of course, not.'

'I can't believe that a brother in our communion is questioning the words,' said Paul.

John looked directly at Paul. 'I have faith. I am a Christian. I know that beyond the words, there is the meaning, God was within us all. God was the best of us. Jesus walked this earth and died to show us that. The truth of Jesus was faith. Faith in Him, and in the God that is in us all, in all of humanity, including the most despised and accursed among us.'

The circle of congregants listened intently. John's warm, soft tones, caressed the words, and they left him and engaged with the others in the room. 'This was before all texts and all words. God's love was not written the same way, in English, in Greek, different languages and alphabets. The first gospels were not written but spoken in Aramaic for forty, fifty, even sixty long years. No word of Christ was written. When it was written, it was in Greek by people outside of the land of Judea. Does it matter to me? No. Let scholars and academics argue and debate... because the meaning is beyond language and beyond words. Love is translated through the heart and its actions, not the alphabets of the world.

'So, yes, I caution against anybody that preaches we know, we understand, we can translate the words of God, we need the actions of sacrifice and love to be the guide to our life, not the vagaries of texts. Even more so when we sit in judgment. Don't let this be your path.' His hands reached out in Paul's direction as if to pull him back in.

Paul's voice carried contempt for weakness, evasion, and doubt. 'If we question the word, if we raise ourselves, our understanding above the word, then this is truly the end of belief. Who are we sinners to question, to debate the word?' He raised his Bible, and held it above his right shoulder. He held it above them, over them, as if it had the power to subdue, and people should bow before it, before him, as the bearer of its power. 'The word was given to us by the Lord himself. We judge not the word. Like the Lord's, our judgment is reserved for the sinners.' He let his raised Bible fall back and moved it toward his chest.

'Paul, my brother, if you value the words above all things, then let these words from Luke be your guide: *If your brother or sister sins against you, rebuke them; and if they repent, forgive them. Even if they sin against you seven times in a day and seven times come back to you saying I repent, you must forgive them.*'

Paul closed his eyes and waited for a moment. He knew the room was waiting, watching. He kept them. He held their gaze and attention with his silence, knowing that every second would give weight to the words he used. 'In his letter to the Romans, Saint Paul, my namesake and teacher, declared, *Whoever resists authority resists what God has appointed, and those who resist will incur judgment.'*

He took a step forward, breaking the circle that had formed, and moved towards the door, stopped, and turned to face the group. 'I will carry out the vengeance of the Lord. I will be his sword and shield. I fear no evil.'

He marched to the door and opened it. Mrs Taylor followed Paul.

John's words followed them. 'Saint Augustine explains: *If you believe what you like in the Gospel, and reject what you don't like, it is not the Gospel you believe, but yourself.*'

Mrs Taylor closed the door behind them.

~

Saints and sinners walked the streets of the Holy Land, and the conflict between them was yet to be resolved.

CHAPTER THIRTEEN

CHARLIE

Friday, January 17th, 2020.

Charlie opened his eyes, as he did every day, to the poster of Mo Salah, the Liverpool FC striker staring down from the wall opposite. Mo Salah filled his eyes, but all he could see was the knee in the back, face pressed into the ground, the wriggling body as police carried Matt to the van. Then the flashing baton aimed at Amina. Here one minute, gone the next; here twenty-three years and then gone. Was that how it worked? What did you do when you lost faith in the place you called home?

Mo Salah and Liverpool were storming the premiership; Charlie's waking sight would usually be his waking thought, but he had been robbed of that pleasure.

He stretched and rolled over. His arm ached as he lifted it to check his phone: 11 am. He should get up in case his dad was going in late or his mum came home for lunch. They hated finding him in bed so late in the morning. It was a reminder that he was going nowhere, physically and metaphorically. He couldn't see the difference; he was home anyway and might as well be sleeping in, nothing else to do.

Job hunting was useless. Half the jobs weren't even jobs. Taxi driver? You had to have your own car, insurance and license. Delivery drivers were self-employed, and paid by the parcel. He tried cycle deliveries in town, but it nearly killed him. Dodging traffic wasn't worth it. He would be a barista, but you had to pay for training. It was all a pile of shit. He was clever enough for university, but he didn't want it.

His mum and dad did.

Bollocks! Tens of thousands of pounds in debt for what? So he could be a barista with a degree? He would still have to pay for the fucking training.

Football was his passion. His dad tried to follow so they could watch a match over a pint, but he didn't really care. His mum didn't even try. He guessed they were disappointed in him. No job, no flat, no life of his own, fucking zero. Jesus, shit, if Liverpool did pull off the league, that would make his year. *Fuck year, that would make my life.*

He closed his eyes. Instead of Jordan Henderson holding the trophy aloft to a roaring Anfield, he saw that kid Matt with his megaphone. Charlie swung his legs out of bed. At least he was meeting the guys in the pub in the evening. That was something.

~

Terry's face was an explosion of glee. 'We fucking battered them.' He had looked sixteen since he was twelve. Charlie knew he always would. His short, dark hair curled, as if trying to escape his head.

Charlie laughed. 'Yeah.' He nodded at the empty chair then asked, 'Where is he?'

'On his way.' Terry took his jacket off and hung it over the back of his chair. 'Do you want a pint?'

'Yeah.'

'Best bit of the match?' Terry asked. 'And not the goal. That's too easy.'

'I don't know. All of it, I guess.'

'Are you okay?'

'Yeah, fine. Are you getting the ale in?' The question was a way of changing the subject.

'As we speak.' Terry pulled out his wallet, held it aloft for a second, then went to the bar.

Charlie looked around. He enjoyed being back in his local. The John Brodie was a proper pub, with old men and dogs as welcome as a group of students on a night out. A big, purpose-built pub, soft carpet underfoot, big screens for the footie, and a quiz night where students embarrassed themselves against the locals.

Charlie and his mates had been coming here since they were seventeen. It was a home from home. He knew the bar staff and more than a few of the other customers. Those he didn't know acknowledged him when they met. Everything was the same and yet...

Terry returned with two lagers. 'How many... nine replacements from the usual team? Five, six of them teenagers, and they beat a full-strength Everton squad.'

'What time's Alan coming?'

Terry pulled out his phone, and his thumbs flashed over the screen. 'He's on his way.'

'I hope you took it easy on him,' said Charlie.

Terry aped a TV commentator. 'And Curtis Jones curls one into the top left corner for Liverpool. Oh no, look at that - the Picford's arms are too short. He can't reach the ball.' Terry laughed. 'So, where have you been, anyway? I thought you would have been the first to rip into Alan.'

Charlie smiled.

'Come on, something's up?' said Terry.

Charlie rubbed his hand over his face. 'I would rather wait till Alan's here.'

'Why? What's it got to do with him?'

'He knows a bit more about it, that's all.'

'He's an Evertonian. He knows fook all.' Terry took a long draught of his pint, then looked up. 'Speak of the devil.'

Alan approached that table. His thin face and short, straight, side-parted hair gave him a serious air. 'I wasn't sure about coming here tonight,' he said.

'I bet you weren't. Ding ding!' Terry mimed striking the bell. 'Round Two of the public humiliation.'

'Okay, you're on a roll.' Alan sat down. 'But Ancelotti's gotta have time to sort the team out. Last week was the low point. There's only one way to go from here-'

'Never mind that,' Charlie said. 'I want to ask you something.'

'Yeah, like how he can show his face,' said Terry.

'No.' Charlie snapped at Terry. 'Leave it out a minute, will you?'

Terry pushed his chair back. 'What?'

'Just hold on.' Charlie's hands moved forward, making a downward motion as if physically suppressing something. 'What do you know about Extinction Revolution?'

'The movement?' Alan asked.

'Yeah.'

'They're climate change activists, into direct action, non-violent. A bit apocalyptic.'

'Apoca... what?' asked Terry.

'End of the world shit,' said Charlie. 'Climate change... global warming...'

'Why, what's all this about?' asked Alan.

'Good question,' said Terry. 'What the fuck. Liverpool reserves beat Everton 1-0 and you want to talk about climate change?'

'I saw a guy get arrested last Monday morning. By Monday afternoon, he was dead.'

'How? Alan asked.

'I don't know. He died in the police station.'

The laugh lines disappeared from Terry's face. 'The bizzies are cunts.'

Alan objected. 'Come on, you can't say that.'

'I just have. After Hillsborough? You're fucking kidding, aren't you?'

Charlie laid his arm on the table and rolled up his sleeve, the swelling had gone, the purple and blues were less intense, but still there.

'Shit, what happened?' asked Alan.

'I saw a guy arrested, then I heard on the news that he was dead. The weird thing was, he was looking directly at me. While the cops had him on the ground. It was like he was looking into me. I don't know. He said, 'The world is burning...' Then they carried him off and threw him into the back of a van. His name was Matt. Later I went to a kind of picket, and a cop lashed out and did that.'

'I think I remember hearing it on the radio,' said Alan 'The death, I mean. You saw it happen?'

Charlie nodded and took a drink of his lager.

'And you didn't tell us?' Alan said.

'You went to a picket on your own?' Terry said. 'What happened to one for all, and all that?'

Charlie looked from one to the other. 'This isn't kids' stuff, we're not Musketeers.'

'But we are supposed to be mates,' said Terry, 'a team.'

'Hang on a minute, did you say Matt?' Alan looked at Charlie and raised his eyebrows. 'Matt?' he repeated.

'Yeah,' said Charlie.

'You know his name? I didn't think they had released that publicly? Not yet, anyway.'

'They haven't,' Charlie said. He picked up a beer mat and began ripping pieces off it.

Alan and Terry waited.

'It gets complicated. I spoke to a girl. A woman at the picket.'

'I knew it,' said Terry. 'A woman. Had to be a woman behind it. What's she like? Is she fit?'

'Jesus, what century are you living in?' Alan asked Terry.

'Give me a break.' Terry snarled. 'You and your woke bollocks.'

'She is, but that's not the point,' said Charlie. 'I think I've got myself mixed up in something.'

'Here we go. Have you shagged her?'

'No. I went to the police and offered to be a witness.'

Terry leaned in over the table. 'That was stupid. What did you do that for? They don't like it if someone gives evidence against them. I'd be careful if I were you.'

Alan looked at Terry as he spoke. 'It's not often I say this, but I think Terry's right. What did you see?'

'It was a bit weird. They had these straps around his body. And around his face, over his mouth.' Charlie lifted his hands to demonstrate how it was applied.

'Spit or bite guards. They're only supposed to use them where they get resistance.'

'You'd better watch your back, mate,' said Terry. 'Have you given your statement yet?'

'No, I went into the station. They said they'd be in touch.'

'They're just putting you off. Kicking the can down the road. I'd forget it, drop the whole thing.'

'You should be careful, whatever you do,' said Alan.

'The fucking woman,' Terry shook his head. 'You're gonna end up in the shit over this; you mark my words. A woman and the bizzies; you tell me, how is this gonna end well?'

'I also spoke to his mum.'

'Bloody hell, you are involved,' said Alan. He paused for a second. 'You did the right thing. Tell them what you saw, then let the process work.'

'It's a mistake, mate,' Terry said. 'You should keep clear.'

'What have you been up to?' The voice was urgent and sharp, and the three guys turned round. Charlie's dad was behind them.

'What are you doing here?' asked Charlie.

'Your phone's dead.'

Charlie pulled out his phone and swiped the black screen. 'Shit, yeah, sorry.'

'The police called the house. They want to speak to you.'

'Oh shit,' said Charlie.

'What the hell is going on?'

Alan and Terry avoided his dad's eyes.

'It's not what you think,' Charlie explained.

'What do I think?'

'I don't know. But really, it's okay. There's no need to panic.'

'Come on, let's get you home.' His dad motioned with his hand.

Charlie took a drink.

'Come on.' The impatience in his dad's voice showed.

'Go on.' Alan stared intently at Charlie, 'But remember we're here if you need us.'

'Did you watch the match, Mr Connolly?' Terry said.

'Not now, eh, Terry,' said Charlie's dad.

Terry turned back to the table.

'Well?'

'Okay, okay. I'm coming.' Charlie drained his pint. 'I'll see you guys.'

'Let us know how you get on?' said Alan

'Yeah, especially with the bird,' said Terry with an exaggerated wink.

Charlie followed his dad, putting on his jacket as he walked out the main door. 'Was that really necessary?' Charlie asked.

'I don't know; you tell me?'

They walked along the street in silence. The charge between them built with the distance. Charlie's dad stopped and turned to face him. 'Come on, what's going on? Tell me now, before we get home and face your mum. Why are the police calling you?'

'I volunteered to give a statement.'

'About what? What have you done?'

'I haven't done anything.'

'Look, you can tell me. I'll understand.'

'Dad, I'm not you. I haven't done anything.'

His dad's eyebrows raised. 'What's that supposed to mean?'

'You told me about when you were a kid. Some of the trouble you got into.'

'Yeah, okay. Thanks for reminding me. So, what's this about?'

'Can we wait till we get home? I don't want to go through it all twice. You know what Mum's like. She'll want it word for word.' Charlie walked off and his dad caught him.

'So, you haven't done anything? Last chance.'

'No.' Charlie smiled. 'You're the only scally in this family.' He hit his dad playfully across the head.

'Come here, you bugger.' His dad pulled Charlie in for a hug.

A stab of pain shot through Charlie's sore arm and he pushed his dad away. 'Oww! What the fuck, what's up with you? Get off.'

~

His mum was at the dinner table. She pointed to the chairs opposite. Charlie took a seat, and his dad moved to the counter and turned the kettle on. His mum lifted the remote to silence the TV and fixed her gaze on Charlie.

Charlie felt like he was in an interview.

'So?' Her question hung in the air.

Charlie gathered himself to explain. 'Last week, going to work, I walked out of Central Station by the Tesco.'

'Yeah, I know it,' said his dad. 'They have that cake shop there, where they do like Beatles cakes, or footballers. Really good, or it was, not sure if it's still there.' He leaned against the counter.

His mum gave his dad a look. The kettle started to boil, and his dad turned to sort it out.

Charlie told them what happened, what he'd seen.

'My God, that sounds terrible,' said his mum. 'Why do they have to be so brutal?'

The noises from the kettle grew as steam poured from the spout. His dad reached for cups and arranged three in a line. 'Who wants one?' he asked.

'Yeah,' said Charlie.

'Yeah, but go on.' His mum urged Charlie on.

'Later, I heard the radio news. It said a protester had died in police custody. I knew it was him. Don't ask me how, but I knew.'

His mum reached out and squeezed his hand, and Charlie flinched at the contact.

'Fuck,' his dad poured water into the mugs.

'Do you have to?' Charlie's mum said.

'What?'

'Swear.'

'Alright, sorry.' His dad turned his attention back to the tea.

'So that's why the police are calling. I went in and said I would give a witness statement.'

His dad placed a mug of tea in front of Charlie. His mum slid a coaster across the table to him.

'Although, now I'm not so sure.' Charlie placed his tea on the coaster. 'What did they say when they called?' he asked.

'They left a name and a number here.' His mum reached behind her and pulled a piece of paper from the counter. 'Superintendent Smith.'

'What are you going to do?' asked his dad.

Charlie stared at the table. 'I want to help. But how can I help him? He's dead.'

'By telling the truth,' said his dad. 'Did the police do anything wrong? Did you see anything?'

'No, I don't think so. They strapped him up pretty good. But they didn't beat him or anything.'

'Then that's what you should say. Just tell the truth.'

'That's what Alan said.'

'Yeah, well, he's a sensible lad. Not like the other idiot... Terry.'

'You think I should give a statement?' Charlie asked his mum.

'I'm not sure.'

'Why?'

'I'm selfish. I don't want anything to happen to you.'

'Well, I do,' his dad said. 'Not want anything to happen to you. I mean, you should give a statement.'

'Why?'

'Because you have to face things. You can't just walk away. Pretend the bad things don't happen. I've seen enough to know that. But you should realise you're not doing it for the kid or for his mum. You're doing it for yourself.'

'That's just it, though. I don't know what I want.'

'It's all well and good saying you have to face things,' said his mum. 'But he doesn't. He didn't do anything here; he's not in the wrong. Not like you and the others.'

'Oh yeah, that's nice,' his dad said. 'Turn this into an attack on me. Yeah, good one.'

His mum shook her head. 'I'm just saying it's different. You guys robbed an old man's house, and he died, whether you were kids or not. Charlie hasn't done anything. You hear all the time about people getting into trouble, being witnesses.'

'Time to get your shit together, son. You saw someone die. If that doesn't make you think about what you're doing, nothing will.' He took a drink from his tea.

'He didn't see him die. He saw him arrested, don't dramatise it.'

'When he looked at me, it went through me,' Charlie said. 'I mean, I think he saw inside me.'

'And what's inside you?' asked his mum.

'That's just it, nothing. I mean, what am I doing? I don't have a proper job. I live with you two. I don't have a girlfriend. I go to the football when I can scrounge the money together. I go to the pub.'

'Don't be too hard on yourself,' said his mum. 'You're young, and you have time to decide.'

'You had me at this age,' Charlie said. 'And dad, you were at university. My grandad had come over from Ireland. What am I doing?' Charlie played with his mug, spinning it and the coaster around on the table.

'What do you want to do?' His mum asked.

'I don't know. I don't know if anything was wrong or not.

This guy Matthew, the guy who died... he was involved in campaigning against climate change. He was doing something with his life. You know what I mean? Why him? Why did he die? When there are loads of us; it wouldn't make any difference if we died.'

'That's a terrible thing to say!' His mum snapped. 'Don't you talk like that in my house.'

'No, I didn't mean it like that, Mum. I know you and Dad would be upset.'

'Upset?'

'Okay, a bit more than upset.'

'Nah, upset's about right,' his dad said, smiling.

His mum glared at his dad.

'What I mean is, he was making a difference. Changing the world.'

'Okay, well, if you want to do something, why don't you go to see Jaime?'

'Who's Jaime?' Charlie asked.

'You met him. Well, a long time ago. At Sammo's funeral. Do you remember?'

'The guy from town?'

His dad took a sip of his tea. 'He's involved in stuff, knows the right people. If you are serious about helping Matthew's family, then maybe you could have a word with him. Do you want me to call him?'

'I'm not sure.' His mum cut in. 'Don't encourage him.'

'I'm not encouraging. I just think if he's going to do something, maybe he should talk to someone who actually knows what the procedures are.'

'Maybe. This girl has been kinda helping,' said Charlie.

'Who is she then?' asked his mum.

'Emma.'

'Where is she from?'

'She's in the Extinction Revolution.'

'No, I mean, where does she live? Where are her family from?'

'I don't know. She's at uni. I think she shares a house in Wavertree,' Charlie said.

'Where are her family from?' His mum asked again.

'I don't know, Mum.'

His mum took a drink of tea. 'Well, are we going to meet her?'

'It's not like that,' Charlie lied.

'Well, if you're spending time with her, I would like to meet her,' said his mum.

'We'll see,' said Charlie. 'Anyway, I'm going up.'

~

Charlie closed the door to his room. His single bed took up one side, and a bookcase took up half the length of the other side, next to a wardrobe. The bookcase was filled with Liverpool Annuals. He had every year since he was ten. Mo Salah was still looking down at him. His laptop was beside the bed. Charlie flopped onto the mattress and swiped his finger across the mousepad; the screen came to life.

YouTube. A list of videos on Liverpool's push for the title. Would this be the year? All his childhood, he had heard of the glory days. He could name the teams and see the faces even though he wasn't born... Dalgliesh in eighty-eight... eighty-three to eighty-four under Bob Paisley... Ian Rush getting the golden boot for the season... Keegan... the Shankly years. Liverpool were the undoubted champions of English football. It was coming back. He felt it. Everyone knew they were so close the previous season and unbeaten so far. Surely nothing could spoil it? He had waited his whole life for this. He clicked on Redmen TV, lay back on his pillow and closed his eyes. As the guys discussed Man United, Liverpool's next victims, the scratchy sound of Matt's amplified voice crept into his consciousness. The world is burning, the words competed with the voices from Youtube; they merged into one question What are you going to do?

~

His wife had gone up for the night. Vinny's anxiety levels were rising. It had been a while since the last crisis over Sammo's death. It was strange for Vinny to see his son struggle with the same dilemma: how to do the right thing.

Charlie needed something, someone to energise him, to give him a reason to care.

Vinny Connolly crossed the living room. As he reached up to draw the curtains, his eyes landed on a slim figure on the other side of the road. He was walking now, but Vinny could swear when he first saw him, he was standing there looking at the house.

CHAPTER FOURTEEN

CHARLIE

Monday, January 20th, 2020.

Framed by the red sandstone of the Anglican Cathedral, Emma tapped away at her phone. She didn't see Charlie approach. Her blonde hair splayed out across her shoulders. He waited until he was in front of her before breaking through her frown of concentration.

'Hey. Miles away?' He nodded at the phone.

'*The Guardian.* My daily dose of misery. How was your weekend?'

'Pretty good, actually. We beat Man United two nil.'

'That's a good weekend, is it?'

'It'll do me.'

'Good to know you're easily pleased.'

He sat next to her. 'How about yours?'

'I've just come from The Hub. There's a pretty big action coming up. We've got a lot of coordinating to do.'

'What kind of action?'

'I can't say too much about it at the moment.'

'A big secret, is it?'

'No, not like that, but if we are doing direct action, then we have to be conscious of security.'

'I thought you wanted people involved.'

'We do, but we have to protect our actions.'

'Strange place to meet,' Charlie looked around suspiciously.

'Is it to throw off your tail?'

Emma punched him softly.

Their bench was outside the enormous Anglican Cathedral on Saint James Mount. Its red sandstone central tower loomed above them. Charlie looked out over the city to the silver line of the river reflecting sunlight below.

'I usually go down into the park but thought it would be easier for you to meet here,' Emma said.

'The graveyard?'

'Yeah, but it's a park as well.'

'It is a cemetery, though. Cemetery first, park second, is the way I see it. No, let me change that. It's a cemetery, full stop.'

'Not anymore. It's classed as a park. It stopped being used as a cemetery decades ago.'

'Try telling that to the dead people.'

To the left of the Cathedral, a path led down behind the outcrop of rock of Saint James Mount, down below ground level to the old Saint James Cemetery. No longer in use, it had become the resting place for tombstones moved from other locations within the city. The path to the park curved steeply and the right-hand wall was lined with gravestones. Tourists and locals would wander among the stones reading the sometimes harrowing tales carved in them.

'You wouldn't get me back down there. My dad used to take me on some sort of weird excursion. Did you know there are catacombs down there? Most of the graves from the workhouse were transferred over from where the university is now.'

'How do you know that?' Emma asked.

'My dad, he's always telling me stuff.'

'Why?'

'He's a historian at the uni.'

'Liverpool Uni'? Oh, really? That's cool. What's his name? I might know him.'

'I hope not.' Charlie smiled.

Emma nudged him playfully.

'Connolly. Vinny Connolly. He's in the history department.'

'So, your dad's a uni lecturer?' Emma seemed impressed.

'Yeah.' Charlie could feel his stock rising. 'He's a lecturer now, but he was raised in Speke. My grandad was from Ireland, a bit of a villain. My dad was a scally as a kid. He's told me some of the stuff they used to get up to, but he managed to get out.'

'You sound quite proud of him.'

'Is it possible to be proud and embarrassed at the same time? I don't know. Maybe I am, in a way.'

'So, you come from a long line of Irish scallies and criminals?' Emma teased.

Charlie laughed. 'I guess so.' He changed the course of the conversation. 'You didn't have to come.'

'I know. I wanted to. I think it's really great that you're doing this.'

'Come on then. Shall we get this done?' He stood up.

~

He was pleased Emma was with him. She was so open it was kind of frightening; it made him more open too. He knew she was with Andy, but she said she was Poly. He'd checked it out, polyamorous - a person who had intimate relationships with more than one partner. Or someone who shagged around, as Terry would say. He couldn't see his mum being happy with that.

The walk from the Cathedral was just a few minutes, along Georgian streets that reminded Charlie of Sherlock Holmes; all you needed to complete the scene was the horse-drawn cab.

It was his second time in a police station in a few days, although he had an appointment this time, and he would be interviewed by Superintendent Smith.

'Mr Connolly.'

Charlie almost missed it. He wasn't used to hearing his name sound so formal. He stood and moved toward the counter.

'If you go over there, a colleague will let you in.'

Charlie crossed the waiting area. Emma followed him. He waited outside a door. There was a square, silver pane of glass in the top part of the door. He guessed it was a one-way window.

There was a buzz and the door clicked. A female bizzy held it open. Her dark eyes flashed between Charlie and Emma.

'Mr Connolly, can you come this way, please?'

'Can I come?' asked Emma.

Charlie wasn't sure she would be allowed but said, 'Maybe it's better if you wait here. I'll be fine.'

'Okay,' she waved, weakly. 'I'll be here for you,'

As Charlie turned to enter, Emma sprang forward and planted a kiss on his cheek. The kiss was a surprise. Her lips were soft and warm, and Charlie savoured the touch.

'Mr Connolly?'

Charlie had his hand up to his cheek.

The dark eyes smiled. 'Sir?'

'Yeah, sorry.' He went through the door.

There was a short corridor with interview rooms on either side. The constable led the way and turned to a door on the right. A sign on the door said, *Interview Room Two.* She opened the door and waited for Charlie to enter. In the centre of the old cell, a grey table held a double cassette recorder. He pulled one of the four chairs out and sat. The officer stepped out and closed the door.

He waited, the grey walls enveloping him. Up high, there was a small window, tiny with thick glass, it rationed light into the room. It was his first time in a cell and he felt the power of absence. Not just of light, but of sight or sound. The senses were denied, in grey walls and floor, painted brick and concrete. He understood the biggest denial was humanity. The walls reflected back his thoughts. The only sounds were those that bounced around inside him, the voice that questioned what he was doing and why. He shivered. *Fuck.*

The door swung open, and a woman in her fifties in a grey trouser suit and white shirt entered and held out her hand. Her hair was bunched and held with black hair grips. 'Superintendent Smith, and this Detective Sergeant Molloy.'

DS Molloy barely raised his balding head in greeting and was concentrated on laying out papers in front of him.

Charlie shook hands with the Superintendent. She indicated for him to sit.

The dark eyed, female bizzy entered the room, closed the door, and stood to the side. Superintendent Smith sat down. She folded her hands and waited.

Sgt Molloy slipped a new cassette into the recorder and pressed two buttons. The mechanism began to turn.

'You know you have the right to legal representation?' she asked.

'Yeah,' Charlie said.

'Okay, how can we help you, Mr Connolly?'

'I am here to make a statement about what I saw.'

'Just to clarify. You are referring to the arrest of Mr Matthew Whitney on Monday the 7th January 2020 in the concourse of Liverpool Central rail station.'

'Yeah, that's right,' he felt a bit stupid he hadn't given the time or place.

'I have to inform you that we will record this interview for future reference and that you will be asked to sign to verify the recording.'

'That's fine.' Charlie spoke clearly but wished he could be somewhere else.

Sergeant Molloy opened official proceedings. 'Monday 20th January, 1300 hours. Voluntary interview between Superintendent Smith and Charles Connolly in relation to ongoing IOPC inquiry MP217/534. Also present Sergeant Molloy and PC Jones. Mr Connolly has been advised of his entitlement to legal representation and has declined.'

'Thank you, Sergeant. Good afternoon, Mr Connolly. What

would you like to tell us? Relax, take your time and just tell us what you remember.' The Superintendent held her pen poised to make notes, her eyes alternating between Charlie and the notepad.

Charlie leaned forward, elbows on the table separating him from the two officers. 'I heard him before I saw him.'

Charlie recounted his story ending with the officer telling him to 'fuck off or he'd be next"

'Okay. Thank you, Mr Connolly. In a moment, my colleague will summarise your statement and read it back to you. You can sign it, and before you leave, sign to verify the recording.' She smiled at Charlie. 'But before we do that, I do have some questions.'

'Yeah, go for it.' He tried to sound relaxed; he had nothing to hide. He had made his statement. As far as he was concerned, the issue was over.

'Why were you in the station at that time in the morning?'

'I was going to work. I was doing a day shift.'

'Okay, I see. So you were not connected to the protest in any way?'

'No.'

'You did not know Matthew Whitney? Have any connection with him?'

'No. Why are you asking?'

'We just need to establish there is no other motivation for your statement.'

'No, none at all.'

'Okay. That's fine. So, just to be clear... you have no connection to either the protest or to Matthew Whitney?'

'No.' Charlie paused. 'Well, I did go and see his mum.'

The Superintendent raised an eyebrow. 'Okay, I see. When was this?'

'Last week. Thursday, I think it was. Is that a problem?'

'No, it's good you have told us. It's a bit surprising.' She was quiet for a moment, and let the silence hang in the air.

Charlie didn't respond.

So she asked, 'You went to see Mrs Whitney?'

'Yes.'

'Why? And how did you know where she lived?'

'Oh, yeah, sorry. A friend of Matt's told me. I heard he died on the radio. Well, not Matt. I didn't know who it was. I just heard on the radio somebody had died. I don't know how, but I guessed or sort of knew it was the guy I had seen arrested. The radio said there was a protest outside the station. Here, actually,' Charlie pointed at the table. 'I didn't go to protest. I'm not sure why I did go, actually. It was at the protest someone told me more about him.'

Her eyebrows arched. 'Who was it that told you more about Mr Whitney?'

Charlie was uncomfortable. 'Someone at the protest.'

'They told you about Matthew and where his mum lived? Why would they do that?'

'Because I saw what happened.'

'Can you give me the name of the person who told you about Matthew?'

'No, not really.'

'You can't or won't?'

'Both.' He didn't want to give Emma's name, but he felt trapped.

'I thought you came here voluntarily to help with the inquiry into the circumstances surrounding Matthew's death?'

'I did, and I have.'

'So who told you where Matthew's mother lived?' The Superintendent leaned forward.

'I think I have said enough now.'

'Mr Connolly, why are you giving a statement today?'

'I told you. I saw what happened.' He leaned back in his chair and folded his arms.

'You also said you had no connection to Mr Whitney or the protest.'

'I didn't.'

'That's not how it appears.'

'I'm not lying.'

'No one has accused you of that. I am explaining that your motivation seems conflicted or, at the very least, confused. You admit that someone from the protest spoke to you about his death, and you spoke to his mother.'

'Yeah.'

'Can you see how that raises questions about the impartiality of your statement?'

'Like I said. That's it, I'm done. I've told you what I saw.' Charlie stood and moved toward the door.

'Please, Mr Connolly, wait one minute.'

Charlie was pissed off.

'Sergeant Molloy will read your statement back to you and you can sign to verify the information you have given.' The Superintendent paused; her voice changed from the warmth of encouragement to an ice-cold threat. 'Before you sign, I have to warn you that it is a criminal offence to provide false evidence, or to attempt to interfere with, or obstruct a police investigation.'

He knew she was trying to scare him, and on some level, it was working. *Fuck, this is crazy.*

Terry's words came back to him. *A woman and the cops - this is bound to end badly.* He might be a cunt, thought Charlie, but he's not stupid.

Sergeant Molloy read out his statement. His monotone delivery made it sound dumb. Charlie didn't care now. He just wanted to get out of there. He signed the form, and the constable opened the door for him.

Superintendent Smith handed him her card. Her voice had reverted to the friendly schoolteacher. 'If you need to speak, if you want to change your statement or give any other information, feel free to call me.'

'Yeah, right,' Charlie had glimpsed behind her friendly

demeanor and didn't like what he saw.

He stepped through the door back into the station atrium, where Emma was waiting. She came across to meet him. Her bouncing step, flowing blonde hair and warmth meant something different, but he wasn't sure what.

'Come on, let's get out of here.' He made his way out, leaving Emma rushing to keep up.

On the street outside he took a deep breath. Despite the traffic and the fumes, the air tasted good. The sun was climbing toward its high point, tussling with the clouds for dominance. The noises of the cars and buses were a shot of reality.

'What happened?' Emma's casual question betrayed the concern in her eyes.

'I made a right pig's ear of that. *Fuck. What an idiot.*'

'How? What happened? You told them what you saw, didn't you?'

He didn't answer. He turned the corner and walked down the hill letting his weight carry him. Emma trailed slightly behind, trying hard to keep up. He'd been a fool. He should have listened to his dad and spoke to a lawyer.

'Wait. Charlie, Wait!' Her voice was higher and more urgent the second time. 'Charlie, wait!'

He swung around. 'What's wrong?'

Emma walked back up the hill towards Hope Street and the police station.

'What's up?' He was now following her.

Emma's fast walk broke out into a jog. Charlie couldn't see what was wrong.

'Emma, what's going on?' he shouted after her.

She didn't reply.

Emma shouted something, Charlie couldn't hear. She disappeared around the corner of Hope Street.

When Charlie caught up to her, she had stopped running and shouted 'Simon!'

A guy in his mid-thirties was crossing the road from the

Philharmonic Hall. He was slim, dressed in black trousers and a black jacket. He looked unremarkable, heading for the police station.

'Simon!' Emma called a second time.

He didn't react.

Charlie looked again. Something about his movement seemed familiar.

Emma waved as if she expected him to stop and talk.

The figure passed the public entrance to the police station and continued. As he turned to go through the secure entrance, he produced a card and swiped for the gate to open.

Charlie saw his profile, the black clothes, the movement. Could it be?

Emma stopped, confused. 'Simon,' she shouted the last time, this time with desperation or disappointment; Charlie couldn't tell.

Simon turned and looked at the gate. He didn't flinch. There was no sign of recognition, the gate buzzed open, and he went through.

It couldn't be, could it? Charlie was confused. 'Who was that?'

'It was Simon. He was in our group.'

'He's police?' asked Charlie.

'I don't know. You mean because he went in that entrance?'

'Yes, that's what it means, if he has a card to get in there. Are you telling me this guy… that guy who just went in the police station was a member of your group?'

A shocked Emma replied. 'Yeah, I think so. No, I know he was. It was definitely Simon.'

Charlie took a step back, shaking his head. He spoke slowly and clearly. 'Those bastards... there's something very fucking odd going on here.' He paused and took a deep breath. 'And I'll tell you something now. I'm gonna find out what the hell it is.'

CHAPTER FIFTEEN

CHARLIE

Monday, January 20th, 2020.

They were on Hope Street. Everything around them was in motion: the traffic lights changed, the cars stopped and started; pedestrians passed by.

'We didn't know.' Emma turned away from the police station and headed the opposite way.

'What do you mean you didn't know?' Charlie caught up to her.

'We didn't know his job. What's the big deal? What's wrong with you?'

'He's police. Emma, it's not normal to have a bizzy as part of your group, or am I wrong? You tell me.'

'Aren't they allowed opinions? Aren't they people?' Emma said.

They turned the corner again and walked down Hardman Street.

'Of course, they are. That's not the point. What was he doing in your group? Was he…I don't know, undercover? Was he in the unit that arrested Matt? Was he the one who killed him? There was something about him. Who is he?'

'His name is Simon.'

'What about his surname, his address?'

'You're being really aggressive.'

'It could be important. Do you know his name and address?'

'Not now, but I have it. It's on my laptop at home. He signed up to the group, so we've got his contact details.'

'Okay. We need to go and check it out.'

~

The house Emma lived in was a Victorian semi. It had been let out to students for many years, so many of the original features were worn and damaged. The coving around the windows was cracked and peeling. The house on Grant Avenue faced Wavertree Park, about twenty minutes by bus from the town centre. The houses were larger and more substantial than the two-up, two-down terraces of Garston or the Dingle.

As long as students handed over cash for rent, these houses were in limbo, no upgrades or improvements. Owners sat back and watched values grow without breaking a sweat. No wonder he had to live with his parents.

He followed Emma through to the kitchen. A large wooden table filled the room, and a line of wine bottles ran down the centre, some recently emptied, others filled with candles, dried flowers, and plants. The windowsill was full of little jam jars used as plant pots; Charlie guessed they were filled with homegrown herbs.

The gas cooker had an old-style kettle with a whistle attached. The Belfast sink had two huge old brass taps and a wooden drainer. Everywhere was full and overflowing; the lack of control was palpable. Books balanced a whisker away from toppling from shelves. Plants hung low off the top of cupboards. Charlie was uneasy. His mum's kitchen was clean and organised. He'd never really considered it before, but it was shocking to see a house where no one took responsibility and everyone was accommodated.

'Do you want a tea?' Emma asked.

'Yeah, sure.'

'Green? Chamomile?'

'Do you have any ordinary, normal tea bags?'

'I think we've got some Earl Grey somewhere. Will that do?'

'Is it normal tea?'

'It's black.'

'Yeah, sure,' said Charlie, not sure at all.

Emma lit the ring under the kettle and the gas flared. Then she disappeared. He heard her clumping up the stairs.

The silence was broken by the sound of the water inside the kettle; he could hear it beginning to boil. The water vapour echoing around inside, then the quiet roar as the water began to move. Both sounds combined and grew. A wispy line of steam came from the whistle but not enough to force it to sing. The sound consumed Charlie. He could almost see the water bubbling and steaming. He felt the same; something was happening, something was growing. He wasn't sure what yet, or what it meant. Even though he listened intently to the growing whine, he was still startled by the brutality of the whistle when it screamed.

Charlie sprang into action and turned off the gas.

'Nice one. Just in time,' Emma appeared from the hallway. She crossed the kitchen and poured the boiling water into cups.

'Have you got any milk? Sugar?' asked Charlie.

'Err, somewhere, let me check.' She produced a handmade clay pot. 'Here.'

He dug into the congealed brown sugar, knowing it was all he could expect.

'Milk?' he asked tentatively.

'Soy,' said Emma opening the fridge.

'Whatever,' said Charlie.

'Come on, let's take these upstairs.' She led the way through the hallway.

He felt awkward going to her room. He fancied Emma, but this situation was weird. He was still angry about the copper. She got him into this mess, asking him to give a statement.

'Here we are.'

The smell hit him first, sweet, sickly. He never understood

why overpowering one smell with a stronger one was supposed to be a good thing. A wisp of smoke spiralled from a joss stick on a cast-iron mantelpiece crowded with coloured candles and more dried flowers.

Her laptop was open next to the bed, which was a mattress on the floor. The room was free of furniture except for a full-length mirror that leant against a wall. There was a big sash window, its frame painted a dark green, which was also the colour of the tall skirting board that ran round the length of the room. The wall had an architrave, again dark green, about a foot from ceiling height. Various chimes and dream catchers hung from the ceiling. A riot of colours screamed from walls full of paintings and posters.

'Wow.'

Emma laughed. 'You like it?' she spread her arms in a sweep of ownership.

'I guess,' said Charlie.

'Sit down.' Emma arranged herself on the bed and placed her drink on the floor. She lifted the laptop and put it on her legs.

Charlie stood by the door, not sure what to do.

'Don't be shy.' Emma patted the bed next to her.

Charlie accepted the offer. He sat next to her. He lifted his tea and almost spluttered the liquid over the bed.

'Okay?' Emma asked.

'Yeah, sure,' he lied. 'Just a bit hot.' He leaned across to put it on the floor.

Emma started typing. 'Let's see what we can find out.' After a minute, she turned the screen towards him. 'This is our membership list. Here we go... Simon Abbot... 16 Isaac Street, Liverpool 8.'

'That's in the Dingle, isn't it?'

'I don't know, but we can check.' She tapped away at the keyboard and pulled up Google maps. 'Yeah, off Park Road.'

'And where does your group meet?'

'Mainly in Woolton, but we have people from different parts of South Liverpool, so nobody really cares where you live.'

'But the Dingle?'

'Yeah, you're right. The Liverpool Central group would be much closer and easier to get to.'

'Does it say his job?' Charlie asked.

'Not on here, no.'

'Do you usually ask?'

'Not really. Membership is just a way of collecting a few quid, and to give people the chance to feel a part of something.'

'This is fucking crazy. Can you check him out? Try Facebook.'

Emma put his name in. Two profiles appeared; the first, a young guy with longer, darker hair. 'That's not him,' she said. The second profile had no photo and no details, just the name. Emma clicked on it, but all the settings were private. 'That could be him.'

'How about Google?'

'Nothing local. Is it worth trying anything else?'

'Probably not. A link would come up on Google anyway.'

'Yeah, true.' Emma let the laptop slide off her legs and leaned back against her pillows and the wall. 'Look, we don't know anything yet. Don't you think you might be over-reacting?'

'We know he's dirty. You don't swipe a card through that gate if you're not.'.

'You're really freaking out about this, aren't you?'

Charlie was surprised she could be so blasé about their discovery.

'Here, let me help you relax. Turn round.'

'What?'

'Turn round,' Emma slapped his shoulder and then physically turned him.

Charlie shifted his position to face the window. Emma began massaging his neck and shoulders. 'Is that better? she asked.

'It is, but it's not relaxing.'

She continued, but the massage became softer, and her hands spread from his shoulders, one stroking his neck. Charlie was getting aroused. Did she know what she was doing? *Jeez.*

He turned; her face was close to his.

'Do you like it?' she asked.

'Very much,' he said.

He moved forward and kissed her. A single kiss, but she didn't pull away, and he felt the pressure of her response. The kiss took its own course, soft, gentle kisses that quickly moved to open-mouthed urgency.

Emma slid down the bed and pushed the laptop aside, and Charlie repositioned himself so he was lying next to her. He was acting on impulse, going with the flow. She was not only responding but leading the way. He was about to have his first shag in months.

The last time was at a party at 3 am, when neither he nor the girl were particularly sober. He remembered waking up first and leaving the room before she woke. This was different. Neither had been drinking. His annoyance with Emma, Matt, and the copper, everything took second place to his urgent desire.

~

Charlie lay back and marvelled at the design around the light fitting. It was scrolls of leaves, maybe vines. Emma had covered herself in a sheet and disappeared to the bathroom at the end of the hall. He swung his legs round and lifted the quilt in search of his boxer shorts. He wasn't sure how he felt. It was good. *Fuck,* he enjoyed that. Sated was the word that sprang to mind. Fulfilled, he hoped she enjoyed it.

'Hey,' Emma reentered the room and closed the door behind her. She sat next to Charlie, careful to keep the sheet covering her. Charlie was boxered up with his back against the wall. Emma held the sheet at chest height with her right hand.

Her left arm was uncovered at her side. Charlie noticed scaly, purplish scar tissue on the inside of her left forearm.

'Shit. What's that?'

Emma looked at her arm and moved it quickly out of sight. 'Oh, nothing.'

'It doesn't look like nothing,' said Charlie

'Teenage stuff, all in the past.' She stood. 'Do you want anything? More tea? I should get dressed.' Emma collected her clothes from around the bed. 'Back in a minute.' She left with her clothes.

Charlie dressed quickly. When Emma returned, he said, 'I should be going.'

'Yeah, no problem,' Emma said. 'Strange day, eh?'

'You got that right.'

'What are you gonna do?'

Charlie assumed the question was concerning Simon. 'I don't know. I need to think about it.'

'Are you okay getting home?'

'Yeah, the bus is easy from here.'

'Call me.'

'I will.'

The stunted exchange filled the embarrassed space between them. When he opened the front door to the street, it felt like escape.

~

'Hey!' Charlie's dad called out as he entered the house. 'What's going on?

'I'm starving.' Charlie moved towards the kitchen.

'Any news?'

'You know...' Charlie opened the fridge.

'No, not until you tell me, I don't.'

Charlie rifled through the fridge and came out with a carton of milk. He opened a cupboard and pulled out a cereal box.

He wondered how much he should say. He didn't want any lectures, but his dad did know shit. He grabbed a bowl from beside the sink, poured the cereal and milk into it, and sat at the dinner table.

His dad was still on the sofa. 'Is it Matt's case?'

Between mouthfuls, he answered, 'Yeah, partly, I dunno. Things are getting complicated.'

'How?' His dad put down his book and raised his glasses.

Charlie paused the almost robotic movements of the spoon between the bowl and his mouth. 'Well, you know I met that girl Emma...'

'Yeah, that sounded interesting.' His dad smiled as he moved towards the table. 'Is there anything going on?'

'Dad...' Charlie objected but couldn't help smiling back.

'Hey, don't be embarrassed.' His dad was close enough to raise his hand for a high five. Charlie lifted his and received rather than gave the celebration.

'What's all this?' Helen entered the kitchen from the garden, carrying a basket of washing.

'Oh, great,' Charlie said, looking embarrassed.

'High fives?'

'Charlie here has a girlfriend.'

'Dad, it's not like that.'

'What is it like, then?' asked his mum. She put the basket on the dinner table and began folding the washing.

'Jeez, I wish I kept my mouth shut,' said Charlie.

'Well, you didn't. So come on, spit it out.'

'Firstly, she's not my girlfriend. It doesn't work that way these days -'

'Okay, I'm sorry, explain what's going on.'

'Secondly, it's about Matt.'

His mum continued to fold the washing, creating three piles on the table.

'It's just this weird thing... one of the climate group members turns out to be a copper.'

'How do you know?' asked his dad.

Charlie recounted his experience that morning. 'He actually swiped his card to get into the station.'

'Wow, that's pretty serious,' said his dad. 'It could mean there was some kind of undercover operation.'

'That's what I thought.'

'Maybe he was just a member. Police can have political views too,' said his mum.

'That's what Emma said.'

'Well, maybe she is right.'

'Really?' said his dad. 'Then why would he disappear?'

'Well, that's pretty obvious. I guess he recognises people might not be... you know, so accepting of his job. Maybe he just got bad vibes from the group. It's possible.'

'Do you know if they are allowed, Dad?' Charlie asked.

'They can be a member of a political party, but they can't join any movement or group that might bring into question their loyalties while doing their job.'

'What does that mean?'

'It means, no, they wouldn't be allowed to join a climate change group, because they might be asked to police that same group a week later. So it does raise questions.'

'What should we do?' asked Charlie.

'Give the information to Matt's family solicitor,' his mum said. 'Let them deal with it.'

'Was it the copper who had his knee on Matt's back?' asked his dad.

'I don't know. I didn't see him properly. If I had, maybe I would recognise him, be able to identify him. Is that what you mean?'

'No, I didn't mean anything. It was just a question.'

'If I could identify him, that would make a difference, though?'

'Maybe, but this is silly. You can't identify him,' said his mum.

'Not yet,' said Charlie.

'What does that mean?' she asked.

'I don't know.'

'Don't do anything stupid,' Helen put the clothes together in one pile and placed them back in the wash basket.

'You mean, do nothing?' asked Charlie.

'No, I'm not saying that. Let people do their jobs. Give the information to the family's solicitor and let them handle it.'

'What do you think, Dad?'

'I think your mum is right. You should give the name to the solicitor. But sometimes, you have to shake the tree to get any fruit.'

'What is that supposed to mean?' asked Helen.

'It means we can't sit around and wait for other people. Sometimes we have to take the initiative,' he said.

'Oh my God, here we go again.' She stood and picked up the basket. 'This is not some fairytale adventure. A young man has died, and you are encouraging our son to get involved in... God knows what. I don't believe you sometimes. This is all about your dad again, isn't it?'

'What about your dad?' asked Charlie.

'You know the story. Your grandfather killed someone in Garston and ran off to Ireland. Your dad here and his girlfriend went gallivanting off to discover his roots or play at being detectives,' his mum said.

'That's not fair.'

'Yeah, well, neither was leaving me with your son.'

'Okay, I get it. Will you guys let it drop?' Charlie moved into the kitchen. 'I'll make my own decisions.'

'Did you speak to Jaime?' His dad asked.

Charlie shook his head.

Vinny tapped the side of his head. 'Maybe you should start using this instead of...'

His mum's look stopped his dad finishing the sentence. She carried the basket toward the stairs, stopped, set it down, and turned up the volume on the TV.

'Are you okay, Mum?'

'Of course, I am. I just want you to be careful, not get into anything you can't handle... have you seen this virus thing in China?'

'I'll be careful, Mum, promise.'

His dad called out. 'Yeah, a new Coronavirus, similar to SARS. It looks pretty serious.'

'Let's hope it doesn't come over here.' Helen turned the TV off and carried the clothes basket upstairs.

'She's not happy,' Charlie finished his cereal and put the bowl in the sink. 'I'm not sure what to do, Dad.'

'Can I tell you a secret?'

'Yeah.'

'None of us are. But we do shit anyway.'

'You know what?'

'What?'

'I think it's time I got *my* shit together.' Charlie turned and left the room.

CHAPTER SIXTEEN

CHARLIE

Wednesday, January 22nd, 2020.

Charlie got off the 80 bus on Princes Road. Liverpool Eight was in the latter stages of gentrification, a process of dispossession well documented in major cities. Just a mile or two from the city centre, the Georgian quarter, as it was now known, was prime redevelopment real estate. For decades, the area had been isolated and abandoned as home to most of Liverpool's non-white population. Liverpool Born Black had become a term of pride and exception, with deep ties to the city and its culture also indicating a cultural difference from newer communities of immigrants.

Charlie dodged and weaved through the building work that was going on all around. A new cycle lane was being installed. When he stood in front of Kuumba Imani Centre, he wasn't surprised by its design. He had checked it out on Google. The Centre stood proudly in Princes Street. The silver lettering that rose vertically along its front was the only signage that celebrated so publicly the African men, women, children, and their descendants who inhabited this area. This very corner of Princes Street was near the centre of the uprising in 1981. The riots were a reaction to the constant police harassment of the young men in the area.

The Rialto, a furniture emporium, and a relatively new Nat West Bank saw flames eat away at their structure just yards away. The centre was the end of a long road of campaigning for the activist group Liverpool Black Sisters.

So much had been going on for Charlie; the statement to the police, the whole thing with Emma. The *poly* thing he just about got; people wanted to be different, show that they were individuals, break some conventions. She was nice, maybe *too* nice. Was there a hint of desperation?

He opened the door and walked into the atrium. The building was new, clean and minimalist. Two things struck him immediately: the bright colours of the artwork on the walls were matched by the headscarf of one of the most striking women he'd seen, and that woman was Amina.

As he approached the reception counter, he tried to look confident, as if he knew where he was and what he was doing. The previous times they had met he had been out of sorts.

Amina was focused on the screen in front of her. She turned to face Charlie and smiled in surprise, 'Good morning. How can I help you?' Her voice was smooth, and her lively eyes held his.

'Charlie Connolly, I'm here to see Jaime Jaware. He's based here. I'm not sure what office.'

'It's okay. I know Jaime. Have a seat for a minute, and I'll see if I can reach him for you.

After completing her call, she smiled and asked, 'How's your arm?'

Charlie flushed, 'Oh, bruised, but nothing too bad.' He was embarrassed looking at Amina. He didn't know what to say.

'I never got to thank you properly,' she said.

Charlie shrugged. 'No need.' He was brought back to earth quickly. A large man was heading towards him with his hand outstretched.

'Jaime?' Charlie asked.

'Yes, Charlie Connolly?'

Charlie felt the strength as he shook Jaime's hand. He was a solid man, in his fifties but still powerful.

'Yeah.'

'Good to meet you,' said Jaime. 'From your call, it sounds like you have a problem?'

'Maybe, I'm not really sure,' Charlie said.

'Okay, let's see what we can do. We can sit over here, if that's okay with you? Do you want a drink or anything?'

'Yeah, that's fine, and nah, I'm good, thanks.'

They had moved behind a partition, still in the reception but a semi-private area. Jaime indicated for Charlie to sit. 'How can I help?' asked Jaime, when they were settled.

'I think there might be nothing I can do, and it might be too late anyway. I'm not sure what to do, if anything,' Charlie said.

'How about you stop telling me what you don't know? Tell me what you do know.' Jaime wasn't wasting anybody's time.

Charlie took a deep breath. He had replayed and retold the events of that day so many times it was becoming like an internal movie, a story he was practiced at telling, but each time he told it, it lost a little reality.

'I saw a guy get arrested, and he died later the same day in police custody.'

'You mean Matthew Whitney?'

'You know about the case?' Charlie couldn't hide his surprise.

'Of course I do. I grew up in this area. Any death in police custody, especially happening after Mohammed Mzee... well, let's just say my ears perked up when I heard the news.'

'Who?' Charlie asked.

'Another young guy who died while restrained in Liverpool One.'

'Oh, right.' Charlie had never heard of the case or the guy involved. 'Is this part of your job then? Watching the police?'

'No. I work as part of Community Health Outreach, making sure people can get the healthcare they need when they need it. I am a campaigner because someone needs to be.'

'Right, anyway, I gave a statement to the police,' said Charlie.

'Okay, let's start again. Tell me what you saw.' Jaime paused for a second. 'Actually, hold on. Let me get someone else in here.' Jaime rose from his chair and walked behind the partition. He came back with Amina.

'This is Amina. She joined us recently. If you don't mind, she will take notes. She is involved in the local Black Lives Matter group.'

'Yeah, we've met.' She smiled. 'It's Mina to friends.' When she smiled it was like someone turned on the light.

'How do you two know each other?'

'We met on an agency job. Then Charlie took a hit for me.'

Jaime smiled. 'Okay. Do you want to start again?' He asked Charlie.

Charlie explained what he'd seen and the events since then, including the police interview.

Mina took notes, and Jaime sat back, listening intently.

'What do you think? Charlie asked.

'Well, in terms of the police action, there is a question over the use of the spit guard. It is a new instrument, but its use has been growing over the past couple of years. Half the deaths in police custody involve restraints. They should only be used where a defendant is resisting arrest. Obviously, placing something over the mouth restricts breathing and has huge potential dangers. So that would be the first thing... why did they use it and was it authorised? By whom, and on what grounds? Then you would have to ask how long was it used for? Is there camera footage to confirm any of this? The custody suite, even individual cells, should all be monitored.'

'I didn't think of any of this,' said Charlie.

'Why would you?' Mina asked.

Charlie met her look and knew it was supportive.

'There is another problem from what you've said. You were taken to see Matthew's mother. By people involved in the protest?'

'Yeah. A woman called Emma. She was there when he was arrested. Well, I think she was. I haven't asked her. I remember she told me they wanted someone outside the group to give a statement.'

'There's nothing wrong with that, but in terms of pursuing action or using your statement to implicate police behavior, it becomes problematic. It gives the impression that your evidence may have been corrupted. Tainted by association with his friends, and his family.'

'Shit.' Charlie looked down at his hands. 'I feel like I've let him down.'

'Who have you let down?' Mina's eyes invited him in. 'Don't think you have let Matthew down. You're here, asking about it. How many other people were in that train station? How many people walked straight past, looked the other way? There are none so blind as those who will not see. Everyone's journey has to start somewhere.'

Jaime laughed. 'Sorry, she just can't help being poetic.'

Mina's eyes swung down for a second and Charlie sensed her embarrassment.

He waited until she raised her eyes and met his. 'Thank you,' he said.

Silence hung in the air a moment before Jaime broke it. 'Okay, so look, back to the point. The bottom line is the police do nothing without pressure being applied. There are three forms of pressure that affect them: political, press, and public. Not necessarily in that order. Without these, this case will disappear. Maybe someone will get a warning, if you are lucky.'

'There's something else,' Charlie said.

'Yeah,' Jaime said expectantly.

'There was a copper in the group. In the climate group that Matt was involved with.'

'Undercover?' Jaime asked.

'We don't know.'

'That's weird. Weird that you found out. How *did* you find out?'

'We saw him going into the police station.'

'What police station?'

'Hope Street. After I gave my statement, we were coming away when Emma saw him.' Charlie didn't know why, but he looked at Mina when he said Emma's name.

'Then he wasn't undercover,' said Jaime. 'If he was undercover, he wouldn't have gone near a police station. They have special handlers. Everything is covert, so whatever this copper was doing it wasn't official undercover.'

'Did you recognise him?' Mina asked. 'From the protest, the police who took Matthew in?'

'I didn't see him well enough. I kicked myself that I didn't get a proper look.'

'There's nothing you can do about that now,' said Jaime.

'So, what should we do?' asked Charlie.

'We?' asked Jaime.

'I don't know what to do? How can they do that? How can they kill someone without anything happening? It was stupid.'

'What was?'

'To go and give my statement unprepared like that. What did I expect to happen, some kind of good citizen award?'

'What else could you do?' asked Mina.

'I could have seen a lawyer, like my dad suggested. I could have spoken to someone used to dealing with the police. I could have found you. Instead, I sat at home playing computer games, watching videos.'

'Rashan Charles, Sean Rigg, Roger Sylvester, Joy Gardner, Cynthia Jarrett, Mark Duggan,' Jaime said. 'These are all black people who died after contact with police.'

'I never really thought about this stuff. Shit, I don't know what's worse, feeling so angry or so stupid.'

'The anger is useful,' said Jaime. 'Hold on to it. Nurture it. Don't let anyone take it from you. If you are not angry when a thing like this happens, then something has died inside you.'

'One of my favourite speakers often quotes Saint Augustine. *Hope has two beautiful daughters, Anger and Courage, and we need both of those daughters in today's struggle. Anger at the way things are, and Courage to change them.*' Jaime was silent for a moment. 'I can't tell you what to do about Matthew. You've given your statement. I can recommend a lawyer. I suggest you educate yourself... find out about similar cases. You should speak to his mum again, see if she has legal representation. I'm sure she has, but if not, we would be happy to speak to her. There must be some form of campaign if they had a protest.'

'I think that was Matt's friends in Extinction Revolution.'

'Okay, well, speak to them?'

'Who, me?' Charlie was surprised. 'What can I do?'

'You've done it. Your head is in this thing now. Here, with us, you have taken the first steps.'

'That's not who I am, though. I'm not a campaigner out on the streets. Matt was, look where it got him.'

'Why are you here, Charlie?' Jaime asked.

'My dad suggested I speak to you,' he answered honestly.

'No, before that.'

'Because I saw Matt get arrested.' He was following Jaime's lead.

'And then?'

'And then he died.' Charlie closed his eyes a second and he sat back. 'I get it. You mean Anger and Courage. The anger is about his death. I'm here because it doesn't sit right with me. The question is, do I have the courage to do anything about it.'

'But Mina is right. You already have, you have given your statement to the police, you are here now talking to us. The question is, why isn't that enough for you?'

'Because of that copper. There's something wrong about this. I can feel it.'

'So, what are you?' asked Mina.

'I don't know. I don't understand the question,' said Charlie.

'You are what you do,' said Mina. 'You will be what you've done.'

Jaime smiled and shrugged. 'I did warn you about the poetry.'

There was not much else to say. Jaime shook Charlie's hand. 'If you need anything, feel free to call.'

'Thanks.' Charlie turned toward the door. 'It was nice meeting you,' he said to Mina. 'Or meeting you again, if you know what I mean?'

Mina was gathering her things from behind reception. 'Actually, I'm just finishing. I can walk you to your car if you want.'

'Bus,' Charlie was embarrassed to admit.

'No problem. Hold on, I'll be with you in a second.'

Jaime disappeared back through the door he'd come out of thirty minutes earlier.

~

It was a cool, clear afternoon and the light was just beginning to fade. Buses and cars filled both sides of the Boulevard.

'Do you want to walk down the middle?' Mina asked

'It looks new.'

'It is. They are still finishing some of it.' She led the way to the central reservation. The dual carriageway was separated by a cycle lane and walkway. Red and white barriers protected the unfinished parts, but they could follow the pavement.

Polished granite sculptures spelt out L and the figure eight at the start, and hardwood benches lined the walkway. Newly planted trees and Victorian-style street lamps added to the aesthetic. 'It's nice,' Charlie said.

'Yeah.'

They walked over Nelson Mandela quotes carved in the pavement. Inspirational images of trees and life.

'You don't sound convinced,' said Charlie.

'No, don't mind me.' Mina waved her hand.

'What? What is it?' he asked.

'You won't be interested.'

'How do you know?' Charlie was mildly insulted.

'Because your life is computer games and football. You told us earlier.'

'Yeah, it was, until my bubble burst.'

'What bubble?'

'Middle-class life. Parents working to subsidise me.'

Mina stopped and threw both hands up. '*Bismillah*, will you give it a break with the guilt.'

Charlie stopped. 'What?'

'Stop the moaning. You've taken the first step, and listen, I was wrong to snap at you on the protest, but now you either have to shit or get off the pot.'

'Shit, or get off the pot?' Charlie laughed.

Mina joined his laughter. 'Come on, let's sit down.' Mina dropped onto one of the benches.

'*Bismillah*?' Is that how you say it?

'Yeah, it kinda means *in the name of God*.'

'Like Jesus Christ, or for God's sake, or my mum's favourite, when she totally loses it 'Jesus, Mary, and Joseph.' He paused for a second. 'You're right, though. I have to stop moaning; either forget it or do something.' He looked at her and for first time noticed a few freckles just above her cheek bone.

'Like I said.'

'Yeah, I know. Shit or get off the pot. So much for the poetry Jaime was on about.'

'I work there. You know, professionalism?' Mina said.

'Actually, no, not in my skill set. Tell me... how does a quiet Muslim girl get to say 'in the name of God' and 'shit' within two sentences. The Muslim girl was a guess, by the way.'

'The same way I was born in Liverpool instead of Yemen. Shit happens.'

'So, go on... what were you going to say?'

'About what?' she asked.

'I said all this was nice.' Charlie waved his hand at the surroundings.

'Oh, yeah. It is, don't get me wrong. I'm not gonna argue when they celebrate anti-racist activity or talk about real history. But it's all a bit superficial.'

'What do you mean?'

'There's Caribbean Centre round the corner that has been closed for years, and people are trying to reopen. Where's the money for that? There's a plaque down the other end, celebrates Liverpool Eight's influence on the Merseybeat.'

'Isn't that good?' Charlie asked.

'It is... but what happened to all the clubs? The Yoruba... Sierra Leone... The Silver Sands... the Gladray... I could go on. All places that were around here.'

'What happened?'

'According to my mum, every one of them, the Nigerian... Jamaica House... all of them shut down one by one, by the council, the police, licensing authorities.' She paused. 'If they were so shitting good, why did they shut them all down?'

'I don't know, but shall I tell you what I do know?'

'Go on then.'

'*Shit* is your favourite swear word.'

She punched him. 'I don't like the others.'

'That's okay with me.'

'Are you going for the bus?' she asked.

'Am I boring you?'

'No, I thought it was the other way round.'

They stayed on the bench talking and realised, although they lived in the same city, they lived in very different worlds.

~

He lay back on his bed and let the events of the day sink in. Whatever road he was on felt better, knowing Mina was on it too. 'I could listen to you all day,' he'd said.

'Well, I can't sit here all day, so I have a bit of advice for you,' Mina said.

'Go for it.' He looked at the Liverpool Annuals in his bookcase and smiled as he remembered Mina's words.

'Go read a shitting book.'

CHAPTER SEVENTEEN

CHARLIE

Thursday, January 23rd, 2020.

'Morning, Mohammed.' Charlie slapped the poster as he opened his bedroom door to leave his room.

He heard his mum and dad in the kitchen below. The smell of fresh coffee assaulted his senses. Tea and coffee divided his parents: his mother enjoyed the full range of lattes and espressos available in coffee shops and did her best to recreate them at home. Dad had raised him on Typhoo and Tetley, anything else was beyond the pale. His dad explained the Pale was a 16th-century limit to English control in Dublin, and to be beyond it was not good.

'Oh my God, what's up with you?' His mum asked when Charlie entered the kitchen. 'Have you wet the bed?'

'Very funny.' He made his way to the fridge and pulled out the milk. His mum handed him the cereal box and a bowl. He sat at the table opposite his father.

'Spoon?'

'Thanks, Mum.'

'Do you want a cup of tea?' His dad's eyes were fixed on his laptop.

'Yeah, sure.'

'Well, you know where the kettle is.'

'Thanks, Dad.'

'Stay there. I'll get it,' His mum moved along the counter. 'So come on, what's the occasion?'

'Nothing. I just have something to do.'

His mum changed the subject. 'Have you heard the news about Wuhan?' She directed this at her husband.

'Yeah, they've gone into lockdown. No one can get in or out. There was a case in Thailand too. A death, I mean.'

'And Hong Kong,' she added.

'It's definitely on the move then,' he said.

'Should we be worried?' Charlie looked up from his cereal.

'Not yet, but who knows.'

'As if we don't have enough going on,' said Charlie.

'Do you want to share?' his dad looked up from his screen.

'Not right now.'

'Okay.' He paused before asking. 'Did you see Jaime?'

Between spoonfuls of cereal, Charlie replied, 'Yeah.'

'I hope it was helpful.'

'Kind of.'

'What did he say?'

'Be careful.'

'Good advice,' His mother put a tea in front of Charlie.

'He said I should speak to Matt's family lawyer.'

'Again, sounds sensible,' Helen left the kitchen, picked her coat up from the hallway and called back in, 'You two keep out of trouble.'

Charlie shouted, 'Bye Mum,' and the front door closed behind her.

'Don't you have to get to work?'

'I do, but I needed to speak to you without your mum hearing.'

Charlie's stomach sank. 'Why? What's going on?'

'Someone was watching the house last night.'

'Fuck.' Charlie shook his head. 'Who?'

'I don't know. I couldn't see them properly. Look, I don't know what Jaime told you but this is serious, scary stuff.' He paused. 'I thought about calling the police, but what could I say?'

'I know. The worst thing is you just don't know whose side they're on.'

'There's already one twenty-three year old dead. I don't want to see another.'

'I know, dad.' Things were getting very real for Charlie.

'I'm not sure you do.'

'Ok you're right... I don't, but I'm learning.' Without telling his dad, Charlie made decision.

~

His dad negotiated the traffic. 'Where do you want to be dropped?'

'I'm going to The Dingle, so wherever you can.'

Cars and buses edged along, the flow determined by traffic lights. The start-stop would continue all the way into town. The *rush* hour was anything but, as people drove cars that cost more than a year's salary through clogged and polluted suburban streets

'I can drop you at the top end of Park Road, if that's any good?, Then I can swing round.'

'Yeah, that's fine.' Charlie relaxed into his seat. He was nervous and scared but also a little excited.

'Do you want to tell me what you are up to?'

'Mmm, not sure...' Charlie stared out the side window.

'Okay, I'm not going to push you.' His dad looked at Charlie. 'I am proud of you, though. This whole thing with the police... not everyone would do what you have.'

'How about you keep your eyes on the road,' Charlie pointed forward before adding, 'It's not a lot, really.'

'No, maybe not. But it's something.' His dad failed to make eye contact with his praise.

'Everyone's journey has to start somewhere.'

Vinny smiled. 'It does indeed, but where did that come from? Sounds a bit philosophical for you.'

Charlie met his smile. 'Mina.'

'Whoever Mina is, she really made an impression on you.'

'Yeah, she did. I don't want to mess it up. The thing is, she knows so much more than me.'

'About what?'

'Everything.' Charlie lowered his window for air, but closed it quickly as the noise and smell came with it. 'Dad, what should I read?'

'What do you mean? It depends what you want to know about? Is it climate change, Extinction Revolution stuff?'

'No, more Black Lives Matter.'

'Well, go online. Do some research. If you want books, I thought *The Autobiography of Malcolm X* was great. There's a film too. Watch that then read the book. Look at some of his speeches. Martin Luther King too, but Malcolm was more exciting for me.'

'I've got so much to learn.'

His dad reached across and slapped his shoulder. 'But don't forget, a whole life to do it in.'

Charlie turned to his dad. 'If it's not too late.'

~

Charlie had Simon's address from Emma on his phone. That was his first step. His road began there. He knew following the police guy was stupid and dangerous... but fuck it. It must have been that bizzy his dad saw the previous night. Who else? Extreme measures for extreme situations. Or was it the other way round? He wasn't sure where he heard that, maybe a tag line from *Fortnite*, but it sounded right. At least he could try and get another look at the copper who had been in the Extinction group. Did he infiltrate it? Was that the word when someone pretended to be something to get information? Jaime didn't think he was undercover, but who knew what the hell was he doing? What was the connection to Matt's death?

So many questions. Charlie's mind had been working overtime since the meeting with Jaimie and Mina, not only because Mina was crazy, in a good way, but all the stuff that was going on. He had started noticing things and thinking. Every day brought new realisations. It was like someone had turned on a light in his brain. He knew the Dingle was not an area coppers usually lived in, though there was nothing wrong with it. It was a locality policed, not *for* the police. It was not leafy enough; the houses were not big enough; the area didn't have the prestige and value of a suburb. It was working class.

He was outside Tesco. Park Road was a well-used arterial road for the city centre from South Liverpool. Shoppers, bus stops, zebra crossing; it was a busy spot, easy to hang around unnoticed. What made it perfect was he had a view straight down Isaac Street. The houses were clean, well maintained, small two-up, two-down with bathrooms. Bay windows projected out into a small walled-off area of street frontage. In the council days, front doors could be blue, red, or green. Now in the period of private ownership, a range of colours were on display.

Charlie saw the house near the top on the right. Now he was there, he was not sure what to do next and wondered who the guy lived with. Did he have a wife and kids? If he was undercover, was that his front? He heard some coppers had partners, even kids, in an undercover life.

Shoppers and buses, cars and bikes, everything streamed by in a constant drone of sound, colour, and smoke. He leant on the wall of the ramp to Tesco and checked his phone for messages from Mina. Nothing. He had thanked her for her help. She had replied, so now they were officially communicating. He smiled and re-read her last message.

Mina: *No probs, h4u.*

'Here for you'. He had never used that. Maybe it was something people did, like wtf... or omg... he would have to check it out, but he liked it.

Oh shit.

The door opened. Charlie's eyes flashed between his phone and the street. He didn't want to look obvious.

Simon came out. He looked in both directions up and down the street before stepping out. Was that security training? He must have had anti-surveillance courses if he was undercover.

Charlie walked slowly down the ramp and stood behind the bus stop. Simon walked towards the main road at a brisk pace. The walk was too regular for Charlie; it wasn't a normal person's walk. It wasn't a scally walk, shoulders swinging, head bobbing. It was a walk influenced by marching -high knees, regular arm action. It wasn't a march, but... it wouldn't take much to stiffen the joints and movements for it to become one.

Simon approached Park Road, stood on the opposite kerb to Charlie and looked straight at him.

Charlie froze for a second, then moved quickly behind the advertising on the bus stop. *Fuck.* His heart rate increased, his stomach flipped. *That was stupid.* What was he doing?

Simon started crossing the road.

Oh, shit, he's seen me! Fuck. Charlie froze, turned his back, pulled his hood up, put his head down, and waited for the inevitable. Instead, he saw Simon's back as he moved past him. He walked straight by him up Park Road.

The air and tension escaped from Charlie's body. He moved to the opposite side of the bus stop to see Simon walking away, and he let out a large breath. *That was close.* Was that luck? *Was this what I am meant to be doing?*

He dropped his hood and ran his hand through his hair. He enjoyed the feeling of escape, of release, the afterglow of adrenalin. He laughed out loud, drawing a grimace from an old lady. *What next? Well, I can have a look at his house now I know he's not in there.*

Charlie checked the road before crossing. Isaac Street ran down towards the river. It was quite a long road, and Mill Street cut across the bottom. He couldn't see the river from there but knew it wasn't far away. The area was once full of people who made a living from the sea: dockers of various kinds, stevedores, lightermen, winch and crane operators, truckers, and carters. All trades, the coopers, metal bashers, carpenters, and warehousemen and their workshops, filled the Baltic triangle between Dingle and the city. Victoria, Albert and Herculaneum Docks had turned into tourist attractions and upmarket housing, but the area hadn't suffered the fate of Kensington or Granby, where Victorian terraces had been boarded up for demolition.

Not sure what to do, he headed past the house. The brass knocker on its glossy emerald green door shone in the morning sun. The house opened into a two-foot walled space to separate it from the pavement. Charlie passed the window but couldn't see beyond the net curtains. There were no signs of kids, no stickers on the windows or scrapes on the door. He walked down to the end of the street for time to think.

Simon Abbot - strange name, Abbot like the old monks. He would feel at home there in the Holy Land. *Okay,* come on, now or never. What was it, Mina said? *The first steps are the hardest.*

He's not in. I 'll just knock and see what I can find out.

Charlie moved slowly back up the street. His nerves were building as he got closer. This was stupid. What if he came back? What if they asked who he was? *I'm from the climate group. We haven't seen him in a while, just seeing if he's okay? Oh, well, fuck it, here we go.*

He stopped at the door and raised the knocker. He was surprised by its weight. It had to be real, solid brass. The raps were loud and resonated. He stepped back, worried it was too much.

The door opened quickly.

'You've got a good knock on you? For a minute, I thought it was the rent man.' The woman in front of him was slight, with fine grey hair. She stared at him.

'I'm sorry. I didn't realise.'

'Don't worry, I'm only pulling your leg. We haven't had a rent man for... for God knows how long, but believe me, if you're looking for a new profession, you've got the basics down to a T.'

'Yeah, sorry.'

She smiled. 'What can I do for you, love? Why has the Lord sent you to us today?'

'Is Simon about?'

'My son? No, he's gone. You've just missed Paul. He's gone to work.'

She must've misheard him, but she definitely said Paul.

'Oh, that's a shame. What time will he be back?'

'I don't know, love. They have them working such strange hours.'

'Oh well, never mind.'

'Have you come far?'

'Not really, Allerton.'

'Oh, that's far enough. Do you want a cup of tea? I don't meet many of Paul's friends.'

So, it was definitely Paul. 'Err, yeah, sure.'

Charlie followed the old lady into the house. There was a phone table in the hallway. Next to the phone were a couple of envelopes addressed to Mrs E Taylor. The hallway led straight through to stairs and continued to a kitchen, but immediately on the left was the parlour or sitting room.

She opened the door. 'Here, make yourself comfortable while I put the kettle on. Paul doesn't really have friends, it's nice to meet you.'

He went in. On his left, the bay window flooded the room with light. A sofa ran the full length of the other wall, and to his left was an armchair with a high back. There was no TV, which was unusual. The open coal fireplace had been boarded up and a gas fire had been fitted. It had a comfortable, if slightly old-fashioned, feel.

Charlie did a quick scan around, looking for anything that could tell him more about this guy. There were a couple of photos on the mantelpiece. One showing what looked like a simple wedding. The woman in the picture was a bit of a looker, dark hair, thin features, high cheekbones. It was black and white and framed in a doorway. Another one showed a teenager blowing out candles on a cake. He must have been around thirteen or fourteen. There were no other children in the picture. The woman from the first picture, he assumed, was the old woman who let him in.

The living room door swung open behind him, and Mrs Taylor appeared carrying a tea tray.

Charlie lifted the framed photograph. 'Nice photo.' He turned it over as he spoke and checked the back. It was marked the 13th April 2003.

'That would have been taken by Mr Taylor. That's me and Paul. He's thirteen, there. That's the year we rescued him, his first year with us.

'You rescued him?'

'Oh, yeah, we saved him,' she said with a wave of her hand, like it was the most normal thing in the world. 'Had to. We adopted him. That was just a couple of weeks after he arrived. His first birthday cake, he told us.'

'He looks happy,' said Charlie.

'Yeah, I think he was. God's gift, that's what he was. We had a couple of foster children before Paul, but he was the one who stayed. A Gift from God. Brought a lot of joy to Mr Taylor before he left us.' She indicated the other photo of her younger self and husband.

Charlie decided to go with the flow. 'He must have been happy to find such a nice home.' He paused before adding, 'You rescued him from..?'

'Saved, it was; we *saved* him. Paradise House. Oh, that place was horrible. Those nuns... call themselves Christians. He settled really quickly. We offered to take him back to Crosby to see his friends and whatnot but he was never interested. He viewed us as his saviours, told us many times over the years.'

'Did you say Crosby? I have an auntie out there. It's nice near the sands.'

'Not this place. Dark.' She shook herself. 'You think I'm kidding. You've seen nothing like it. A real house of horrors. A big place, not too far from the river. We went there once to see him before he came to us. Oh my, a frightening place.'

Charlie felt guilty. She seemed like a nice old lady; crazy but harmless.

'And how long have you known Paul? Are you a policeman too? Such strange hours he has to work.'

'Er, no, no, I'm not in the police. I am part of the group Paul joined. We haven't seen him for a while, and I thought I would just check up on him.'

'Oh, what group is that, then? I didn't know about a group.'

'Climate protection. You know... stop global warming.'

'Oh, really! I never knew he was interested in that. Of course, it was all forewarned. We know it is God's will.'

'Yeah, of course,' Charlie replaced his teacup in the saucer. 'That was really nice, thank you, but I better be going now.'

'Oh, that's a shame.'

Charlie stood and moved towards the door. She followed him. He opened the front door and was closing it when she asked, 'What did you say your name was?'

He closed the door without answering and marched up the street as quickly as he could.

For the second time, he was buzzing. It worked. It actually worked! He'd found out who the copper was, that he was adopted. His mum was some kind of fundamentalist. He was a loner, not many friends. Not married. No sign of a girlfriend.

There were new questions, too. Was Taylor his real name? If he was adopted, did he take his adoptive parents' name?

It felt good. Charlie was being active and proactive, and he wasn't sitting around worrying. *Making things happen*, Mina would be proud.

Should he tell her? Maybe wait a little. Whatever the next steps were, he knew they would be on the road to Paradise House in Crosby.

CHAPTER EIGHTEEN

PAUL

Thursday, January 23rd, 2020.

He stared into the mirror sideways on, a white polo shirt and beige chinos, the epitome of respectable attire. 'My life is to deliver the will of the Lord.' Paul turned to face the mirror full on. 'I am the will of the Lord.' In the reflection, he exaggerated a sign of the cross.

His bedroom window was propped with a book, enough for the cat to slip in and out. The sash was loose, and the window had a habit of crashing down. The cat would be back soon, after its long night of prowling. He didn't know why he kept it. Maybe there was something in its independence, its carefree existence, beholden to nothing or no one.

Its black head slipped inside, its neck extended under the window.

'You'd better move. If that window drops, it will have your head off.'

The cat looked at Paul and disappeared. From the sill, it was an easy jump down to the wall that divided the Taylors' backyard from the neighbour. The cat reappeared, darting under the window frame into the room, as if it sensed the danger. When Paul looked, a brown package was deposited on the floor. He leant down to inspect it, and the cat watched him, its head at an angle.

It was a sparrow, a dead sparrow. Its feathers had a natural camouflage pattern of soft and darker browns. Paul touched the silky feathers of its wing. His finger traced down the curve, and he pulled gently to extend it. He felt it pull, and as the wing flapped, the sparrow's eyes flashed open, its beak parted, and a sharp trill pierced the air.

Paul let go. The cat had been watching and pounced, its claws protracted. They sank into the bird. The sparrow wobbled and struggled but couldn't get enough space to extend its wings and fly. The cat's claws sunk in the flesh of one wing, the other slapping the floor in desperation. Its trills sharp and loud, the cat held on to its victim as it flapped and staggered. The cat could finish it at any time but didn't. It lay, one paw extended, watching its prey struggle for life.

Paul smiled. *This was nature, as God intended.*

The cat raised its other paw, unsheathed its claws, then slammed it down on the bird. It pulled the animal towards itself and lunged forward to take the sparrow's head in its mouth. There was a final desperate flurry of wings before the cat's jaws closed and the wings went limp. A paw reached up, claws sank in, the body was pulled away, then the cat opened its jaws and the head dropped out. It was over. If decapitation was good enough for his namesake St Paul, it was good enough for anyone or anything. The cat waited for praise.

Paul bent, picked up the body and head, and threw them in his waste bin. The cat meowed, jumped back onto the windowsill and slipped out again.

He knew the cat had no soul; it was not conscious of good or evil and, therefore, could commit acts of neither. It acted without conscience or pity in the way designed by God. If pain and death could be delivered conscience-free to an innocent animal, how much more deserving were the guilty sinners who placed themselves outside the bounds of God's law and, therefore, His mercy? He would be the same, unbeholden, unobligated.

~

Paul strode through the streets, suspended but called in again. Another interview, another round of denials and assertions. If what he'd done were discovered, he'd deal with it. He knew what he was doing and was secure in the path he had taken. Let them scrabble at his feet. Let them question and challenge; he would stand firm.

The shout cut through the city sounds. A woman's voice. He turned sharply and recognised the blonde haired figure. Whipped now by the wind, her hair covered her face, and she hadn't seen him turn. *Ignore her.*

'Simon.'

The voice had an edge of desperation, he slipped his hand in his jacket and pulled out his I.D. A quick swipe and he would be inside. As he swiped, he looked again.

They saw me. He knew Emma and the street rat had seen him enter the station. Had they recognised him? *I know she had; she was bound to. No, he couldn't have.* The uniform, the helmet... he would never have seen enough of his face. He knew nothing, she knew something. But was it enough?

~

'Thanks for coming back in.' Superintendent Smith smiled at him.

The polite demeanor didn't impress Paul. 'I had no choice. There is no need for thanks.'

'You have it anyway. Despite what you think, Sergeant, I am not here to find fault with you, or any of your team. I simply want to establish the facts and be able to report those facts to allow for a determination if the policies and procedures of Merseyside Police were in any way breached or otherwise contravened. If not, we can all go back to our primary function of protecting the British public.' She paused and turned a sheet in front of her. 'I would like to do two things this morning;.. first, review the videotape, and secondly, to discuss the decision making on the day in question. Do you have any objections?'

Paul's Federation rep answered for him. 'We have no objections.'

'We have retrieved the video footage from Central Station.' The superintendent pressed a remote control and a TV screen attached to the wall sprang to life.

Paul looked at the grainy black and white footage. It was a busy morning, hundreds of people passing by every few minutes, and some protesters were mingling with the commuters offering flyers or trying to get them to sign petitions. Another group gathered around Matthew Whitney, the megaphone was raised to his mouth, and his other arm beating the air in time to words that were no longer audible, but Paul knew them by heart: *The world is burning*.

'Do you recognise this scene?'

'Yes, of course. I viewed this footage in real-time and responded to the situation appropriately and in accordance with Tactical Support Unit training.'

'Is there any disturbance in this scene, Sergeant? Is there any commotion? Is anyone being obstructed?'

'The protesters are on private property, at the high point of rush hour. They are trespassing and causing potential life-threatening incidents.'

'How, Sergeant? Explain how what we are looking at, a normal Monday morning rush hour, is life-threatening.'

'I'm sure the superintendent is aware of our duty to consider public safety at all times. If there were an incident of any kind, these protesters and campaigners would obstruct evacuation routes and could be the cause of panic, resulting in injury or harm to members of the public.'

'Those are very tenuous grounds for a physical intervention, Sergeant.'

'Quite the contrary, ma'am. Public safety is among the highest priorities in the management of crowds. Prior removal of the ringleaders is a tried and tested method of crowd dispersal. It is what we were trained for.'

'We may differ on the circumstances requiring the use of those methods, Sergeant.'

Paul said nothing.

'Whose decision was it to deploy the TSU?'

'It was the Duty Inspector's decision.'

'I have a statement from the Duty Inspector, who reports that you requested deployment of the TSU.'

'The decision to deploy the TSU is the duty inspector's,' Paul said.

'Why did you request deployment on what appears to be a perfectly peaceful scene?'

'It is part of my responsibility as TSU team leader to monitor police reports and respond appropriately to information received, or requests for assistance.'

'Did you receive a request for assistance from the Central Station Manager?'

'We received a report of a political protest, trespass, and a potential public safety problem, and responded with the correct authority.'

'The advice and training for the Emergency Restraint Belt requires that it be used to restrain resisting or aggressive detainees. Mr Whitney appears to be neither of these. Why did you use the ERB? And we have statements from the other officers at the scene that it was your decision to use the ERB.'

'Of course, it was my decision. As you can see from the video, the station concourse is packed with hundreds of moving people. It is not serious to suggest that we should have transported a detainee through that crowded area and left the potential for the detainee to struggle, kick, punch, bite or otherwise injure members of the public. My priority was public safety, and the ERB's were used to that end.' Paul sat back. *They didn't know. If they did, they would have said by now. Fools. It might just work out. If I can make sure the whore and the rat stay away, victory is possible.*

Acting under instructions from Paul, the Police Federation representative now applied the only form of leverage available to him. 'We are aware that it is your responsibility to act with appropriate efficiency, that there be no undue delay in delivering your report. I have been advised that you have received statements from the officers present. I have been made aware that you collected witness statements. You have clearly reviewed the video evidence, so I am formally asking you on behalf of my client when we can expect an end to this unnecessary inquiry.'

'I have made a note of your concern, and of course, we will act without undue delay. You can be assured of that.'

'I would like to add to the record that my client's suspension is having a detrimental effect on himself and his family. His elderly mother, for whom he is the sole carer, is aware of his suspension and is, of course, extremely worried about her son. This worry will undoubtedly have an effect on her already fragile condition.'

'I repeat, I have noted your concern. If I can turn back to the video, Sergeant Taylor.'

Superintendent Smith pushed the start button. 'When you detained Mr Whitney, applied the ERB belts to his arms and legs, there was no application of the spit guard. Yet when you appear in the courtyard of Hope Street Police Station and Mr Whitney is removed from the van, we can see that you, Sergeant, are controlling the spit guard over Mr Whitney's face.'

'The detainee had become abusive and aggressive on route to the station, and as a result, in line with TSU training, I applied the spit guard in the interests of the safety of myself, my officers and, ultimately, Mr Whitney himself.'

'Okay, Sergeant, can we cut through the formalities here?'

'If you like,' said Paul.

'At no point in Central Station or in the police station yard is Mr Whitney struggling, being aggressive, abusive, resisting. I repeat: at no point.'

'TSU training requires that officers-'

'Cut the bullshit, Sergeant. I am asking you why you restrained a non-resisting detainee?'

'Because he was a detainee, Superintendent. I don't know how long it is since those lily-white hands of yours have been on a suspect, but here we take no chances with prisoners, with detainees, with anyone. In arrest, in questioning, we take no chances. If you had seen the number of injuries sustained by my officers, through punches, kicks, bites, scratches, you name it, you would understand why we take no chances. If you want to condemn me for that, then go right ahead, but you will be condemning every officer who puts on a uniform and goes out into the streets. If you want to crucify me for doing my job, then go for it. I welcome your disapproval. Are we done here?'

'One final question, Sergeant.'

The superintendent wound the film forward. 'Here, we can see two officers laying Mr Whitney down in the holding cell. The officers remove the ERB's and withdraw from the cell. Can you confirm that is what you can see?'

'Yes, I can see it.'

'And that is you, crouching next to Mr Whitney's head?'

'Yes, that is me.'

'The spit guard is wrapped around Mr Whitney's face.'

'Yes.'

'How long has this restraint been applied to Mr Whitney at this point?'

'I'm not sure, from shortly after we got in the van.'

'As you would expect, we have checked the timestamps. We

work it out to be approximately nine minutes. Nine minutes of restricted breathing, nine minutes of reduced oxygen, the last nine minutes of Mr Whitney's life.' She paused. 'Can you see, Sergeant?'

'Yes, I can see.'

'You are talking, Sergeant.'

'Am I?'

'Yes, you are.'

She pressed a button on the remote control, and the picture zoomed in. 'We can see your lips moving, Sergeant.'

'As Mr Whitney lays dying. What is it you are saying, Sergeant?'

'I don't know. I can't remember.' Paul looked down at the table.

'The last words Mr Whitney would hear, what were they, Sergeant? And don't tell me you can't remember the last words you spoke to a dying man.'

Paul sat up straight, raised his eyes from the table, and looked the superintendent in the eye.

'What were you saying, Sergeant?'

'I was praying for his soul.'

'Here,' she pointed at the screen, 'you stand and remove the spit guard. There is no movement from Mr Whitney. Did you know he was dead or dying when you left that cell?'

'No, I did not.'

'Why were you praying for his soul if you thought he was still alive?'

'I pray for the souls of the sinful, dead or alive, Superintendent.' Paul pushed his chair back and stood. 'Shall I add you to list?'

~

Paul walked home slowly through the busy streets. Late January and a cold drizzle refreshed him. He let the droplets build upon his face. It was clarifying, cleansing after the hypocrisy he had just experienced. Paul had come to like this area; it was honest and forthright. The pawnbrokers took your valuables and gave you money, an honourable tradition. The second-hand shops allowed the poor a chance to buy what they couldn't afford. The discount supermarkets stacked it high and sold it cheap. The betting shops gave you one last chance for that big break. The newsagents sold you a range of truths and your nicotine of choice. The bargain off-license sold multipacks of diversion. That was the reality. How in this world of decay could they question him?

~

He lay back, the cat at his side. He stroked the smooth, black fur as he thought of the video footage. Paul didn't need the usual defence for officers confronted with video evidence; what happened before the film footage, what was *not* seen? *What you see is not what you see. We have become very good at telling our eyes what to see, rather than our eyes telling our brain what is happening.*

The film showed the efficient transfer of a subdued prisoner. Inside the van, he had to be restrained for his own and the safety of the officers involved. They would see a concerned officer kneeling to administer care to a prisoner.

Would they put the two together as one person? Paul and Simon? They might, but didn't everyone know the story of the conversion? The epiphany, on the road to Damascus? St Paul hearing the words of God? His favourite depiction of this event was the Carravagio conversion of Saint Paul. The weight of the horse screamed through the oils, the darkness and light battling for the soul of Saul, also known as Paul, as the transformation took place. Paul struggled to emerge from under the dead weight of the animal, to free his human from the animalistic and diabolic. *I can't let that young street rat get in the way.*

'The Lord kills and brings to life,' Paul said aloud.

People had to be punished for their sins, and those who belonged to God would be with Him forever. Both were present in the same act, the punishment and the salvation. That was the beauty. In Him, Paul would trust. Through Him, all things came. Such was Saint Paul's message; one the earthly Paul would follow. *Time and time, let me deal with the issues of this world and have faith in Him. The solution and the path will be shown and will be clear, and the only question: will my faith be strong enough to implement the will of God?*

'Paul, are you coming down to eat, love, or shall I put it outside your door?' His mother's voice strained with effort, not the effort of sound, but of connection. She was always reaching out to him.

He raised his head from the pillow. 'I'll come down. Give me a minute.'

'Righto. It's ready.'

He heard the results of her unsteady gait, a plate in one hand, a saucepan lid over the meagre offerings. She would be turned sideways to negotiate the stairs, her left hip stiff and awkward.

Paul waited till the hobbling descent was over. Then joined her in the small but neat kitchen. His plate of potatoes, carrots, broccoli, and a single lamb chop lay lukewarm and unappetising before him.

'Your friend seems nice. It's been so long since we've met any of your friends.'

Paul's head spun round. She was standing at the sink, wiping dishes as she spoke. 'Friend?' Paul controlled his voice despite his growing anger.

'From the climate group. He didn't say his name. A nice, well-spoken young man from Allerton.'

The wannabe street rat. 'What did he want?'

'He just had a cup of tea, said he would call you. Did he call?'

'No, he didn't.'

'How strange.'

He watched as her shoulders swayed with the movement of her arms. Between the floral pattern of her pinafore straps was her thin, wrinkled neck. How stupid could she be? It wasn't her fault. He knew that she was innocent, unprepared for the ways of this world, for the struggle ahead. Soon she would be happy with her husband. She would go to live with Christ in Heaven. If necessary, he would deliver her soul to the happiness she deserved.

~

Later, Paul lay back down on his bed. The rat was playing with danger, a bird on the ground. He pushed the cat aside, it meowed its disapproval.

CHAPTER NINETEEN

CHARLIE

Thursday, January 23rd, 2020.

Charlie closed the front door behind him. A couple of steps, and he was outside the gate. The house had a bay window and a tiny space in front protected by a small wall, just enough to put a couple of pots out.

He turned left toward Allerton Road. The pub was a five-minute walk. He tried to work out the difference between where he was and the Dingle; it was weird, wider streets and some trees, but that was about it. The shops and cafes, the houses, everything was so similar, yet the difference remained.

Even here, things were changing. Bargain Homes was opposite Enisworth Road, and next door was Barnardo's, a better class but still a charity shop. The grip on status for individuals and areas was so tenuous that the slip, once it started, was difficult to stop. Empty shop units were rare in Allerton, but one or two were taking longer to let.

Charlie was changing too. His brain had been re-wired or repurposed. Neural networks devoted to calculating points and games, tactics and strategy, were now recognising poverty and discrimination. Would he still be a part of the collective Liverpool experience if he saw this stuff?

He shook his head and strode forward. The John Brodie was on a corner, a mix of modern and traditional, a flat-roofed rectangular brick building at the end of a row of shops.

The lower fascia was painted wood panelling, as if it were a medieval inn. Brodie was the celebrated designer of the tunnel under the Mersey, the longest underwater tunnel in the world when it was opened in 1934.

'Hi, Charl, haven't seen you in a couple of weeks. Keeping busy?' Joey, the barman, was an artist, studied art history and was a decent painter. Charlie had been told this, although he had never seen any of his work. Joey was a quiet, slim, tidy guy; the opposite of the bohemian artist stereotype.

'Something like that, yeah.'

Joey began pulling Charlie's pint.

'Have you seen the others?' Charlie asked.

'Not in yet.'

~

Spaces in front of the TV were filling up. Sky Sports were showing the pre-game for Liverpool against Wolves in what looked like the unstoppable progression toward Liverpool's first League title for thirty years.

'What's up?'

'Hey.' Terry was next in. 'Not got a table yet?'

'Thought I'd wait for you,' said Charlie.

'Alan coming?' asked Terry.

'He said he was.'

'Coming for more torture?'

'You can ask him yourself,' Charlie greeted Alan as he approached them. 'Hey, Alan,'

They bought drinks and were seated, waiting for the game to begin. Sky was doing its normal pre-match build-up, interrupted by advertisements every couple of minutes.

'So, who's he playing? What's your lineup?' asked Terry.

Alan jumped in before Charlie could answer. 'Never mind that. What's going with this copper stuff?'

'Yeah, and the bird?' said Terry.

"Bird?' Fucking hell, you're getting worse,' said Alan.

'Shit, I don't know where to start.'

'At the beginning,' said Terry. 'Usually better than at the end, unless you are Tarantino, then you can start where the hell you like cos no one knows what the fuck is going on anyway.'

Charlie took a drink and put his pint glass on the table. 'I gave a statement.'

'To the police?' asked Terry.

'Who else?' Alan leaned in. 'How did it go?'

'Okay.' Charlie shrugged. 'Well, they didn't slap handcuffs on me, so that was a nice surprise.'

'What do you mean?' Terry said. 'You've done nothing wrong.'

'I know but bloody hell, if I don't have to step foot into police station for a long time, I'll be more than happy.'

'Come on then…' Alan was waiting.

'I gave my statement. They were kind of official but friendly. Basically, they said thank you very much, now go home and forget all about it.'

'So, of course, you didn't,' said Terry.

'Bingo,' Charlie replied.

'And the bird?' asked Terry

'Bingo again.' Charlie smiled.

'You dirty bastard. I knew it. As soon as you said there was a woman involved. Okay, let me guess. Was she there when you gave your statement?'

'Yeah, but it wasn't like that.'

'So, you got your reward for being a good boy,' Terry said. 'That could be bribery.'

'How do you work that out, idiot,' said Alan.

'Instead of getting cash for giving a statement, he got his end away.' Terry shrugged. 'Okay. We're off.'

The game started, and all attention was turned to the screen high on the wall. Liverpool was expected to win, although the

Wolves had surprised many people by performing well in their first season back in the Premier League.

'So, the woman,' Alan's eyes remained fixed on the screen. 'Anything going on there? I mean, anything longer-term?'

'No, no chance.'

'Why?'

'She's polyamorous, anyway.'

'Puts it about, you mean.'

'Yeah, thank you, Terry,' said Alan.

'So not for me.'

Liverpool dominated the early part of the game, then a corner. A cross fired in from Trent Alexander Arnold. 'There it is!' said Terry.

There was an outburst of cheering and clapping, a few half-hearted chants of 'Jordo, Jordo' as Jordan Henderson, team captain, put Liverpool in front with a header.

Charlie could relax a little with Liverpool in the lead; it was unlikely they would lose the game. They were so dominant in the League, people were talking about record points, a record number of straight victories and all kinds of records were made and broken. But Charlie only cared about the trophy; get the league in the bag and he would be happy.

The first half came to a close, Liverpool lost Sadio Mane through injury, but it didn't look too serious. Wolves had looked threatening, especially Traore on the wing. There were still forty-five minutes to play, but the odds were on a Liverpool win.

Just before the halftime whistle blew, Charlie said, 'Okay, my round, same again?'

'It's okay. I'll get it.' Terry stood up. When he returned with the drinks, the TV pundits replayed significant moves from the first half.

'Come on then, spit it out,' said Alan. 'No more holding back.'

'Okay, well, to get to the main point,' said Charlie.

'Yeah, what was she like?' said Terry.

'No, it turns out this Matt was in a climate group, right?'

'Yeah, XR, you told us,' said Alan.

'It looks like a copper was also in the group.'

'What do you mean,' said Terry. 'Like, undercover?'

'No, that's what I thought. I mean, he gave a false name, but his real address. He wasn't undercover.'

'So, he was just a copper who wanted to fight climate change?' said Alan.

'Then why use a false name? And they are not allowed. It's against their rules.' Charlie had their attention. 'But here's the thing... I think it might have been the copper who arrested and killed Matt.'

'Whoah, that's fucking serious.' Alan raised his hand palm outward. 'Whoah, if that's true, I mean, this would be all over the news.' He thought for a moment. 'Do you know how big this is?'

'Yeah,' said Charlie.

'I don't think you do. An undercover cop involved in a death in police custody? There have been major public inquiries about less. In fact, there's one going on right now.' Alan got his phone out and swiped the screen. 'Here... the Pitchford inquiry.'

'I kinda heard about that. Isn't that where these coppers were shagging protesters?'

'Yes, Terry, trust you to reduce a major civil rights violation to sex. But...you're not that far from the truth. Undercover cops had relationships. In one case, I think even had a kid, all while using false names and reporting back on everyone around them.' Alan said. 'They have been spying on people, especially people who fight the government for years.'

'But we know it's not that. I went to see an old mate of my dad's.' He said, 'He wouldn't be in a police station. If he was undercover, he wouldn't use his own name or address, so he is not undercover, not Special Branch, or any of that stuff,' said Charlie.

'They're coming out,' Terry pointed. On-screen, the two

teams filed out for the second half. The conversation died down as they watched the teams line up. As the second half kicked off, Charlie thought about Alan's reaction. He was right, he had to be more careful, but he wasn't giving up, not just yet.

Alan leaned into Charlie. 'What if you're right? That he's not operating as a police officer, isn't that worse?'

'How?' asked Charlie.

'It could be even more dangerous. A loner, vigilante?'

'Why, though?' This was the question Charlie couldn't answer.

'Who knows? A Dirty Harry complex?' said Alan

'Dirty who?' asked Terry.

'It's a Clint Eastwood movie,' said Alan.

'Well, we can make a new one. Never mind Dirty Harry, we've got Dirty Charlie here shagging anything that moves.' Terry laughed.

There was a sudden silence and a mass intake of breath when Adama Traore crossed the ball for Wolves, and Raul Jimenez managed to get enough on it to steer it into the net. There was a collective groan as Wolverhampton Wanderers were level with Liverpool just six minutes into the second half. For Charlie, that was not the way it was supposed to go. For the next period, Wolves dominated the game as they seized the momentum and pushed for a winner.

'This is worrying,' said Charlie.

'No sweat,' said Terry. 'We'll pull it out the bag,'

'I think you've got more to worry about than Liverpool,' said Alan.

'Don't be stupid,' said Terry. 'What could be more important than the League?'

The weight of Alan's concerns played on Charlie's mind. He might as well tell him the rest. 'I had his address from Emma.'

'I'm not going to like this, am I?' asked Alan.

'So yesterday, I went. Just to have a look at the house...I don't know... anyway, while I was there, he came out. He didn't see me, but he went off somewhere. So, long story short, I knocked, went in and had a cup of tea with his mum.' He rushed the last part as if it would make it less important.

Alan laughed. 'This is so fucked up. This is worse than some bat shit script off the telly. You are taking the piss - tell me you didn't really do that?'

Charlie winced. 'I did.'

'Well, got to give it to the kid,' said Terry his attention between the screen and the conversation. 'He's got a full set of balls in there somewhere.'

'I don't know where to start,' said Alan. 'This is so crazy.'

'Look, I know. The cup of tea part wasn't planned, but I found two interesting things. Firstly, his old lady is a bit cuckoo, proper fundamentalist Christian. Secondly, he was adopted.'

'What have either of those things got to do with anything?' asked Alan.

'I don't know... yet.'

'But…let me guess, you're gonna find out,' said Alan.

'Maybe, look, instead of taking the piss, why don't you guys do something constructive?'

'Like what?'

'Help, maybe?'

Charlie's phone beeped. 'Hold on.' He swiped the screen.

'Who's that?' asked Alan.

'Mina.'

'Who's Mina?' asked Terry.

'Err... and before I say anything.' Charlie pointed at Terry. 'You keep your mouth shut.'

Terry mimed a zipper across his mouth. 'My lips are sealed.'

'She's from town. She's part of Black Lives Matter. We met last week. She's pretty cool.'

'Cool or pretty?'

'Both,' said Charlie.

'And he's scored! Terry raised his arms in the air. The pub

broke into celebration. Bobby Firmino had scored with just minutes of the game remaining. 'What did I tell you? This team, this manager, are going to do it.'

'You're right. We can do it; so can we, guys. We can find out what the hell is going on.'

'So, you want us in your team, then?' asked Terry.

'As long as you behave yourself.'

'This is getting good. Do you want me to organise with that woman from the climate group?' asked Terry.

'No, I don't,' Charlie said. 'You keep away.'

'Alan, are you still in the government's computer system?' asked Charlie.

'He works in the passport office, not MI5,' said Terry.

'But the government system is all connected, isn't it?'

'Kind of. There are different servers for different departments, different platforms, but they all use the same coding, same architecture.'

'Okay, can you find out as much as you can about Paul Taylor, including any adoption records?'

'What are you going to do?'

'I'm off to Paradise.'

'Is that supposed to make sense?' asked Alan.

'It was the kids' home he was adopted from,' said Charlie.

'What do you expect to find?' asked Alan.

'Who knows?'

'What's my job?' asked Terry.

Alan smiled. 'You can get the ale in.'

The final whistle was greeted with claps and cheers. Liverpool were unbeaten in the Premier League for the last forty games. Surely, they were on to a winner. Charlie and Terry high-fived across the table.

'They're making it harder and harder,' said Alan. 'Wolves were unlucky,' said Alan.

'It's the final score that counts. Victories like this, where you have to struggle all the way; they make it all worthwhile. We can't win every game three nil, so we have to win these scrappy ones.' Terry spoke more fluently about football than any other subject.

'The League is ours. It would take something, I don't know, out of this world, to stop us now.'

'The impossible is only impossible until it happens,' said Alan.

'Who said that? Klopp?' Charlie asked.

'No, Mandela,' said Alan.

'Who does he manage?' asked Terry.

'Nelson Mandela,' Alan sounded out the name as if to an infant.

'Okay, okay, I get it. It could have been Klopp, though.'

~

Charlie swiped the screen to see the message from Mina. The room was spinning, or was it the world? The way things had been going, nothing would surprise him. The text had told him to look up Stephen Lawrence and Anthony Walker. He would, but not right now.

The names sounded familiar, but he wasn't sure why. For now, he would enjoy the post-match chill. It was a feeling he had lost recently. In fact, since he saw Matt's arrest, he had been on edge. It was like he had some secret knowledge; he saw something no one else could see even though there were loads of people in the station.

How could a single moment change a life? It seemed so absurd, but in reality, it was the only way things happened. We were used to seeing things in movement -as growing, building, evolutionary. But life itself was revolutionary; the goal was scored when Bobby Firmino's foot impacted the ball. From that point on, the goal was going to happen. It might have taken years of training, but that was the moment.

Charlie's head hurt. He didn't know where those ideas were coming from. Ever since that day in the station, he had seen the world differently. That moment of eye contact with Matt, when he felt the chill, saw into him. An epiphany. Whatever happened, his life would never be the same again. Now he had a purpose, and Mina.

~

He googled the names Stephen Lawrence and Anthony Walker. What he found shocked him. The two cases had many similarities, despite being so far apart in time, one before he was born and one when he was eight. Where was the progress in between? Two young men hanging with friends were attacked first at a bus stop and then isolated and killed by racists. The ice pick and the knife that murdered them were the instruments, not only of ignorance, as widely claimed, but of the system that refused to recognise its own bloodied hands.

Charlie was surprised by what the local Labour Member of Parliament said; although there was a "certain surface comparison" between the two murders, Walker's killing was "random, exceptional and representative of absolutely nothing."

Mina's words came back to him *There are none so blind as those who will not see.*

CHAPTER TWENTY

CHARLIE

Monday, January 27th, 2020.

Charlie had to stop reading. The last few days, he had been cocooned in his room. He was halfway through *The Autobiography of Malcolm X*, he'd downloaded the film, and that had helped him understand it. It was James Baldwin that really spoke to him. This small, well-spoken guy used words like *a razor in a knife fight*. He cut through excuses and bullshit. The funny thing was, he talked a lot about how racism destroyed the humanity of white people. They could not be fully human, he argued, in their denial of the humanity of black people. Charlie saw Anthony Walker's open, smiling face and had to look away. He turned back to the reports of the match the day before.

The afterglow from a win, depending on the importance of the game or the opposition, lasted from a few days to a few weeks, or even months. The unease after yesterday's 2-2 draw would last until the next League victory. It was an FA Cup game, and fair play to Shrewsbury, they would get a replay at Anfield. No one expected them to win, but the fact that the Liverpool machine hit a bump in the road was concerning. After any game he would read match reports, watch the various pundits' analysis, Sky... BBC... ITV... and then there were the blogs and podcasts. Redmen, The Anfield Wrap, Maych TV. If you wanted, you could fill your world with football.

2005 was a big one, not so much on the blogs or match

reports then, but definitely the TV stations. He was eight at the time of that amazing night in Istanbul, the night Steven Gerard became a living legend and Liverpool won their fifth European Cup. From three-nil down at the end of the first half to three-all at the end of extra time. Liverpool won it on penalties, and the young Charlie danced around the room.

Why didn't he know about the murder of Anthony Walker? He checked the date, July 2005. He would have been in the afterglow of that amazing night in Istanbul.

He closed the browser, got up and dressed and made his way downstairs. His dad was bent over his laptop, a piece of toast in one hand and his mug of tea on the table next to him.

'Morning,' he said

'Morning,' Charlie answered.

'What are you up to today, no work?'

'Nah, Christmas sales are over, everything will be dead in the shops for a while.'

'Nothing else likely?' His dad looked up.

'Not at the moment. The agency will message me if they get anything in.'

'Are you okay?'

'Yeah, I guess.' Charlie flicked the switch on the kettle.

'Strange result yesterday. Did you watch it in the pub?'

'Nah, I listened live on the radio.'

'You need a couple of quid?'

'Nah, well, yeah, but no, that's not the problem.'

His dad pulled out his wallet. 'Here.'

Charlie took the Twenty-pound note.

'Don't tell your mum.'

He poured the hot water into his cup, making the tea on autopilot.

His dad lowered his laptop screen. 'Come on. What's wrong? Sit down.'

Charlie pulled a chair out and flopped down. 'Anthony

Walker.'

He closed his laptop.

'Why didn't I know about it?'

'You were a kid at the time.'

'His murder must have been on the news?'

'It was.'

'So why don't I remember it?'

'Who knows? But... another question is, why are you upset about it now?'

'A local kid gets an ice axe in his head and you want to know why I'm upset?'

'No, come on, I didn't mean that. I meant, why are you upset *now*?'

'I don't know.' Charlie took a drink of tea and placed his mug carefully on a coaster. 'That's not true, I do. Mina told me to look him up. I guess she knows more about me than I do.'

'You shouldn't feel guilty; it was a horrible crime. A young lad killed because he was black.'

'How could they have done that? I think his dad was from Jamaica, Liverpool would be nothing, all those big buildings in town, the docks, the city, it all came from exploiting them.'

'You've been doing your research.'

'People go mad about Liverpool, how they love it. They don't know it. It's pissing me off because I'm one of them.'

'Give yourself a break. You're a smart lad.' He got up and walked around the table to put his mug in the sink. As he passed Charlie, he ruffled his hair.

'Daaad,' he protested.

'I'm proud of you, maybe I don't say it enough, but I am.'

Charlie exhaled loudly. 'Believe it or not, that's the second time in a few days.'

'Okay, but it's hard out there, and you are dealing with it.' He turned and looked at Charlie. 'Okay, so what's going on with police stuff?'

'The climate group Matt was involved in; you know there

was a copper in it?'

'Yeah, you said. I mean, they have lives as well, I guess.'

'No, it wasn't like that. He didn't tell anyone he was a copper.'

'Maybe he was just being, you know, private. It wouldn't be the most popular job, especially among campaigners.'

'Nah, he was up to something.'

'How did you find out? What have you been up to?'

'Never mind.'

'I do mind, though. You should be careful. What was he up to in the group?'

'I don't know yet, but if he was a copper, is a copper, and he gave a false name, doesn't that show that something was going on?'

'It definitely looks suspicious. Are you going to call the superintendent?'

'No. Not yet, anyway. Look at what happened when I gave my statement. Within minutes, they had me thinking I'd made it up because I'd met Matt's mum. The police cover shit up. I'm not giving in that easy. I can't moan about other people doing nothing and do nothing myself.'

'So, what's next?

'If it wasn't official? Then maybe I've got a chance to find out what's going on.'

'If it wasn't official, then it's more dangerous. You've got no idea what this guy is up to.'

'That's what Alan said.'

'Or if he was involved in Matt's death. This is serious. You need to think about what you're doing.'

'I have, that's all I've thought about the last few days, and I won't do anything dangerous.'

'Promise?'

'Yeah, promise.'

'So what's the plan for today?'

'The next piece in the jigsaw.'

CHAPTER TWENTY-ONE

PAUL

Monday, January 27th, 2020.

Paul waited. Allerton Road was busy, and it provided good cover. He sat in a cafe with a newspaper and a tea. He could see Charlie the street rat's front door. Black, like the colour of his clothes; even unconsciously, naturally, this man chose darkness when all around could be light. Paul had no fear; he had faced darkness before and triumphed.

'Would you like anything else?' The waitress hovered beside him.

'No, thanks, I'm fine.' Was she trying to get rid of him? He had only been there half an hour. 'Actually, sorry, yeah,' he called after her. 'Can I have another tea and maybe two pieces of toast.'

'Sure, no problem,' she smiled.

He knew his life was temporary; as long as it suited the Lord to have him do his work, then he would remain on earth.

'Oh, and butter. Natural. No margarine.'

'Of course.'

'Toasted both sides.'

'All our toast is.' She turned back towards the kitchen.

'That's good,' he said to no one.

As Saint Paul said to the Philippians, of life and death, *I do not know! I am torn between the two: I desire to depart and be with Christ, which is better by far; but it is more necessary for the people that I remain in the body.* He was ready for the path that was chosen. His path was to combat evil and defeat the enemies of the Lord, and He would take him when he was ready.

The waitress returned with his toast.

A few moments later, the front door opened and Charlie Connolly stepped out. *Yes, I know your name, and I know who and what you are. A fake, wannabe, plastic, hoodie-wearing street rat. We know of your sins and failings, for they are the sins of the multitude. Claiming to be wise, they remain fools, as God has shown himself, yet they refuse to see.*

Paul stood, eyes fixed on the men getting into their car. The father, Vinny Connolly, minor convictions as a youth, nothing serious. Either he had changed his ways, or he had been clever. *Which is it?* False father that refused to teach the son.

My father was true and yet false. True in following the saviour, false in blood. He accepted me into his house and family, where others were true in blood but false, and offered nothing but rejection.

'Your toast, love. Butter not margarine.' The waitress held his plate out.

'Not now.' He walked towards the door.

'You asked for toast, here it is. Are you gonna pay for this?'

'Yes, yes, of course.'

'Don't get shitty with me, love. You asked for toast. You got toast. Two pieces, done both sides, with butter, not margarine, that will be fifty pence... please.'

He dropped the coin on the counter and turned to leave. Then he stopped, grabbed the toast and left.

Paul watched them get into their car, a blue Fiat Punto, quite old. Now was the difficult part, to get behind them without attracting their attention. Toast in hand, he raced across the road, dodging buses and cars. He had parked his BMW 2 series wisely. After a few yards, he turned left and was in their street. He got in his car, turned the ignition on, and moved out, taking the first left into Enisworth Road.

The Connollys were waiting to take a left at the top of the

road. The road was short, no more than two hundred metres, so he approached the end slowly. They turned, and he accelerated. He forced himself out into the traffic and was behind them.

Plain sailing, they would have no idea he was there. Why would they?

He followed them along Mather Avenue heading South. *Where are they off to?*

Paul wanted to build up a picture of the rat Charlie's activities. See what he did, who he was. He needed to know his weakness to bring him down. Whatever it was, he would find it. Most young people on estates smoked marijuana these days, but it was still illegal. Enough of a reason to hold someone, search their room, computer, who knew what he might find. Charlie was connected to Emma, he had seen them at the police station together. She was into drugs. That house was a rathole; they could break up that little group of theirs any time they wanted. See how long the old ladies, solicitors, and housewives stayed around the climate group if they knew its leaders were all druggies. But that was one for the back burner.

This is the bastard. He gave a statement; why did he do that? Then he went to my house, my *house.*

He recalled the words of the prophet Matthew. *As for me and my house, we will serve the Lord. My house will be called a house of prayer,* and this was the truth to Paul. *You have made it a den of thieves.* Charlie had brought down *his* house, he had dirtied and sullied *his* house, and he would pay the price.

He followed Charlie to the bottom of Mather Avenue, swinging round into Garston train station, or Liverpool South Parkway, as it was now known. *Where are you going, boy? Not leaving us already, are you; running away from the hornets' nest you have stirred?*

The father dropped the son at the entrance. Paul pulled into the car park. He left his police gym membership on the dash; it was usually enough to escape any tickets. He watched as the father pulled away.

Paul sprinted across the car park, through the bus stops and into the station. Access to all platforms went through one main barrier. He approached the guard, flashed his Police Federation card and the guard opened the barrier.

'A minute ago, black jacket, grey hoodie, and Adidas trackie bottoms,' Paul said to the guard.

'Went through to Platform Two. Train due just about now.'

'Where to?'

'Liverpool and Southport!' the guard shouted after him.

Paul crossed the footbridge and made his way down the platform. The guard was right; the train was just pulling in. There he was; he'd boarded the train near the end. That would make Paul's job easier. *Perfect, going into town, are you, son? To meet Emma, or Andy, your new radical mates?*

CHAPTER TWENTY-TWO

CHARLIE

Monday, January 27th, 2020.

The train rolled out of Garston. Charlie put his ear pods in to get the match reports. He wanted to get back into it and settled down, allowing himself to luxuriate in the sound. Redmen TV and The Maych were his favourites. He used to be able to lose himself for hours in these, enjoying every second. Now they were a distraction from the thoughts of Anthony Walker and the material he had been reading.

CHAPTER TWENTY-THREE

PAUL

Monday, January 27th, 2020.

Paul sat near the front of the train. His plan was simple. At each stop, Paul got off the train. He knew what carriage Charlie was in, so he stepped onto the platform to watch for him. It took seconds for people to clear the train. Cressington and Saint Micheal's were no problem. Around a dozen people got on and off. The train rumbled on, Paul was nervous. He didn't want to lose Charlie or be spotted.

They reached the short underground part of the journey. There were only six stations in the underground loop. Central Station was one of Liverpool's busiest. He stood by the door, ready to be one of the first to leave the carriage. Near the stairs, he would hide and wait for Charlie to make his way along the platform, then use his surveillance skills to follow him.

Passengers began to gather near the door. The train swayed and juddered as the brakes were applied. The light came on, and a beeper sounded to keep people clear of the doors. Paul was among the first off. He moved to the centre of the platform and hid behind an advertising board. There was no sign of Charlie yet, but bodies were packed on the platform, people shuffling on and off the train. Where was he?

Paul moved from behind the hoarding to get a better view. Charlie wasn't there? *Damn. He didn't get off earlier. Where the hell is he?*

He panicked. He heard the doors beep and moved quickly towards the train as they started to close. He thrust his arm in the gap, an alarm sounded, and the doors reopened. He stepped back on the train, and the doors closed behind him. *What is happening? Where is he going?*

He moved through the train. Had he missed him? Did Charlie get off earlier? He traversed two more carriages before he reached Charlie's. There he was, feet up on the seat in front of him, eyes closed. Was he asleep? Had he missed his stop? No, he had earplugs in.

Paul moved back quickly. At least he hadn't lost him. The train was heading North out of Liverpool Centre. The train line was a mile or so inland from the river but parallel with it. The Mersey came and went into view as the train rushed past buildings. The miles of docks were also visible; docks that once employed tens of thousands of men stood empty. Occasional mountains of rusting scrap metal like angry pimples against the backdrop of the river.

At the very least, he would learn a little more about Charlie, where he was going, and who he was visiting. It could all help; intelligence was not looking for a single piece of information; intelligence was taking in everything he could find then sifting it, letting it flow through the sieve until what remained was key. Football and women were the two obvious interests; they might sound innocent enough, but who knew? Connections to football violence... pornography? Paul would find something, and when he did, he would discredit Charlie and stop him poking about in things that did not concern him.

Bootle, a suburb largely rebuilt after devastating wartime air raids, came and went. Liverpool was the most bombed city outside of London. Four thousand people died in the summer and autumn of 1940.

The further the train went away from the city towards the more prosperous destination of Southport, the more anxious

Paul became. He didn't like the area. For others, it was an escape from the poverty and tension of the city -the golden sands and blue skies of the river estuary, the destination for tens of thousands of city families, a short ride to another place.

For Paul, the space and light were emptiness, a refuge against the shocks and jabs of pain. He would escape into that void. He would leave his body and walk the cold, damp sands, feel the sea spray on his face, one step after another, through the low grey clouds, the misty mornings, the damp, wet air, clawing his way to that emptiness, denying the slaps, the blows of the nuns.

He shivered. Those days were over. He had been saved. The Taylors were sent by God to deliver him from evil. The women in black denied the love of Christ in everything, soiling his name in their mouths. They lived for the antichrist. They destroyed the true Church. They put themselves -priests and nuns, bishops and pope- between believers and God. Who were they to interpret His word, claim the right to speak in His name, and act on His behalf? *Come on, Charlie boy, where are you taking me? What's in Southport?*

Paul was disciplined and followed his strategy. At each station, he left the train and looked along the platform, ensuring Charlie didn't get off early. But with each station, the anger and dread, grew. The Bootle stations passed, Seaforth then Waterloo. The next Station was Blundellsands and Crosby. *No... he couldn't be?*

Charlie disembarked, head down, hoodie up. He walked along the platform. Paul reacted quickly; he kept well back but made sure he didn't lose sight of him. His body was disciplined and controlled; at a steady pace, he found cover in the people and objects before him, but his mind was boiling. It felt like he had been dropped into a pool of hot water. *He knows, the bastard knows! He's leading me to Paradise.*

CHAPTER TWENTY-FOUR

CHARLIE

Monday, January 27th, 2020.

Charlie followed the map on his phone. Paradise House was a mile or so walk from the station. He had only been to Crosby town once before. His dad kept going on about the statues, so they had a day out. He didn't mind it. They got to spend time together, went to the beach, then to Southport afterwards, played mini golf, walked on the promenade and went to the amusement arcade. He and his dad loved it, but his mum wasn't too keen. His dad brought him back to the statues a few times. It was a special place.

Paradise House had the feel of the classic haunted house. It was huge, a mish mash of shapes. The original structure was Victorian gothic, three storeys high, with a central angled roof, and large, pointed attic windows to break up the roof space. Four massive, flat-sided chimneys stuck out. In the centre was a large arch with a cross on top. In an alcove beneath the cross lurked a dark grey statue. Charlie couldn't make out the figure.

Two other buildings were attached to the first one, in a similar style, but these had roofs and gables at all angles, producing a chaotic and jumbled appearance. They looked newer but not by much. They, too, had brick exteriors with decorative wooden trim beneath the gable ends. Each had a plinth mounted on the first storey in the centre of the building, and on the plinth, a statue of Our Lady, painted white, so she was unmissable.

The overall effect was imposing.

Three distinct buildings in different styles combined to serve the one purpose. Three different statues were arranged to reinforce the obedience, poverty, and chastity that were the mottoes of the order of nuns that ran the place.

He walked up the drive and passed the sign at the entrance; *The Sisters of Paradise.*

CHAPTER TWENTY-FIVE

PAUL

Monday, January 27th, 2020.

How does he know? How much does he know? Paul's head was spinning. It was as if someone had rolled out his life like a rug, and Charlie was walking all over it.

It must be a sign to revisit the place from which he was delivered. He kept back and followed Charlie. It wasn't hard to do. Charlie walked straight ahead, hesitated momentarily at street corners but, checking his phone, marched forward. Paul's anxiety was building as they got closer and closer. Those picturesque, leafy streets were the route to his despair. The semi and detached houses, drives with new cars, and gardens with flower beds led to the walled estate. The red sandstone walls, stone gateposts, and the long gravel drive that led to Paradise House.

The children walked these streets in pairs, in white vests and blue shorts. Whatever the weather, the nuns believed in strength in adversity; they would walk to the sands, receiving pitying looks from middle-class housewives. Paul and the other kids were the deserted, the abandoned, the destitute. The physical education teachers were priests from the local parish. They would exercise on the beach.

Charlie walked ahead and showed no fear. Was he organising for Paul to go back? Is that it? Were they planning his fall and his return to the sisters? Paul shook himself. He would have to stop those thoughts. If God was leading him there, there must be a purpose. Was He showing the nature of Charlie? Was this God's way of exposing the evil to him?

Charlie entered the grounds through the stone gate posts and walked up the drive and through the portico doors.

Paul looked up; he could count the windows to his room. He shared that room with five other boys, all from Liverpool. The nuns said they were the children of harlots and ne'erdowells. He didn't know what those names were, but it didn't take long to find out. The boys and girls showed how they were the sons and daughters of harlots and ne'erdowells.

The nuns said they beat the devil out of the children, but Paul knew they were beating him in. They became the instruments of the devil, and they transferred him to the children. Every stroke of the leather belt, every welt and bruise, every stab of pain was the seed for hatred and anger against the nuns, against each other and the world. They beat the devil in, and he would be on slow release for the rest of their lives. Beginning with the other kids as they beat each other, they used fingers in holes and bums and touched and squeezed. The devil was everywhere, and the nuns brought him in. The doors of Paradise House, once closed to the world, were open to Satan.

The beach was his refuge, the emptiness drawing him on, the cold, wet reality. The wind, mist, and spray would swirl around him, cleaning him, refreshing him.

CHAPTER TWENTY-SIX

CHARLIE

Monday, January 27th, 2020.

Once through the main doors, Charlie knew he was in an institution. The atrium was wood panelled, with a partitioned cubicle immediately to his left. A lady sat reading a book. The flowers and image of a windswept woman on the front indicated a romance.

'Hi. I spoke to a Clare Dowling. Do you know where I can find her?'

The lady put the book down and removed her glasses. 'Hello.'

'Hi, I spoke to a Clare Dowling. Do you know where I can find her?' Charlie repeated.

'Oh, yes, of course, dear. You want Clare from the office.'

'Yeah, I guess so.'

'Give me a minute.' She raised her palm. Charlie could feel her painful concentration. She lifted the receiver, looked into the earpiece then placed it next to her ear. She raised her right hand and pressed the buttons of the phone, holding each one down for half a second before releasing it and pressing the next. The numbers were one, two, and three. 'Hello? Hello dear, it's Margery here. I'm at the reception office, and there is someone here.' She listened in silence, nodding, her head turned to Charlie. She held her hand over the mouthpiece and asked, 'Who are you?'

'Charlie Connolly.'

'What do you want?'

'To speak to Clare Dowling.'

Margery's attention returned to the telephone. 'Okay, will do, my dear.' She stood up, removed a blue cardigan from a hook on the wall behind her, and put it on carefully before she opened the little glazed door to the cubicle. Charlie stood back, expecting Margery to lead him to the office.

Margery closed the door behind her and pointed to a corridor on the other side of the entrance. 'There, first door on the left.'

'Thanks.' Charlie nodded and moved off.

When he reached the office door, he looked round to see Margery removing her cardigan and taking her seat again in the reception cubicle. He opened the door. 'Hi, we spoke on the phone. Charlie Connolly,' he introduced himself.

'Yes, Hi,' Clare said. As Charlie entered, she stood and held out her hand. She wore a white blouse with a light grey jacket and skirt, pale pink lipstick softened the look. Around the same age as Charlie, she looked comfortable and in control.

'Come in, sit down.'

'It's a huge place,' Charlie said of the building as he sat where she indicated.

'Yes, I know. Really it's three buildings in one. The first block, or main house, if you like, was built at the turn of the twentieth century, and the other two sections added later.'

'How long have you been here?'

'Not quite that long,' Clare joked, as she sat behind her desk.

'No, of course.' Charlie laughed.

'Just over a year now.'

Charlie looked at the brass nameplate resting on the front of her desk, *Clare Dowling, Business and Administration.* 'Very impressive,' he said.

She smiled.

'It must be a huge responsibility.'

'Actually, it is. The sisters provide the palliative care, and, of course, there are regular medical visits. But for everything else, contracts, maintenance, employment, that's all down to me.'

'You live local?'

Clare leaned back in her chair. She could have redirected the conversation back to immediate matters, but didn't. 'That's a strange question, if you don't mind me saying.'

'Sorry, I didn't mean to be too personal. I was just curious.'

'Actually, yes, I am local; went to school round the corner, Merchant Taylor for Girls.'

'Sounds posh, all hockey sticks and gymslips.'

She laughed. 'It was a bit.'

'It's nice though, the sands, the whole town. It kinda has that holiday feel about it, do you know what I mean?'

'I do, compared to Liverpool. We have the fresh sea air, open spaces.'

'*Another place.*' Charlie referenced the famous modern art installation on the local beach.

'Very clever, Mr Connolly, and here I was about to ask if you are a proper Scouser.'

'Mmmm, so the implication is a proper Scouser wouldn't know about the Gormley sculpture?' He narrowed his eyes in a feigned scowl.

'Okay, you got me. What is that, cultural superiority?'

Charlie smiled. 'Am I a proper Scouser? That's a good question. It all depends on the definition, obviously. Let's see, born in Speke but moved shortly after to Allerton. Support the reds, so there is that, a retro music fan, love the Beatles. I think guilty as charged.'

'No guilt involved.'

'Okay, and as for Gormley, my dad is nuts about the statues down at the beach. I'm not sure how many times he dragged me out here as a kid.'

The air between them was fizzing. It was weird for Charlie, he wasn't sure what it was, but ever since that thing happened to Matt, he was doing well with women. He felt guilty, but also said a mental thanks. Was Matt helping out from the other side? *Don't worry, mate. I got you too.*

Clare interrupted Charlie's moment of silence and brought him back into the room. 'Sorry, to get down to business.' She leaned forward on her desk.

'Yeah, of course.'

Clare picked up a pen. 'You are looking for a relative?'

'Not really.' He had prepared this. 'I know there are protocols about information that leads to reuniting parents and children. This is not about that, nothing to do with that.' He wanted her to know he was not asking for anything illegal.

'Okay.'

'I know there is a register for contact between biological parents and children. This is kind of... it's a bit confusing. I am here for my auntie. She adopted a young boy. My cousin, Paul. I didn't know he was adopted. Paul Taylor, 16 Isaac Street, Date of birth 13th March 1990.

'The thing is, Paul is in trouble. It's sad... my mum, the whole family is upset. Unfortunately, Paul had some mental health issues, got into a bit of trouble and he ended up on the streets. You know... living rough. We would see him from time to time, try and help him out.'

'I'm sorry to hear that.'

'Yeah, I know. What can you do? Well, part of this was he took the name Taylor when he arrived. But my aunt swears she was never told his real family name. They didn't tell you that back in the day. Everything was secret; not like now, where things are much more open. Because of his issues, we believe he's using his family name again. We want to try and help him, but we're having difficulty finding him.'

'That does sound difficult, but I'm afraid I'm not sure how we can help.'

'He was here, you see. I have his full information. I am not looking for his parents' details or anything private. Here,' Charlie handed over a piece of paper with Paul's details. 'It's even got the date my aunt collected him from Paradise House.'

Charlie sat back and hoped he had done enough. 'I guess there are old files around somewhere.'

'Everything is electronic now. All the old files have been transferred. It's all on a database.'

'All I need is his original family name. It would mean so much to us, Clare. I don't know if you can help, but I would really appreciate it.'

Clare leaned back, and her left hand moved through her tight, jet-black bob. She looked at Charlie without saying anything. Her right fingers tapped the keyboard.

She stood and turned the screen toward Charlie. 'If you're interested in the history of the building, I think we've got a brochure somewhere. Give me a couple of minutes, and I'll see if I can find it.' Clare walked towards the door. As she did, she let her hand rest briefly on Charlie's shoulder.

Charlie heard the door close behind him. *Fuck.* He sprang around the desk to get at the keyboard. A blinking cursor was waiting for an input, and he typed in the name Paul. Within seconds, the page was full of Pauls. Each line a disrupted life, each name a child without parents. *Shit.*

His eyes scanned the columns, date of birth on the right. He moved his finger down the screen, turned the next page, and the page after, and there, halfway down, *DOB 13.04.90 Paul Kane.*

He tapped away at the escape button until a box came up to close the database and pressed, *Yes*, then turned the screen and returned to his seat when Clare re-entered the office.

Charlie stood as she handed him a brochure on the Paradise Sisters. 'There you go. I knew we had one somewhere.'

'Thank you,' Charlie turned towards the door but stopped. 'If I ever need a guide for the Gormley sculptures *Another Place*, would you know anyone?'

Clare slipped open a drawer and retrieved a business card. She handed it over to him. 'Always willing to help the disadvantaged.'

'Thank you,' Charlie made his way out. He waved to Margery as he passed. He grabbed the door handle and pulled to open it but felt resistance. He tried to push the door when he realised somebody was on the other side. He let go of the handle and stepped back.

The door opened, and a figure cloaked head to toe in a black nun's habit appeared in front of him. Charlie smiled. There was no smile in return, just a cold empty stare. He stepped aside, and the figure passed him.

Charlie exited the darkness, relieved to be in the cool fresh air.

CHAPTER TWENTY-SEVEN

PAUL

Monday, January 27th, 2020.

Paul had followed Charlie to gain control, to find something he could use. Instead, he found himself unraveling. Who was chasing who?

His stomach turned as he watched Charlie enter Paradise House. He checked his watch; it was a few minutes before 4 pm. This guy was out to destroy him, but it wouldn't work. He could consort with evil, sup with the devil. Paul had faced worse and overcome it. He would not be cowed.

He checked his watch every couple of minutes. The double wooden doors remained resolutely closed. Nothing was visible. The building was constructed to conceal, not reveal. How much of his past would Charlie uncover? If he was here…if he had followed the breadcrumbs… then the next step would be the woman who bore him; he wouldn't use the term *mother* because it carried with it the duty of care, care he did not receive.

Charlie was treading a dangerous path; it was *his* road, Paul's, and it did not belong to anyone else. *No, you could not walk a mile in my shoes. You have not suffered enough, you do not deserve them. They are not made for you. They will not fit you.*

A rage was growing as he waited and watched the window from which he once stared out at the light. Nothing came from outside to help until the Taylors. They were sent to deliver him from evil, and he would not be returned to those same forces.

Although they spoke the Lord's name in vain, and they clothed themselves in the language of love and devotion, those black-clad demons knew nothing of Jesus. They worshipped at the altar of order and control, and they did so in service of a commercial machine. Look at the house, bigger than any local Lord or Earl, a millionaire would struggle to own such a property, and there, those practitioners of poverty earned thousands, tens of thousands, for every child they battered and abused, those practitioners of chastity.

If Charlie was choosing that side, then he would pay the price. Do we not have to pay for our sins? *You will pay, Charlie boy. Your time is coming. Mine is to live or die for the Lord at a time of His choosing. My life is spent at His will. I neither desire it nor repent it. I use it in His name, to His purpose.*

One in black went in, and Charlie came out, and his fate was sealed.

Charlie, you have crossed a line. Like Matt before you, you cannot and will not steal my life. I give it voluntarily only to the Lord.

CHAPTER TWENTY-EIGHT

CHARLIE

Monday, January 27th, 2020.

Charlie left Paradise happier than when he arrived. The forbidding exterior, with its turrets and statues, opened to the pleasant and helpful Clare. Paul Kane, born Friday the 13th April 1990, was delivered into Paradise in August of the same year. Jesus, there were so many ironies. Messages? Simon or Paul? Paradise? It was all a bit weird.

There was no address for his parents. His mother's name was listed as Mary Kane, but no father was indicated.

He walked back to the train station. The light was just beginning to change as the winter sun lost its power, and the evening grew in strength. *Friday the thirteenth, unlucky for some*, thought Charlie.

He wasn't sure what he could do with the new information, or how it would help him, but 'If you don't try, you don't get,' was becoming his new motto. Charlie worked through his thoughts: *Simon Taylor, who we now know is Paul Kane, was attending the Woolton-based climate group, where he met Matt.* He stopped walking for a moment. Paul had infiltrated the group and had later arrested Matt and caused his death.

What came first? The group or Matt? Did he join the group and meet Matt? Then took his aggression out on him during the arrest? What if it was personal all along? What if he joined the group *to meet* Matt?

Why the fuck would he do that?

'Did you find out anything useful?'

Charlie turned. Paul was standing behind him. Paul also known as Simon, copper, infiltrator. Murderer?

'What?' Charlie was confused, shocked. He didn't know how to respond.

'Simple enough question, did you find anything out in that *place?*' The way he spat the word *place* made Charlie bristle.

'I don't know what you mean, mate.' Charlie started walking again. His stomach was doing somersaults. He didn't know what to do or say. He wanted to run. He wanted to get out of there.

'You can't get away from me so easily.' Paul marched beside him, keeping pace. 'So, what did you find out?'

Charlie ignored the question.

Paul lurched forward and blocked Charlie's path. Charlie could see the train station. He just had to get inside. He would be safer; there would be guards or staff around.

Paul put his arm across Charlie's chest and stopped him. 'Don't make me angry. Don't act the innocent with me. I can smell the evil off you.'

Charlie pushed Paul's arm away. 'I don't know what the fuck you are on about. Get out my way, or I'll call the police.'

Paul laughed in his face. 'Think that will help, do you? Really? I'd love to see you try. But you know who I am, don't you?'

Charlie checked out his chances of making a run for it. Could he get across the road and into the station before Paul caught him?

'Yeah, I know who you are. So, you'd better back off. You're in enough shit without this. What do you think Superintendent Smith would say about this, eh?'

'You don't know what you are getting yourself into, Charlie boy. You're playing with forces beyond your control.'

'No. You, mate. You've fucked up. The days of people keeping quiet and looking the other way have gone. I saw what you did, and Matt died.'

'Ha! The gift from God, Matthew, was returned, as we all will. I am my brother's keeper and will save him from evil in this life or the next.'

'You're a fucking nutjob, mate. Cuckoo, fuckin' doolally.' Charlie spun his finger round beside his temple. 'And you know what? You're not getting away with it.'

He pushed Paul out of the way and ignored the blast of horns as he ran across the road and dodged the traffic. He didn't look round but heard a shout that started as a 'No' but turned into a cry of rage. 'Noooaaaaaaa!'

Fuck.

As Charlie entered the station, he saw the sign for Liverpool trains and took the stairs down to the platform two at a time. His legs were like jelly, and he was scared he would slip. A few other people were waiting, but he couldn't see any railway staff. *Fuck.* What if he really was crazy?

The Liverpool train was waiting on his right. He jumped on and moved through the carriages, willing the train to move.

Shit, how stupid am I?

He was on the Liverpool train. It wouldn't be difficult for Paul to find him. Would he do anything? He was a copper. Surely that would stop him doing anything stupid... illegal? But the fucker was crazy. *What if he did kill Matt, and now here I am sniffing round his house and his old home. That would piss anyone off. Fuck.*

Charlie passed through every carriage till he reached the end. He could just about see the stairs through the side window.

Shit, he could see the black boots and beige chinos descending the station steps. *Fuck.*

Paul looked from side to side. He got on the train, and it would only take him a couple of minutes to get through it. Charlie had to think quickly. *Fuck.* There was nowhere to hide.

He checked his watch. It was time the train should leave. He ducked behind some seats, and an old lady gave him a quizzical look. The door buzzers sounded and he looked up to see Paul coming. He had entered the carriage. *Fuck. Fuck!* Paul was closing in on him.

Paul shouted, 'Stop! Police!'

Diving from the train, Charlie stumbled as a guy stuck out his leg to trip him. Fuck, he wouldn't make the stairs. A guy in front dropped his bag and was setting himself to tackle Charlie. Charlie had no choice; he looked right it was just a meter down to the track. He swerved right, picked his spot and jumped off the platform. He landed on the ballast, the loose stones beside the track. Was the track electrified? People on the platform were shouting and Paul was coming. Charlie crossed the first tracks carefully then looked back and saw the oncoming train.

CHAPTER TWENTY-NINE

CHARLIE

Monday, January 27th, 2020.

Charlie dived clear. The train's horn blared, and the rush of its wheels, with the noise and smell, filled the air around him. His hands were bleeding from where they broke his fall, the sharp stones cutting into his palms. *Fuck.* The train thundered on. He needed to move. He picked himself up and jumped the next tracks to reach the bank. He struggled up through the vegetation and climbed a wooden fence, then scrambled across a neat well-kept lawn to a garden gate. Back on the street, he collapsed against a garden wall. His legs were jelly, his bleeding hands shook. His head was full of the noise, the shock and awe of the train. Fuck, he had to move. Getting to his feet, he took the first left along the main road and ran. He kept moving, looking back to make sure no one was following him.

He bounced along the road towards the shore, constantly checking behind his relief grew with distance. *Dick. Not so clever now, eh?*

He'd gotten rid of Paul, but there was a growing awareness that he was in deep shit. Charlie stopped and looked behind. Paul had not followed. He pulled out his phone, and swiped the screen. The call was answered quickly.

'Dad, I've fucked up. Can you come and get me?' He told him where he was and where to meet. Charlie didn't want to go anywhere near the train again today.

He crossed the final road separating the town from the riverside, then crossed the park that led to the dunes.

The wind was chill, and it blew in gasps, sending swirls of leaf debris spinning through the air. It buffeted and rocked him, but he accepted it, head down, hood up.

He walked through the push and pull of the wind, a small battle in the overall scale of things; one that reminded him of the constancy of resistance. 'Whatever we do, however we do it, there are forces that push and pull us away from our goal.' It sounded like a quote from Klopp. Maybe it was. He had internalised so much of the language and images.

He put his ear pods in and started to listen to Redmen TV. He knew his dad was on his way. He needed to think of something else.

He didn't listen for long and turned it off. It was a distraction. Football had been his life, not a hobby, an interest, but a part of him. He had stood in the crowd when they sang, *Fields of Anfield Road.* He had seen tears in the eyes of many during *You'll Never Walk Alone.* Tears for the ninety-seven who died from the Hillsborough disaster. People sang because they wanted to win something; a cup, a premiership, but they also expressed pain and sorrow, and they did it with thousands of others in the hope that things would get better. That was football.

Charlie remembered Jaime talking about Saint Augustine. 'Hope had two daughters; anger and courage. The anger to see what was wrong, and the courage to change it.'

Hope itself was a killer; it killed ambition, it killed drive and engagement, it meant passivity and…hope. *Fuck hope.* Things needed to change, and hope would wander the world impotent, while anger and courage fought for change.

His phone rang.

'Hey Dad, I'm on the sands. Where are you?'

'I'll park up and come and find you,' his dad replied.

'No, it's okay. Just tell me where you are.'

'I'll find you,' his dad answered.

The phone went dead. 'For fuck's sake,' Charlie swore into the wind. He knew his dad wanted to see the statues.

A few minutes later his dad clambered up the dunes. Charlie went to meet him. 'Hey, Dad, thanks for coming.'

'It sounded serious.'

'Yeah, I think it might be.'

'What the fuck happened? Look at the state of your hands.'

'When we get in the car, okay?

'Okay, fine.'

His dad stood at the top of the dune, looking out over the river. The tide was coming in, but the water was still far from the shoreline. The famous statues by Anthony Gormley were spread over a kilometre of the beach. The human shapes made of iron were submerged and revealed with the ebb and flow of the tide. Rusted and barnacled, they now formed part of the riverscape. They were a poignant marker of the millions of individuals who passed through the Mersey estuary. Numbers so huge it could be difficult to envision. These statues individualised that great movement. Each stood alone while remaining part of the great narratives of immigration, emigration, slavery, and famine.

'I love this place,' his dad said.

'I know. I get it, Dad. You are closer to the people who came and went, like your dad. I understand, but for me, it's different.'

'How?'

'I do understand. I liked it when you brought me here as a kid with Mum because we were doing something. It was a good day out, because we were together, not the statues. Maybe because you could never be together with your dad. These statues represented something missing, something that would go with the tide. But my family was with me. I had you and Mum.'

'You're right. You're so smart sometimes, do you know that?'

A tear welled and fell, it rolled down his dad's cheek as he spoke.

'Come on, let's make a move.' Charlie reached out and put his arm around his shoulder.

~

They drove back toward Liverpool. 'Okay, come on, what were you doing out here?'

'I was checking out a place called Paradise House.'

'What for?'

'It was the home Paul Taylor was adopted from.'

His dad's concentration flipped between the road and Charlie. 'Paul Taylor?'

'That's the copper's name.' After a beat of silence, Charlie asked, 'You think I'm stupid?'

'No, it's not that. It's not stupid to do what you think is right. I'm just not sure what you can get out of it, or how dangerous it might be.'

'Neither am I. But I did find out a couple of things.'

'Like what?'

'His name, original name, was Paul Kane. He was adopted into the Taylor family just before his thirteenth birthday. The home he was raised in was part of Operation Care, an investigation into historic child abuse.'

'Wow, you have been busy. But how does this help? I mean, how does it help in working out what happened to Matthew?'

'I don't know yet. But I do know that Paul Taylor is fucked up. He chased me through the station. He's pretty scary. I told him he was crazy, and I think he might be.' Charlie left out nearly being hit by a train.'

His dad slowed the car. 'For fucks sake, Charlie, he confronted you?'

'Yeah, and the way he was talking, it was all this religious stuff.'

'Your mum will go mad if she hears this. What was he saying?'

'That Matthew was a gift from God, and the gift was returned. 'I am my brother's keeper.' He said that, and something about whether he lived or died. Everything was in this language of good and evil. God and the devil, all that shit.'

'He sounds messed up.'

'He is.'

'Okay, well, look, we're gonna have to talk about this. You can't just go off doing stuff on your own. You do realise that you can't resolve this yourself?'

'What do you mean?'

'You're not going to be some hero who comes in to save the day.'

'Is that what you think I'm doing?'

'No, I'm just making sure you know what you are getting into. It's not about you. You can't solve social questions individually. You know that, right?'

'I guess…'

'It's part of a wider thing, how the police treat people.'

'Yeah, it is, I know, Jaime and Mina-'

'Mina?' Vinny interrupted.

'I told you about her, the woman who works with Jaime. She organises with Black Lives Matter.'

'Jeez, what happened to the Fortnite playing teenager, who would only come out of his room for football?'

'He's still in here somewhere,' Charlie said. 'One thing, though. The statues on the beach... I know why you like them.'

'You do?'

'Cos that thing with your dad. You know that you missed him, but it's also because they see everything, I think you are one of them.'

'Thanks. You mean rusty and stuck in the mud?'

'No, I mean, time washes over you. You're a history professor, but for you, history is as much now, yesterday or this morning, as one or two hundred years ago. Those figures are like that. Timeless.'

'I like that, really. Who is it? Emma or Mina?'

'Who is what?' Charlie asked.

'Who is it that is bringing out the poetic in you?'

'Ha, I guess that would be Mina.'

'When do we get to meet her. I think I like her already.'

'There's nothing going on, Dad. We're just friends. Anyway, you might not like this next bit.'

'Go on... what?'

'The statues see but don't do anything. They don't change, while the world around them does.'

'That's not technically true. They get rusty, barnacles grow on them, and they sometimes fall over after storms or if there is a movement in the riverbed...but in essence, you are right.'

'That's like you and history; you understand, and you can learn from history, but you aren't doing anything to change it.'

'Jesus... well, how can I say this? You have actually just proved yourself wrong.'

'How? Charlie asked.

'What has happened to you? Over these past few weeks, what has changed in you?'

'I saw the arrest, I met Emma, and then Jaime and Mina.'

'You met people who opened up your world, or maybe they showed you their world. And you said Mina had given you stuff to read?'

'Yeah.'

'Well, that's what I do every day. How many of my students will do nothing with the knowledge they gain, I have no idea, but my hope is that some of them will.'

'Hope?'

'Yeah, what else can we do?'

'That's what I'm trying to work out.'

CHAPTER THIRTY

CHARLIE

9am, Thursday, January 30th, 2020.

'Hey,'

'Thanks for doing this.'

Emma looked beautiful and serious. She hugged then air-kissed Charlie, brushing cheeks with him. He wondered if she had missed him, even thought of him, since they had slept together. Everything seemed so instant, of the moment. Was it because of her commitments to climate change? An understanding that the future was threatened? Was it conscious, was she living for and in the moment because she had no faith that humanity had a future?

'Come in a second.' She retreated from the doorway and Charlie followed her into the kitchen. Emma moved from place to place around the kitchen, collecting keys, phone, and bag. 'We are really busy organising for Friday.'

'What's on Friday?'

'Have you forgotten already? February?' She looked disappointed. 'First weekend.'

'Valentine's day?' Charlie was confused.

'No, it's the climate change strike, the school strike.'

'Oh yeah, right, of course.'

'Kids have been contacting us all week. There will be a march and rally in town.'

'That sounds great.'

Emma lifted her bag strap over her shoulder. 'Why do you want to see Matt's mum again?'

'I just have a few questions. I want to see if I can find out a bit more background.' Charlie had asked Terry to use his council computer access, but he hadn't gotten anywhere yet. 'Are you ready, then?'

'Yeah, I'm ready, but background for what?'

Charlie walked back to the front door. He wanted to get out. The house smelled. He hadn't noticed on his last visit, but the combination of joss sticks, weed and herbs; the whole thing was sickly. 'I don't believe the police. I think there might be a cover up.'

He opened the front door and inhaled.

'You're probably right.' Emma was behind him.

'Whose car is it?'

'Dad's,' said Charlie

A light drizzle left a film of moisture on everything, the air was chill, and the grey sky completed the picture of wintry gloom. Charlie started the engine and turned on the heater. The fan's noise filled the car for a moment before settling into a mild drone. 'You don't seem too concerned? About the situation with Matt?'

Emma clicked her seatbelt into place. 'No, I think it's great that you are interested.'

'It sounds like there is a "but" coming.'

'Well, on Friday, we will have kids from all over Liverpool in town demanding climate change.'

'Yeah, and...' Charlie reached the end of the street and turned left onto the main road. As he turned, he automatically checked the mirror and saw a silver BMW pulling away from the kerb.

'Well, you know, they are campaigning. *We* are campaigning to save the planet.'

Charlie swung his head left to look at her. 'And this is just one person who died?'

'No, it's important that we find out what happened, but it's not going to bring him back, is it?'

Charlie shook his head. 'And hundreds of kids waving placards and holding hands is going to stop Esso drilling for oil, or loggers cutting down the rainforest?'

Emma looked out of the side window. 'That's so cynical.'

They drove along Smithdown Road. It was a busy and he had to keep his eyes open.

'So, trying to find out how a member of your group died in police custody is not worth it because it's not going to bring him back, but I'm the cynical one?'

Emma turned to face him. He met her look. 'I'm here to help you, okay? There's no need to be aggressive.'

'I'm not being aggressive. I'm just saying...'

'You're trying to impose your framework on me. I am allowed to have my own thoughts.'

'Of course you are. I never said you couldn't.' Charlie negotiated the road better than the conversation.

'No, but attempting to intimidate and dominate is not acceptable.'

'I disagreed with you, that's all.'

'See what I mean? You are trying to shut down my opinion.'

'Alright... can we go to see his mum? Are you okay to do that?'

They were coming up to a complicated junction between Allerton Road, Queen's Drive, and Mather Avenue, where there were traffic lights and a roundabout. Charlie checked the mirror as he drove along Menlove Avenue. The silver BMW was still behind him. That was weird. It had lots of options at the last junction and roundabout, but it was still there.

Charlie was watching both the road and Emma; she folded her arms and looked straight ahead. 'Yes, as long as you know, I retain the right to withdraw if I feel threatened.'

'Yeah, of course. Come on.' He reached with his left hand to pat her but thought better of it. He was beginning to wonder why bringing her was a good idea. Whatever spark existed between them had fizzled and gone out.

He took a sharp left up Woolton Road, over the hill and down towards Halewood Road. He turned left at Macket's Lane. They finished the drive in silence. He pulled up to the kerb. 'I didn't mean to upset you.'

'Who's upset?' Emma got out and slammed the door.

Charlie scanned the road. All clear. He followed Emma up the path.

~

'Hi, thanks for seeing me again.' Charlie tried to sound upbeat.

Mary didn't. 'Come in.'

Before he stepped through the door, he looked one more time along the road. There it was… the silver BMW stopped about a hundred yards away. *Fuck.*

He tried to settle himself. He needed to sort this out, then he would deal with the copper, if it was him in the BMW.

It had been a couple of weeks since Charlie had last seen her, and Mary looked thinner and more drawn. Her face was lean, her cheekbones more pronounced. 'How are you?' he asked when they were all seated.

'You know, getting through.' She opened a pack of cigarettes and offered him one.

'Not for me, thanks.'

'I shouldn't, I know.' She put the pack down. As if to prove the point, a chesty cough erupted that rattled her frame.

Charlie stared at the photo of Matt on the mantelpiece; there wasn't much else to look at. He found it difficult to look at Mary's face for too long.

'There's going to be a huge demonstration on Friday,' said Emma. 'Schoolkids from all over the world are going on strike for action on climate change. It's just the kind of thing that Matt would have wanted.'

'That's nice,' Mary said.

'We've been getting messages all week. It's so exciting.' Emma beamed to Charlie's embarrassment.

'I hope you don't mind,' Charlie said. 'But I wanted to find out a bit more about Matthew.'

'What for?'

There was a connection the last time they spoke. Mary's grief allowed her to reach out to others, to share the sadness, revel in Matt's memory, and to share his life. Now she was flat, Matt was dead, there was no point clinging to the things he did. It wouldn't make him less dead. If anything, it highlighted it.

'Matt had no siblings,' said Charlie.

'That's right,' said Mary.

'No cousins?'

'Why are you asking?' Mary's eyes had a spark of life in them for the first time since they entered the house. But the light was sharp, accusing, threatening. 'Why are you asking that?'

'Anyone called Paul? Paul Taylor?' He was also conscious that the guy could be sitting right outside.

'No, I told you, no one. Maybe you should be going.'

'13th April 1990.'

'What?'

'13th April 1990. What were you doing that day?' Charlie was taking a chance.

'Who are you? You're not the police. You can't question me.' Mary fumbled for her cigarette packet, took one out, and lit it.

'Paul... 13th April... 1990.' Charlie separated the points, and they weighed heavier because of it.

'You bastard!' Mary shouted. 'Who told you?'

Emma's face was white. 'What's going on? Charlie, what are you doing?'

'Who told you? I don't know any Paul Taylor.'

Charlie hammered the question home. 'Who was Paul, 13th April 1990?'

Mary pulled hard on the cigarette. 'How do you know?' The smoke enveloped her words as it escaped her mouth.

'Know what?' Emma stood up.

Mary shouted at Charlie as she stood up too. 'How do you know? Who told you?'

'Your maiden name was Kane,' said Charlie.

The strength left Mary, and she collapsed back into her seat. She didn't exhale and the smoke escaped her mouth and curled upwards, it found its own way to nestle beneath the ceiling. Mary leaned forward, elbows on her knees, and pulled heavily on the ciggie. This time she exhaled a cloud. She spoke in short sharp sentences, a staccato of justification, pain and regret.

'My boyfriend was sent to jail. He got five years. It was easy for him. If it wasn't for him, I wouldn't have been using. We could have kept the baby and everything. It all just went to shit.'

The smoke spread throughout the room. Charlie waved it away but couldn't do the same with the heavy silence.

Emma pushed his arm, her eyebrows raised.

Charlie waited.

Mary smoked.

When she spoke again, the words were softer, slower. 'They took him because of the drugs. There was nothing I could do. I didn't want them to, but what could I do? I called him Paul. They told me they would keep the name.' Mary turned toward Charlie. 'Who is Paul Taylor? Is that him?' Her eyes drilled into Charlie.

'I have to go.' Charlie stood up.

Mary stood too. 'He came here. Someone came here. He was crazy, talking about Jacob and somebody, is that him? Tell me... is Paul Taylor my son? Is that his name?'

Charlie wanted to get out, he'd caused this and now didn't know what to do. He stopped by the door when he realised. 'He was here?'

'Someone was, I didn't know it was him. He was talking

about God and raving like a lunatic. I chased him. Told him I would call the police.'

'What a mess.'

'That was him, wasn't it? You know something, you bastard. Tell me.'

Charlie couldn't say that he thought one son killed the other.

'Is Paul Taylor my son? I didn't know how to contact him. I chased him away.'

Charlie answered her question. 'I think so. But you should talk to your lawyer. I'm sorry. I really do have to go. Give the name Paul Taylor to your lawyer.' Charlie opened the door.

'What fucking lawyer? Look around you? Does it look like I could afford a lawyer?'

'Oh, shit.' He stopped at the door. 'I will try and get you one. I know someone who can help.'

Mary flopped back into her seat. Emma followed Charlie out through the door.

Back on the street, Charlie took a lung full of fresh air and scanned the road. The BMW was gone.

'That was horrible,' Emma said

'Yeah, it was.'

'You used me.'

'Just like you used her? I asked if you wanted to come.'

'You didn't tell me what you were going to say. Did you know Simon... Paul, whoever he is, was Matthew's brother?'

'I wasn't sure. I had an idea but I couldn't be sure until she told me.'

'I think what you did is disgusting. You tricked that poor woman.'

'The man who killed her son might have been his own brother. That's disgusting. This situation is disgusting.' Charlie stopped before he opened the car. 'You didn't get her a lawyer?'

'Me?' Emma asked.

'No, not you personally. The campaign?'

'I don't know.' Emma opened the passenger side door.

'You don't know? For fuck's sake.'

Emma slammed the door. 'You're really pissing me off, do you know that?'

'Get in. I'll drop you home.'

'Don't bother. I'll get the bus.' Emma turned and walked away.

'Emma!' Charlie shouted but didn't follow her.

~

On the drive home, he checked the mirror constantly, and although his heart fluttered a couple of times, he never saw the BMW.

The house was empty when he got home, and he was glad. He needed time to think and to make a phone call.

He flopped down on the sofa and pulled his phone out.

'Mina.'

'Hey, how are you?'

'Good, thanks. What you up to?'

'I need something.'

'Sure, what can I do?'

'Matthew Whitney... it turns out his mum doesn't have a lawyer. There's no one representing her. Jaime said that maybe he or you, someone, could help?'

'I think so. Yeah, I'll have to make some calls. Can you send me her details?'

'Yeah, sure.'

'Okay. I'll see what I can do. When I've got something, I'll give you a ring. Maybe we should meet up?'

'Yeah, that would be great. Thanks, Mina, I really appreciate it.'

'Inshallah, no probs, bruv.'

Charlie kicked his shoes off and lay back on the sofa.

'*Inshallah,* no probs, bruv.' He loved the sound of it; something about the combination made him smile.

~

'You could have put your shoes away.'

Charlie woke with a start. 'What?'

His mum was in the kitchen unpacking shopping bags. 'Your shoes.'

'Right, yeah.'

'Have you called the police?'

'What for? Charlie sat up.

'Superintendent Smith called.'

'Oh right.'

'What are you waiting for?'

'Okay. I'll do it. Give me a chance.'

'Tea?'

'Yeah.'

He got off the couch, dropped his shoes in the hallway and climbed the stairs. Superintendent Smith's card was on his desk somewhere.

He heard the front door, so his dad must also be home. Charlie found the card and went back downstairs. 'Okay. I'm gonna call.' His mum and dad sat at the table. Charlie paced next to it. 'It's ringing…bloody voice mail.'

'Leave a message.' His mum waved at him.

'Hello, yeah, it's Charlie Connolly. I'm ringing to let you know that Paul Taylor, one of the officers at Hope Street Police station, was a member of the climate group Matthew Whitney belonged to. He was also half-brother to Matt. Paul was taken into care as a baby, so there are strong links between Paul Taylor and Matthew Whitney. I think you should do your job and investigate this. Thank you, Bye.'

'That sounded a bit off.' His dad lowered his laptop screen.

'What?'

'Do your job?'

'He's right, though. Why is he the one finding out this stuff?' His mum said.

'Okay, I know, but he could have been a bit more tactful, that's all,' said his dad.

'Good job, it's not an emergency. Bloody answering machine,' said Helen.

'Voice mail,' his dad said.

'Same thing,' said his mum. 'How did you get on today then?' she asked Charlie.

'A bit of a mess, to be honest.'

'Why?'

'Mary, his mum, got upset.'

'What's this about them being brothers?' asked his dad.

'Yeah, half-brothers; same mum, different dads.'

His mum shook her head. 'That's weird. There's something definitely going on there.'

'She said someone came to her door a while ago. My guess is it was Paul. He was ranting and raving and she sent him away, said she would call the police. I don't think she knew it was her son, the one that was taken from her.'

'Poor woman,' his dad said.

'Jesus,' said his mum. 'A baby taken away, then a second dying, no wonder she's in a state.'

Charlie's phone rang.

'Who is it?'

Charlie swiped the screen. 'Merseyside Police'

'Go on then, get it, put it on speaker,' said his dad.

'Hello, Mr Connolly, this is Superintendent Smith, returning your call. I should tell you, Mr Connolly, this call is recorded.'

'No problem.'

'Regarding the call you made a few minutes ago... can you come in and make a statement? We would like to get everything down on paper.'

Charlie rolled his eyes. 'Is that really necessary?'

'I'm afraid so, Mr Connolly. We need a signed statement of the information you provided and, of course, how you came by that information.'

'No, you don't,' said Charlie's dad.

'Excuse me?'

'This is Professor Connolly, Charlie's father. 'What you need to do is act on the information my son has provided. There are two witnesses here that my son gave you information on the background of one of your officers. We don't know if he was involved in Mr Whitney's death. But I am telling you, this officer has been following my son. So, I suggest you get a grip of your investigation and the officer in question.'

'Professor Connolly, we are conducting our inquiries, and as a part of that, require that your son make himself available to give a statement.'

'I am telling you, Superintendent, my son has been followed and threatened by one of your officers. If you do not take action immediately, I will inform the press that a peaceful protester died in police custody in the same station that his half-brother operated from. If that doesn't make you sit up and take notice and start asking serious questions, I know a few reporters who would be more than interested. Thank you, Superintendent.'

Charlie tapped the phone to end the call and raised his hand. 'Nice one, Dad. But what happened to tactful?'

His dad shrugged, and completed the high-five. 'That should put the cat among the pigeons.'

CHAPTER THIRTY-ONE

PAUL

Thursday, January 30th, 2020.

'Are you going to eat the toast this time?'

'I ate it last time. What I pay for is mine to consume.'

'Whatever.' The waitress rolled her eyes and put his plate down. 'Two toast, both sides. Butter, not margarine.'

Paul sat in the cafe, watching Enisworth Road. All was quiet on the official front. He hadn't heard from Superintendent Smith or the inquiry again. That was good news. He didn't trust the superintendent. She went at him pretty hard, but she had nothing and would find nothing; she had no interest in digging.

Who did Charlie think he was? He was a know-nothing, unemployed street rat, putting himself between God and the law. But then, all forces found an expression in physical things. Good and evil were not concepts, not spirits. They were physical forces in the earthly world. The rat had been in Paul's home. He had been to Paradise. He was getting closer, there was no doubt, but... he hadn't yet found the key to unlock the story of Jacob and Esau.

The devil was working hard, pushing and guiding his evil hand, but the Lord would not give in, would not bow down, would not accept defeat. As was said in Romans 13, *The one in authority is God's servant for your good. But if you do wrong, be afraid, for rulers do not bear the sword for no reason.* I am happy to be the bearer of that sword, and will use it without mercy when the time comes.

The day was full of signs. As Romans was running through his mind, the street rat appeared. Paul had eaten his toast in time, tea was comfortably drained, and the bill paid. He could leave without attracting attention.

Paul's eyes were glued to the Charlie. Paul was calm. He knew he could cross the road and get in the car at the bottom of Enisworth in plenty of time.

'Thank you,' the waitress called out. 'And a good day to you too.'

He stared at her. *Was that impudence? Was she being sarcastic?* He held his head high and left.

With Charlie using his dad's car, it would be no problem, the roads were not too busy. He could afford to stay back a little. The small, blue Punto was waiting at the top of Enisworth to turn left into the flow of traffic on Menlove Avenue. *Where to*? Paul followed Charlie through the junctions to Allerton Road. Paul realised before they were halfway there that Charlie was heading to Emma's. The Magdalene, with her touching and hugging, was a corrupter of flesh.

He drove past Charlie as he pulled to the kerb, parked, and used his mirror. He watched Charlie knock on the door and go inside.

Paul hoped he wouldn't be waiting while they committed sins of the flesh. He'd allow fifteen minutes, then go and look around the back. If they were using marijuana, he would call it into the local station. Not a big deal, but enough to disrupt their plans. If the officers made a search, what else would they find inside?

He waited five minutes, then got out and crossed the road. He could walk inside the park and still see the house. It would give him cover to watch the upstairs windows.

The door opened. Paul moved quickly. They were too engrossed with each other to notice him. He reached his car about a hundred yards away before they left.

Charlie was just turning into Smithdown Road when Paul pulled away from the kerb. He was heading away from town. *Where to now?*

Was he taking her home to meet his parents? *Where else? Surely, they will see through the fallen woman.* Anticipation was an important part of tracking, getting inside the character you were trailing. What would they be looking for? Where were they going? If he wasn't taking her home, what else was this side of the city?

When they took a left up toward Woolton Village, his anxiety rose. Then they crested the hill to Halewood Road. They turned right, Paul's stomach churned and he knew. The dread and rage began to build. The bastard... step by step, he kept coming. He had been to his home. He had been to Paradise. What was left to complete the picture? Mary... the source of his rejection and the original sin.

The bastard knew.

He followed them right onto Halewood Road and down through Macket's Lane. He didn't know why he was following. There was no point. He knew where they were going.

Charlie pulled up at the kerb outside her house. Slowly, Paul drove by and watched them enter. Mary the original sinner, another Eve, let them in. The door that was slammed shut in his face was open to them. The rat boy bastard had found the key, unlocked and revealed his pain. He turned round, parked up and collapsed over the steering wheel, his hands rubbing his eyes and face, but there were no answers. Eyes closed, he replayed the moment of his revelation.

It was months before, in the Spring, when new life abounds and all things seem possible. He took it upon himself to question God's plan, and now he suffered the consequence. He had decided to find his biological mother, even though it was clear that God had separated them, that there was a plan at work. He was nervous, not sure where the butterflies in his stomach came from. He had wrestled for years, then given up, then occasionally returned to the idea. But no matter how deeply he buried it, the need to know his real mother was always with him. It was God's will that he be separated and made special. He was chosen to suffer, and by suffering be made strong. And yet...

He walked slowly up the path; it was the right house, he had checked. He knew all about her, Mary Kane, and later Whitney, her partner jailed for possession with intent to supply; a junkie dealer, a junkie couple. A junkie baby?

But to see her, talk to her... his vision blurred, his stomach wrenched, his feet lost grip. He was above the abyss. He stopped, bent double, breathed hard and let the oxygen in the damp morning air pass through his lungs into his blood supply. He could do this. He had to do this. Paul raised the brass knocker and felt the reverberations as he rapped it. Normality and reality passed by. He could hear the cars from a different dimension in the road behind him.

He was speechless for a minute.

The woman in front of him pulled at her cigarette, blowing smoke in his face. 'Yeah? What do you want?'

He tried to speak but choked. Nothing came out.

She tilted her head and took a step back.

He coughed out, 'No, wait.'

She closed the door a couple of inches.

The words came tripping out, like a damburst to wash over her. 'I am back. I am here... I will absolve you of your sin... it wasn't your fault... Let me heal...'

'Who are you? What do you want?'

He reached forward to hold the door open. 'I've returned, to you, Mary.'

'If you don't get off my doorstep, I'm calling the police.'

'No, it's me–'

'You're fucking crazy!' She slammed the door.

'Your son.' Paul sank through the floor into the abyss, and yet he stood and stared; the door remained closed. He raised his fist and

banged. 'I'm yours... yours.'

The curtain to the living room window opened, and her face appeared shrouded in a net curtain. The mouthed words were clear. 'Fuck off!'

Back in his car, Paul didn't know what was coursing through his veins; anger, rage, the power of God? But he felt it, the strength it brought him. God had saved him from that destiny; his mother was that foul-smelling bag of bones. Was this why God had removed him, taken him to his trials and tribulations in Paradise to be rescued on the cusp of manhood? Was this his task, his role, to bring his justice?

In the following weeks he watched and waited, not knowing what else to do. Of all the scenarios in his head, that wasn't one. She had chased him. This Eve rejected him not once but for the second time. Then he saw the traitor, the one who had stolen his birthright, stolen his life; Matthew. Maybe ten years younger, a slim, unkempt mess.

Everything he seemed to be in that first sighting, he was. After that day, Paul tracked the Jacob. The second son who had stolen the place of the first. He was Esau to Matt's Jacob.

His time would come, but he grew tired of watching and was drawn near, like a flame that attracts until it burns. He was the moth darting around until he confirmed what he had always known. Paul knew the smug arrogance of upstart youth in that first instant, rebelling against the world as God created it.

He was right to wait and watch. The bad had replaced the good, the evil had taken the place of the pure, and he was a communist devil. Even in the home of rebellion, amongst the liberals and anarchists of the climate group, he argued, he wasn't satisfied. He wanted God's creation overturned. He was the son of the devil, the son of the revolution. God was the God of Power.

Paul started his car; there was no need to wait for them to

come out of the house. He knew what would be discussed and discovered inside. Now he had to be open and pray for God's plan.

He drove home slowly through a city of movement and sound. It was a wonder how God could watch His world be consumed by materialism and greed. The flash of SUVs speeding by were, for Him, the incarnation of Mammon. All around was the worship of wealth. It was the credo of society: success and money were the sign of God's favour, poverty and hunger were a moral and intellectual lack, the strivers and shirkers. *You will be judged not by what is in your heart but by what is in your wallet.*

That was how far they had fallen. Everyone knew the end was coming. The fires and floods had started, God was bringing His plagues, diseases were spreading from Godless China across the globe. Only those who followed His plan would survive.

He checked his phone. Nothing. Nothing from the station. Could he stop Charlie before he spoke to the traitor Supt Smith?

Paul was back in Isaac Street. He locked the car and took the few steps to his front door. Everything he did now had an unworldly feel. The storm was brewing, and the first winds were gently blowing. Charlie would find out everything from Mary. He would, at some point, report what he found. Then the world would fall upon Paul with all its force.

He opened the front door.

'Hello, is that you love?'

'Hello.'

'Strange, this week. They've got you coming and going at all times.'

'Yeah, a special project.'

'Come in here. You must be hungry. I can have eggs and bacon on a plate in a jiffy.'

'Thanks be…'

'To God,' she finished the sentence with him.

His was not to question why, but that was Madonna without a child, pure of heart and happy to serve. She bustled from the fridge to the cooker. She delivered a mug of tea.

'You look tired?'

'Heavy times. We live through the end of days.'

'It's starting, a plague is upon us…God willing.'

Paul knew Mrs. Taylor had accepted her fate. If the rapture were to come at that moment, she, like all true believers, would raise her arms and open her heart, and willingly leave the earthly world of sin. That was love, devotion, motherhood.

The bacon sizzled and the smell wafted over him. The Lord would choose the time and place, but deliverance was coming, the cleansing was coming. It was in the air, and those who remained faithful would rise from death. The resurrection was assured, and death was a temporary and welcome rest from this world of struggle. A rest she deserved. She had suffered enough for him. An inquiry? Discipline? Media? Gossips? Her world would be turned upside down.

She placed his plate on the table and sat in her chair. Paul picked up two cushions from the sofa and he handed one to her. 'You should have support.'

'Such a thoughtful son,' she placed it at the small of her back. Paul held the other between his hands and brought it down over her head. Standing behind her, he moved it over her face. Her head was pulled into the back of the chair. There wasn't much struggle. Her legs kicked weakly for a minute or so, but Paul held firm. He watched the minute hand on the clock above the mantle. Three minutes should do it, probably less given her age and weight, but better safe than sorry. He waited, and a plate of bacon, eggs and toast waited for him. *Just how you like it. Done both sides. Butter not margarine*. She had said.

CHAPTER THIRTY-TWO

CHARLIE

Friday, January 31st, 2020.

Charlie's dad filled his mug from the kettle. 'You should stay at home.'

Charlie poured milk onto his cereal. 'Why?'

'Because there's a crazy copper on the loose. How about that for a reason? We don't know if they're out there looking for him?' He spooned sugar into his tea.

'Like the movies, they've probably put an 'All Points Bulletin' out on him.'

'This is not funny,' his dad said.

'I know. How many sugars are you putting in that tea?'

'Oh shit,' his dad pulled a face. 'This guy is serious. If you're right and he killed Matt, then he killed his own brother. Do you have any idea how messed up he would have to be to do that?'

'Half-brother,' said Charlie.

'Oh, right. That makes a difference, does it?'

'Dad, I'm going to be in town, surrounded by thousands of coppers,' Charlie sputtered through a mouth full of cereal.

'That's what worries me.'

'Anyway, I won't be on my own. I'm meeting the guys and Mina. You think I'd be safer sitting here on my own?'

'You wouldn't be on your own. I'd be here.'

'I can't stay locked up forever. I'm sure the police are looking for him. They might even have him. Can we call them?'

'Yeah, why not. Give me your phone.'

'Let me get the number.' Charlie swiped the screen. 'Here you go.' The phone was on speaker. It rang out. No answer.

Charlie picked it up and ended the call. 'The same happened yesterday. Maybe she'll call back.'

Within a minute, the phone rang.

'Superintendent?

'Yes.'

'This is Mr Connolly. I'm calling to see if you have Paul Taylor, in custody?'

'No, Mr Connolly, the officer in question has been suspended since our inquiry began and has been called in for questioning, but he is not in custody.'

'Called in? Does that mean you have him in the station?'

'I am not at liberty to give you details, Mr Connolly, but I can assure you we are following up on the information provided by your son.'

'Let it go, Dad.'

'Superintendent, Officer Taylor should not be on the streets. I am warning you, if anything happens to my son, I will let everyone know that you are personally responsible. Do you understand?'

'I understand your concerns, Mr Connolly, and can again assure you that we are actively pursuing all lines of inquiry.'

'Thank you, Superintendent.' They closed the call.

'You've done all you can, Dad.'

'I know you can't stay home forever, but for today?'

'No. Especially today. This was Matt's day. He was building up for this. He wanted a big public display of support, mass actions. I'm not going to sit at home while the rest of the group and hundreds of schoolkids are out there demonstrating.' Charlie finished his cereal. He lifted the bowl to drain the last of the milk. 'And I'll be with the guys, so I'll be fine.'

'Terry and Alan? Is that a joke?'

'Not sure, to be honest, but anyway, I won't be on my own.'

'If you're gonna go, you'd better leave before your mum gets home.'

'Where is she?'

'She's gone the Asda. It's going to be bad enough when I tell her where you've gone.'

Charlie put his bowl in the sink. 'Thanks, Dad.'

His dad reached out and put a hand on Charlie's shoulder. 'For fuck's sake, be careful. Keep an eye out.'

'I promise I will,' Charlie said.

'Stay with Mina and the others.'

'That's my plan.'

'If anything looks dodgy, call me.'

'It'll be fine.'

~

Charlie was on high alert at the bus stop. He scanned the street, on the look out for the BMW he'd seen in Macket's Lane. Paul had followed him before, so Charlie knew he had the skills. He told his dad he was fine, but he wasn't. His arse was going. *This isn't normal. Paul isn't normal.*

He remembered what Paul said outside the station at Crosby about Matthew being a gift returned to God. Life was nothing to him. If everything was eternal, our lives didn't matter. It didn't matter to him that Matt was dead. Life didn't matter. That was scary, the bastard didn't care about his own life. He would welcome the chance to be closer to God.

Charlie shook himself; he had to keep things together. He told his dad this was for Matt, but it wasn't. It was for himself. He wanted his life to mean something, not just to his mum and dad, but something more than the family.

The sights and sounds of Allerton Road, shoppers, students, and pensioners going about their daily routines; that was real.

When the bus came, he was more relaxed. There were a couple of kids with placards on the bus, excited to be going to the demonstration.

He sat downstairs near the front, close to the doors. He wanted to be ready for anything. It was a fresh morning and the sun popped out between clouds like a kid playing hide and seek, wanting to be caught.

Traffic was heavy, and the bus crawled along between traffic lights. The kids' stuff was supposed to start at lunchtime, but XR had some stalls out early and he was meeting Mina.

There were two separate marches from different points on the outskirts of town, and the schoolkids would converge on the pier and head for a rally. It was all chaotic, yet highly organised on different apps. XR and other climate change campaigners had thrown their weight behind the events, helping with speaker systems for the rally, giving space on websites, and publicity.

~

Charlie stirred his tea. 'I feel like my head's exploding.'

They were in the Starbucks at the corner of Catherine Street. Mina cradled her espresso, occasionally lifting it to her nose. 'Why?'

'All this with Matt and the copper. Then there's the climate stuff today - and now this virus.' He pointed at her coffee. 'You're not drinking that?'

'Oh, I will. I just enjoy the smell. Yeah, I guess it can seem overpowering.'

'The smell?'

'No, politics, the world.'

'Just a bit.' He smiled. 'How do you stay so... I don't know... not calm... maybe focused?'

'Because for me it really is simple; there are two things,

humanity and solidarity. These are the two things from which all others flow.'

'What do you mean?'

'If we accept everyone's humanity, then we don't accept attacks on that, whether it's someone in a dinghy crossing the channel, using a food bank, or suffering racism. It's all the same problem.'

'Ha, that sounds so simple.' As he said it, Charlie saw Terry and Alan approaching. He stood to greet them. 'Hey.'

'What sounds so simple?' asked Terry

'Mina's philosophy. Mina, this is Terry, and this is Alan.

'Hey.'

They arranged themselves in comfortable armchairs around the table.

'So, what is it then?' asked Alan.

'Humanity and solidarity.'

'Does that apply to Everton supporters?' asked Terry.

Mina laughed. 'And idiots.'

'Whoah.' Terry raised his arms in feigned karate chops. 'This woman has got some serious moves.'

'You'd better believe it,' said Charlie.

'So, what's the plan?' asked Alan.

'Are you guys getting a drink?' Charlie asked.

'I spoke to Jaime yesterday,' said Mina. 'There's a lawyer we work with. She'll contact Matt's mum to make sure she's represented.'

'Who's paying for that?' asked Alan.

'We'll see. There are a few places to get grants. We'll help with the applications.'

'I thought you just helped Black people?' said Terry.

'No, it's just that more Black people need our help.'

'Yeah, I get that.'

'Is this guy still out there?' asked Alan.

'As far as we know,' said Charlie. 'My dad rang them this

morning, they wouldn't say if they'd arrested him, but it didn't sound like.'

Small groups of young protesters were making their way past the coffee shop and down towards town, some carrying homemade placards and banners.

'Feels like before a game,' said Alan. 'You know, the pre-match nerves, the expectation-'

'And the defeat,' said Terry.

'Yeah, well, hopefully not today, eh?' Alan indicated towards Charlie.

'Yeah, I didn't mean-'

'I know,' said Charlie. 'Look, I appreciate you being around. The guy does freak me out.'

'We got your back, bruv,' said Mina

'So, what is the plan?' Alan asked.

'We go down, try and stick together, just enjoy the day,' said Charlie.

'I'm speaking at a couple of places, along the way and at the Pier Head, I think,' Mina said.

'Wow, cool,' said Terry. 'Doesn't that freak you out?'

'Nah, I'm okay with it now. Terrified me in the beginning, but you get used to it.'

'What's the Bible story about brothers? Anyone know? I should've asked my dad. He normally gets that stuff,' said Charlie.

'Jacob and Esau,' said Alan. 'Jacob steals Esau's birthright, steals his inheritance.'

'Two brothers?'

Alan nodded. 'Yeah, and Jacob is the mum's favourite.'

'Isn't that what's going on here? Paul is given or taken away, then along comes Matt, who gets a proper life. For Paul, Matt is living his stolen life,' Charlie said.

'So, he takes it from him? I guess. I mean, yeah, it's pretty sick, but it does have a kind of logic.'

'Only if you're a fucking nutter,' said Terry, shaking his head. 'You should've given this one a wide pass, mate.'

'I had to do something. I couldn't just walk by,' Charlie said.

'That's your problem, right there. Nothing wrong with walking on by. Do my work, have a pint, watch the match, bit of slap and tickle and that's me done, mate,' said Terry.

'If we were all like you, they'd still be sending kids up chimneys,' said Alan.

'What? You mean they're not? Lazy little bastards.' Terry laughed.

'I can never tell when you're serious,' said Alan.

'That's the point.' Terry winked.

Charlie drained his tea and stood up. 'Come on, then, let's get this show on the road.'

~

They walked down Hardman Street, then Bold Street. Small groups of students were in high spirits, shouting slogans. The atmosphere was of liberation and an unexpected day off school. The closer they got to town, the more police were around, not sirens blaring or lights flashing, but two or three vans, down side streets. Tactical Support Unit officers in protective gear with helmets and riot shields stood by the vans. Meanwhile, relaxed groups of three or four uniformed officers were spaced every hundred yards or so along the street-the two faces of the force in full readiness.

'Looks like they're prepared for anything,' said Alan.

'It's schoolkids,' said Terry.

'It's a demonstration. It's about power,' said Mina.

Charlie said, 'I just hope our guy isn't in uniform somewhere.'

'That's crazy,' said Alan. 'He can't be. He's suspended.'

'No, *he's* crazy, and I wouldn't put anything past him,' Charlie said.

They continued down Bold Street and crossed the road.

'Hi guys,' Charlie greeted Andy and Emma, who were behind a stall.

They were at the top of Church Street just outside the Lloyds Bank; it was a wide-open pedestrian area. A few people were giving out leaflets and Emma and Andy were chilling behind a trestle table covered in climate literature. It was a sunny, clear day and sounds carried through the chill air. Occasional noises of people collecting at the top of Bold Street could be heard.

'Hey, Charlie.' Emma moved in for a hug.

Charlie took a step back. Emma continued forward, and Charlie accepted the hug without much enthusiasm.

'What's up?' Andy asked.

'All good. These are my friends, Alan, Terry, and Mina.'

The area was always busy with shoppers, buskers, and beggars. Today, climate protesters making their way towards Pier Head added to the usual crowds. Lots of school-age kids were darting about. XR campaigners collected signatures and brought people over to look at the literature.

'Emma told me,' Andy said.

Charlie wondered what she had said.

'About the copper,' he said.

'Yeah, it's all a bit strange.'

'We're his bodyguards,' said Terry.

'Guess he's in a lot of trouble then,' said Julia.

'Hey, grandma, show a bit of respect?' said Terry smiling.

Emma introduced them. 'Charlie, this is Julia. She was quite close to Matt.'

'I heard you gave a statement,' Julia said. 'Thank you.'

'You're welcome. I only told them what I saw.'

'He was special, you know, something about him. He could have made a real difference.'

'Maybe he already has,' said Charlie.

'You know, you might be right. That other fella was a weirdo.

Nothing was right about him.'

'You knew him, then?' asked Charlie.

'Yeah, of course,' Julia said. 'He was in the group, hated Matt. Matt wanted a different kind of organisation. The other fella was your mate, wasn't he, Andy?' Andy shuffled his feet. 'No, no. I mean, I knew him. I was just being polite.'

'Anyway, if you see him,' said Charlie. 'Keep your distance. The guy has lost the plot.'

'It's actually quite dangerous here,' said Alan. 'I think we should find somewhere safe to watch what's going on.'

'We could go up to the start of the march,' said Terry.

'Which one?' said Alan 'There are two, aren't there?'

'Yeah,' said Mina. 'One starts by Saint George's Hall, the other at the top of Duke Street, by the Chinese gate.'

'It's fine,' said Charlie. Then looking round, added, 'What's going on here?'

'Pretty quiet at the moment, but we'll have our rally before the main march starts. Then we'll march down and join them. Are you here to help?' Andy asked.

'Of course,' Charlie replied.

Julia gave Charlie's sleeve a gentle tug. 'Come on. You can help me for a while.'

'Sure, what are we doing?'

'Trying to get signatures for a people's convention.'

'Did you campaign in the election?' Alan asked.

'No, we're not a political party,' Emma said.

'So you're okay with the Tories running things?'

'The climate is more important,' said Emma.

'Who do you think will be making decisions for the next four years?' replied Alan.

'That's why we want a people's assembly,' said Andy.

'You're not impressed?' Mina asked Alan.

'Not really, you?'

'The same. We need to pressure whoever is in power.'

Mina, Alan and Terry moved a little distance from the stall. Charlie helped Julia and joined the conversations with people she stopped. Charlie was enjoying himself. Julia was good at talking to people. She listened to what they said; she didn't just repeat speeches or talk at them.

Mina approached Charlie. 'I've got to go and meet some people. Are you okay here with the boys?'

'Don't you worry, love, I'll look after him. And I promise I won't steal him from you.' Julia winked.

Charlie and Mina smiled at each other. Julia had given voice to what he had not yet admitted.

'I'll catch up with you at the Pier Head.' Charlie waved.

Mina walked off with her phone glued to her ear.

Julia nodded toward the retreating Mina. 'You're punching above your weight there, kid.'

'Yeah, I know.'

There seemed to be more XR people milling around. A van had pulled off the road, and they were setting up a few boxes near the table.

Andy stood on the boxes and looked like he was preparing to speak. 'Today, we will see hundreds of students protesting against the destruction of the planet.' Andy's voice drew more people, some of the students heading for the march stopped and others began to appear from different directions. 'We in Earthquake are with them every step of the way.'

There was some activity at the back of the van. Julia pulled at Charlie's arm. 'Quick, get out of the way.'

Charlie allowed himself to be pulled further down Church Street. 'What's going on?'

'Wait, you'll see.'

'We can't trust politicians,' Andy announced. 'We can't wait for Parliament, we are speeding into climate trigger points. Direct action is required to stop this nightmare. Business as usual is death.' Andy raised a whistle he had around his neck and blew it sharply. The high-pitched noise was amplified by his loudhailer.

Things happened quickly; a group of people unfurled a large black banner across the road. It was emblazoned with Andy's last statement, white letters on a black background *Business as usual = DEATH.*

The traffic lights turned green, and car horns blared. The banner was chained to the traffic light on each side of the road, creating a barrier. Five protesters in orange overalls lay down in the street while two others spray-painted around their prone figures. A driver was out of his car and tried to drag one of the prone figures off the road.

The noise of horns grew louder and more impatient with every second. Uniformed police officers appeared and they struggled to remove the banner. They failed and turned their attention to the protesters on the ground. Another driver was out of his car and tried to rip the banner.

Alan and Terry were near the traffic lights in the middle of the crowd.

Sirens blared as police vans appeared, driving up pedestrianised Church Street. Shoppers broke in all directions to get out of the way. More and more uniformed police and TSUs were arriving. They formed a cordon and threw a line around the scene, officers linking arms. The TSU officers pushed people outside the ring.

'They're being kettled,' said Julia.

'What's that?' asked Charlie.

'They keep them there, don't let anyone move.'

About two hundred people, including the XR activists, schoolkids, and shoppers, were trapped inside the police cordon.

'How long do they keep them there?'

'Can be hours.'

'What's it for?'

'Detention... punishment... who the hell knows?'

'Jesus.'

The police cordon had pushed people off the road, and the whole group was corralled on the pavement.

'Did you know this was going to happen?' asked Charlie.

'Yeah, but we have to keep it secret. It's kinda one of the rules. No one can speak about an upcoming action.'

'My mates are stuck in there. The traffic will be backed up all over town,' Charlie said.

'Yeah, that's the idea... disruption,' Julia said.

'Of who, though? There are protesters and normal people in there?'

'Yeah, that kinda sucks, I know.'

'You don't get involved?'

'Not in this stuff. I can't, can't afford the fines, or to be in jail overnight.'

'This is it? This is the way to re-organise society?'

'They're making a point.'

'I'd rather they made a difference.'

'Matt wasn't convinced either.'

~

Charlie waved to Terry, and he waved back. Terry and Alan tried to make their way through the crowd to the police line. Charlie walked over and stood on the other side. People were arguing with the police, begging to be let go. A woman was crying that she had to collect her child, and she wasn't involved in the protest. The police didn't even respond. No engagement.

Alan reached the edge with Terry just behind him. 'Hey, mate. We weren't part of this.' Alan stared at the officer in front of him. 'Hello?'

The noise grew. Car horns from the traffic backed up through Hanover Street, Renshaw Street, and Lime Street, joined in the mayhem. The kettled crowd began to chant, 'Let us go. Let us go.'

Charlie was shocked to see a line of police moving like a black snake towards the cordon. The cordon opened, and officers went into the crowd and emerged, half carrying, half dragging Andy. Within seconds in he was in the back of a van and sirens blaring it pulled away.

'Oh shit.' The sight of the police operation sent Charlie's heart rate soaring. He was sweating and dizzy.

'Are you okay, son?' asked Julia.

'I don't know.' Charlie stumbled.

Julia held him up and half carried him to a bench. 'Here.' She produced a bottle of water from her bag.

Charlie raised the water to his lips. He looked over at the kettled crowd.

The noise, the pushing and shoving with the crowd, everything was chaos. He searched among the faces for Alan or Terry, but instead found Paul.

There! The bastard was in the crowd. Charlie stood to get a better view. Was he mistaken? The face had disappeared. Then Charlie saw him again. Everything around him was moving, a swaying mass of people, but Paul's eyes were immobile, fixed on Charlie.

Fuck.

CHAPTER THIRTY-THREE

CHARLIE

Friday, February 1st, 2020.

Fuck

There he was. Paul was moving through the crowd toward the police line. Charlie shook his head to clear it. *I should get out of here. This is stupid.*

Then he saw banners moving down Bold Street. These weren't hand made efforts but the tall, broad, colourful banners of trade unions, railworkers, fireman, transport workers, and other banners he didn't recognise. They marched straight down Bold Street toward the kettled junction with Church Street. The 'Let us go' chant, was joined by a 'Let them go' response from the unions.

The police rapidly withdrew the kettle and scurried to the other side of Church Street to regroup. A huge cheer went up as the two crowds merged. Charlie knew that in among the chaos of banners, bodies and movement, Paul would be searching for him.

'Are you okay, love?' Julia asked.

'Yeah, but I've got to go.'

Charlie turned. Hopefully Paul would be stuck in the crowd.

He walked away. After twenty yards, he turned to see what was happening. Paul had reached the edge of the crowd. He waved at Charlie.

Shit. Charlie looked back to the crowd and briefly made

eye contact with Julia, then she was gone, He moved down Church Street. He would try to lose Paul among the shoppers. He ignored the first turn towards Saint John's Market and kept going downhill. Marks and Spencer was on the right. He turned left through Peter's Lane into Liverpool One.

He texted Mina. *Wer r u?*

Within seconds his phone buzzed.

Mina: *cmng dwn Duke St.*

Great. A few twists and turns through the narrow, upmarket alleyways and up Seel Street, right at Slater Street and he would come out halfway down Duke Street.

Charlie couldn't see them but heard the marchers, their songs and chants filling the narrow streets, bouncing between the buildings. It was a joyous and urgent noise.

When he emerged into Duke Street, he saw it coming down the hill. Banners flying and voices crying, it flowed around parked cars on and off the pavement, covering everything it touched. Shoppers and assistants stood in doorways marvelling at the energy and commitment of these schoolkids, who had travelled from all over the city to be heard.

In the face of the huge numbers of marchers, the police were low-key, walking alongside one every twenty feet or so, making no attempt to control what was a peaceful and good-natured river.

The front of the march passed him and Charlie waited, eyes peeled for Mina. He saw her, and he took in a sharp breath. She was among a small group of people, but he could only see her, and he could see everything about her: the softness of her hair, slim, elegant figure and graceful movements.

He waved as he made his way through the marchers. 'Mina.'

Her face lit up when she saw him. She linked his arm when he reached her, in what, seemed the most natural and affectionate gesture ever. She beamed with the energy of the marchers around her. 'Where are the boys?'

'They got kettled. They're somewhere in Church Street.'

'Never mind, I'll look after you now.' She smiled and squeezed his arm a little tighter.

Charlie was still conscious of Paul; he didn't want to worry Mina and looked around as they moved down the street slowly.

'Mina?'

Charlie and Mina turned as a couple of teenagers approached. 'We're stopping at the next junction for a quick rally.' One said 'Can you say a few words? We've got a loudhailer and everything.'

'Yes, sure.'

'Come on,' Mina pulled Charlie. 'We have to get you to the front.'

'No, you go. I want to listen to you from the crowd.'

'Okay.' She leaned in and kissed his cheek. 'If you lose me, message.'

'Will do.' Before he knew it, she was gone, dodging among the marchers ahead.

The movement slowed and then came to a standstill. The people from behind were still moving forward, it wasn't a crush, but it was getting tighter. Charlie stood on tiptoes to see forward.

He heard the normally soft, now strident tones of Mina's voice. 'And God gave Noah a warning... no more water, the fire next time.' Mina's voice rose above the tumult and demanded attention. 'This was a warning... and now we have the fires. We have the fires in the Australian bush.'

Charlie looked around anxiously.

'Worse wildfires year after year in California. This summer saw the worst wildfires in The Artic for sixty years.'

He was listening but his eyes scanned the back of the crowd nervously.

'These fires are devastating plant and animal life, and speeding us toward catastrophic trigger points for climate change.' Her sentences were short and direct, her delivery punchy.

'The other fires we face are the fires of outrage and anger - as Black people continue to face the injustice of racist violence. Immigrants face death in the Channel, and Palestinians suffer under occupation.' There was applause and cheers from the crowd.

'These fires come from the same source, and we extinguish these with the same force. Remove power from the polluters, remove power from the racists. It was the pursuit of profit that created slavery, and racism, and it is the pursuit of profit that is destroying our environment.

'We say no more Mark Duggans.

'No more Stephen Lawrences.

'No more Anthony Walkers.

'And we give a warning to the fossil fuel companies, the billionaires, their governments, and their media.

'No more water, fire next time!'

Charlie had no right to, but felt proud of Mina, and then his stomach flipped as he saw Paul moving towards him through the crowd. Charlie turned and edged through the bodies. He wanted to get away, get out of town. He'd had enough of this cat and mouse shit. He took the first left off Duke Street. It looked familiar, and he realised he was just around the corner from the Hub, the squat used by Andy and Emma. He could wait there till he made contact with the guys or Mina.

He turned into Henry Street, found the hole in the fence, climbed through the window and moved quickly up the stone stairs. The sound of his footsteps bounced off the brick walls. The place was empty now.

Charlie had to shake Paul off. *This is getting stupid.*

He stopped climbing the stairs on the second floor, sure now that he had lost him. He would wait ten minutes, then get back out. He needed to be around people. He could hear the echo, the voices from a street away. In the empty warehouse they could have been ghosts. This area, like many others, had seen demonstrations of dockers and transport workers. Liverpool's history was full of struggle and death; the lonely silent death of the hungry, or the violent death of those who fought back. As far back as 1911, troops opened fire and shot dead John Sutcliffe, a transport worker, and Michael Prendergast, a docker. Seventy years later, David Moore died at the hands of police in Liverpool eight. The state has always been prepared to kill to regain control of the streets.

As soon as he stopped running, Charlie knew it was a mistake.

He swiped his phone and saw messages from Alan and Mina.

He pressed his dad's number. 'Dad, can you give me a lift home?'

'Yeah, where are you? What's going on?'

'I'm in The Hub. It's a kinda squat.'

'Where is it?'

'Just off Duke Street. I don't know the address.'

'Okay, I can meet you somewhere, but the radio said traffic's messed up.'

'Yeah, it is.'

'Are you okay? Who's with you?'

'We got split up.'

'Shit, you're not on your own, are you?'

'Yeah, but I'm okay.'

'Okay, look, I'm on my way. I'm leaving my office now. I'll be in town in ten minutes. I'll walk. It'll be quicker. You can give me directions. No, wait... call the guys. Tell them where you are.'

'They're stuck in Church Street. They got kettled.'

'Where's Mina?'

'She was speaking, but yeah, I'll call her now.'

'Call me back straight after, okay?'

'Will do.' Charlie ended the call.

The door below screeched as it was dragged across the stone

floor, the iron screaming out Paul's arrival.

Shit. Charlie waited, hoping it would be one of the squatters.

He heard the footsteps slow and steady as they climbed.

'Char... lie…' the voice was taunting, melodic.

'Char... lie…'

It was Paul.

Charlie leaned back against the wall. The footsteps grew louder. He turned and ran up the next flight of stairs. His pursuer was speeding up. He ran into the main space on the third floor.

'Charlie?' Not taunting this time, insistent, angry.

Charlie would face him. He would fight him if he had to. He scanned the room. There was no obvious hiding space. The window was open, and he remembered the walkway. Maybe he could get to the next building and back down to the street. He crossed the room and stepped onto the iron bridge between the buildings. The alley was below him. Out in the open air, he could hear the chants, the drums, and the sounds of the march in the streets below.

Charlie crossed the bridge quickly and tried the door. It was locked. *Shit.*

He moved back towards the window slowly, the walkway creaking underfoot. Then he heard it again. The voice, an out-of-tune taunting sing-song. 'Char...lie, I know you're here, Char...lie.'

Charlie moved forward cautiously to get a look. He wanted to see if he could get past Paul and back to the stairs.

'Char...lie, you can't run away this time. Come on out, Charlie, you know you can't hide from the Almighty. He sees you, He sees your sins, He knows you. He knows your sinful soul, but don't despair Charlie. He is kind. He is forgiveness. He welcomes back the lost sheep. I know you can hear me, Charlie.'

The voice got louder. Paul was getting closer. He had to be moving towards the window. Charlie ducked to better see inside, The opening was from floor level but the sash window was halfway up. He inched forward, crouching. He could see inside the room.

'There you are!' Paul almost screamed the words.

Charlie leapt back towards the locked door.

'You've got me wrong, Charlie. You've got nothing to be afraid of.' Paul was in the centre of the room. He had stopped. 'I know what you think, but you're wrong. Matthew was my brother. Why would I harm him? Charlie, look... hands up. I'm not going to hurt you.'

Charlie bent and looked through the open window. Paul had his hands up, palms open.

'I was trying to help, not hurt him.'

'What do you want? Why are you following me?'

'Come on, Charlie, be fair. It was you who went to my house, went inside, and spoke to my mother. I just want to talk to you.'

Charlie squatted on the metal walkway. He could see into the room.

'I'm staying here, but can I put my arms down? This is not easy.'

'Yeah, but don't move. My dad is on his way, and the guys will be here soon.'

'That's fine. I've got nothing to hide.'

'Why did you arrest Matt?'

'It's my job. I couldn't not arrest him because he was my brother.'

'What were you doing in the climate group?'

'I was trying to get to know him. I went to see my mother, Matt's mother. I should have realised, but I guess it was a shock for her. She couldn't handle it. I should have known, I mean, she couldn't look after me in the first place, but she rejected me. I wanted to get to know my younger brother. I'd never had a family. The Taylors were good to me, but we all knew they weren't real family. I was a charity... they were doing their bit for the deprived.

'I joined the group to spend time with him, get to know him, and he died in my arms. Can you imagine that, Charlie? Knowing you were rejected as a child. Your own mother gave you away. Then coming back and being rejected again. Finally getting to know my brother, and he dies in my arms.' Paul raised a hand to wipe his face.

'Why did you lie? Why weren't you honest?'

'A copper in that group? Come on, Charlie, it was full of anarchists and liberals. How long do you think it would have taken before they threw me out? We're not like them. They have a different lifestyle.'

'Don't put me in with you. I'm not like you.'

'You're more like me than you know. What do they think they're achieving with their protests? No one cares.'

'That's not true.'

'Grow up, Charlie. People get on with their lives. It's okay for Emma and Andy, they've got no responsibilities, no mortgage to pay. Middle-class kids playing at rebellion.

'You have your religion, your football, and I have my truth. We are the same, Charlie. Look, there's no need to tell Superintendent Smith. You've done brilliantly, putting it all together the way you did. That was really smart. Do you really want to destroy my career, my life? I can't look after Mrs Taylor, my mum, if I lose my job. Come on, Charlie, you've met her... doesn't everyone deserve a second chance?'

'I don't have a religion.'

'Football is all you care about.'

'You're wrong. I thought I'd lost Liverpool, because of bastards like you. But listen, out there... that's us... fighting. I've already told Superintendent Smith everything.'

Paul raised his hands to his head. 'What did you do that for? You stupid, stupid... I was willing to give you a chance... but you don't deserve one.' His voice rose with his anger. 'Don't you know authority comes from God? Rebellion is sinful. You'll pay the price. You'll all pay the price when God's vengeance comes. You ungrateful…'

Paul pulled out his police baton and snapped it to full length. He sprang forward within reach of the window. Charlie fell back. When he looked up, Paul had tripped on the metal studs in the floor and was falling forward, face down. As he fell, he reached out for purchase, trying to grab anything he could. He pulled out the stick that propped up the sash. His head was just outside the window, his neck immediately below the falling frame.

Paul fell, his neck hit the windowsill. At that moment, the cast-iron structure slammed down. The full weight of the glass and metal whooshed down and the iron edge of the casement acted as a guillotine and sliced through his neck.

Paul's head dangled by a thread of skin or sinew outside, and his body was inside. Blood pumped out of his neck onto the glass. A small pool gathered on the ledge outside before dripping into the street below. The head swung to and fro.

Below, a group of kids marched chanting, 'Who's future? Our Future!'

SIX MONTHS LATER

CHARLIE

August, 2020.

Mina gave directions. 'In the middle, no. You need to go to the left, just a touch... yeah, you're good.'

Charlie sent two screws whirring through to fix the sign. The smell of pastries wafted in from next door. The doorway was between a Sayers bakery and a souvenir shop, complete with wobbly headed Beatles in Richmond Street off Williamson Square.

'God, it's going to be a nightmare if I can smell those pasties all day.' A flight of stairs led up to one room with a toilet attached.

Charlie spotted his dad approaching from the square. 'Hey, Dad.'

'I still don't know why you need an office.'

'I don't, I need to get out the house, and this is free.'

'As long as you look after it.'

'You'll be amazed, Mr Connolly.' Mina beamed.

'You sure about the name?' His dad asked. 'It might be another thirty years till you win the league again.'

Charlie frowned. 'You trying to wind me up?'

His dad laughed. 'You only supported Liverpool to have a go at me.'

'And look how well that worked out. Premier League champions.' He pumped his fist in the air.

The street was quiet. Merseyside was coming out of the

Covid lockdown. Restrictions had been lifted to allow for small gatherings and the summer sun drew more people out every day.

Mina stepped forward into Charlie's embrace, he welcomed the contact.

'So, are you going to show me what you've done with the place?' his dad asked.

Charlie led the way. The stairs opened into a square room, and a window overlooked the shopping street below. A large sofa lined the right-hand wall. In pride of place was Mo Salah and now, alongside him, was a poster of Malcolm X. On the left was a counter with a sink, a microwave and a kettle. Charlie's desk and chair from home were in front of the window.

'You do know you can't live here? It has no residential clearance.'

'I know, I know, it's just a base, that's all. Terry and his dad fixed the walls, and Alan is building me a website.'

'Helloo,' a shout came from below.

'You expecting someone else? His dad asked.

'Yeah,' Mina replied.

Emma was first into the room. She moved forward to hug Charlie but stopped midway.

'Never get used to this.'

Charlie held up his fist for a bump.

'It all looks good,' said Andy. 'We might need to get your mates down the Hub to see if they can fix things up for us. And I liked the sign. You'll be like the alternative to the police. We've had enough bad apples.'

'It's not the apples,' Mina chipped in. 'It's the barrel.'

'I thought the sign was about football? Liverpool, the reds.' His dad said.

'It is, but-'

His dad finished for him. 'It's also about the city.'

Charlie nodded. 'Yeah.'

'With all this Covid shit it's been so long since we've been able to do anything. It all feels like years ago. Matthew and his brother; God, how weird does that sound? Both buried.'

'Have you seen their mum?' asked Charlie.

'Yeah,' Emma said. 'She's not doing so well, but she's a got a lawyer helping her with Matthew's inquest.'

'Things might start heating up again,' said Vinny.

'Why? What's going on?' asked Charlie.

'I got a call this morning from Superintendent Smith. They will issue a report at the end of the week. She was giving me some warning. The press might pick up interest. Especially with all the George Floyd protests.'

Andy shook his head. 'Shit never stops, does it?'

'So what's in the report?' asked Mina.

'As far as the IOPC are concerned, there was no breach of rules or protocol in the arrest of Matthew. They will recognise that Officer Taylor acted in an unprofessional and unsanctioned way in the climate group. But in terms of the arrest and detention, neither he nor the police can be held responsible for Matt's death.'

'Surprise, surprise.'

'Did you expect anything else?' Vinny asked Charlie.

'Not really, but it's still a shock to hear it.'

'Another cover-up,' said Mina.

'They won't find one of their own guilty,' Andy replied.

'He was crazy,' said Charlie.

Mina responded, 'The chosen people, that certain type of fundamentalism is currently on the rise. Christians, nationalists, conspiracists.'

'And the inquests?' asked Charlie.

'They'll probably drag that out for years,' said Emma.

'My guess is, there will be open verdicts, the police might be criticised, but nothing will happen,' said his dad.

'Nothing will change, you mean?' said Charlie.

'The media were right about one thing, though.' His dad smiled.

'What's that?' asked Charlie.

'You. You did a hell of a job putting all the pieces together. You've earned that name.'

'Why did they start calling you that?' asked Emma.

'After the story came out, the only photo the press had of me was wearing my Liverpool shirt.' Charlie winced. 'Not sure if I like it.'

'A bit late now. You've just put a sign on the door.' Mina nudged him.

'I know.'

~

Ten minutes later, Vinny Connolly walked down the stairs. He closed the door behind him and turned to look at the sign,

The Red Detective
First Floor

ACKNOWLEDGEMENTS

I have said before and it remains true, that writing a book is a singular activity, but it could not have happened without the support and perseverance of my wife Agnes. However, the heavy lifting is done by the small team at Northodox Press who have made giant strides in the few years they have been in the business, developing a genuinely exciting list of established and new writers. So if you haven't checked out my stable mates be sure to do so.

I want to thank Jo Peggrem, Paul Cooney, Rhi Foynes, Meeta Tailor, and Dr Tahaney Alghrani, who all read drafts and whose comments have affected the outcome, great thanks to Ted and Leila Kirkconnell whose edits always improve my work - special thanks to Mike Simon who has taken the time to help with local insight and research.

I see my writing in the tradition of socialist literature that runs through the likes of Jack London, Upton Sinclair, B Travern, Steinbeck and of course Robert Noonan better known as Tressell, while not claiming their skill or talent I do share the aim of writing to express the lives and struggles of working people. When I was twelve or thirteen my older shop steward brother gave me a copy of the Ragged Trousered Philanthropists to spread the word about the fight for a fairer society. We are still in that fight and as a reader you have a part to play. I hope my books can be shared among families, friends, and colleagues as grains of sand thrown in the gears of oppression.

NORTHODOX PRESS

FIND US ON SOCIAL MEDIA

www.northodox.co.uk

@northodoxpress

@northodoxpressofficial

@northodoxpress

@northodoxpress

@northodoxpress.bsky.social

www.northodox.co.uk